D1739144

Contents

ACKNOWLEDGMENT

Let's just keep it real, most of the time YOU will be the only one that believes in YOU! For those of *you who said, I couldn't do it, THANKS!*

To: Julie, Raé, Ki, Ricky, Chris, Trena, the Cousins (you know who you are), I love you, appreciate you; and value your love, friendship, and advice. Who would have ever thought, right?

Prologue

BOOK – BLACK TESTAMENT

Beep…. beep…. beep…. beep…. What the hell is going on? Why is everyone looking at me like I'm some sort of test monkey? Hey! Hey! Hey, you guys, what's going on? Nobody moves or acknowledges a single word I am saying. Now I'm really starting to get pissed off. E, E, answer me, bro! But everyone just continues talking in those hushed tones like people do at funerals or a damn hospital…. Beep…. Beep…. Beep…. That's me! Wait, wait a second! That's me looking at me, but there's no mirrors in this fucking room!

This isn't my room. This isn't my house. A panic comes over me, but there's no way to let it out, release it, or give it escape. I guess it could be described as "butterflies", but it seems that I'm the butterfly, because I'm "me", hovering over "me", talking about "me," while watching my family look and stare at "me." Nigga this is some freaky shit! I'm, I mean me; or whoever the fuck I am, is in a hospital bed.

The bed looks comfortable except for the tubes in my mouth. I have a mask over my face that reminds me of the one I used to have attached to a bong. There are IVs sticking in each of my arms with thin lines of tape stretched across my eyelids sealing them closed. Beep.... Beep.... Beep. This is some deep shit bra. Am I hallucinating or high? Beep.... Beep....

Somebody cut that fucking machine off. I can't hear myself think. You guys, hey, you guys, what's going on? Babe!! Babe!! Why are you crying, babe? I'm still here; I'm right here! Bro, what's up? Say something! What the fuck!

He does, as a middle-aged white man, with white hair, in a white coat, walks in with a clipboard. Hopefully, he'll clear this shit up!

"Hey Doc," said my brother E. "Any news on the test results?"

"I do," said the doc. The doctor averted his eyes momentarily before going on. I have a duty and an obligation to be honest and upfront with you and the family, and it's not good! His heart is still beating because of the machine and ventilator that we have him hooked up to, but we can't detect any brain activity." The doctor looked my brother in his eyes to see if he understood the magnitude of what he had just been told.

What the fuck nigga, I'm right here! I'm right here, listening to you mutha fucka. Bro, don't listen to him!

"Okay, so what do you suggest, doc?" The doctor shook his head, looked down for a moment, then he looked at my brother in his eyes.... "I'm sorry.... There's nothing we can do for him; perhaps you should call the family in to say their goodbyes."

My fiancé, Juju, collapsed, hitting the ground with a thud like a sack of groceries, screaming, "No, no, no, this can't be, no!!!!!" The doctor patted my brother on the back and walked out coolly.

E bent down to console Juju, his own eyes moist with tears. "It's ok, Juju; he wouldn't want to live like this. I know my brother. He was too full of life to want to be maintained on life support. He wouldn't want to be forced to exist like this as some sort of vegetable. I'm going to step out for a minute so that I can call the rest of the family to tell them to come to say their goodbyes. I'm going to give the hospital permission to pull the plug tomorrow."

"Pull the plug?" said Juju as E exited the room. Juju walked over to the bed, to me. The me in the bed anyway. She put a caressing hand on my chest and then gently kissed my forehead.

Juju, wait, baby, I'm right here! We can get through this! I know I said cut the machine off, but I didn't mean it. I didn't understand what was going on. Come on, babe, we've been through worse. This can't be it. A nigga like me can't go out like this. I pull plugs, mutha fucka's don't pull my plug. Plus babe, what happens after they pull the plug? I'm not going to lie, I'm scared! Babe, can you hear me? Stop staring at that fucking body; I'm right here in your ear.

I try to grab her, push her, hug her... no response!! Finally, with tears streaming down her face, soaking the hospital gown they have draped over my heavily tattooed body, she says, "I love you," then proceeds to start to walk out the door. I tried to block her way, but she walked right through me; yet for some reason, I couldn't exit the room with her. I'm stuck with this body, so I'm stuck in this place. Stuck in this hospital room! All alone, scared and confused. Plus, they're talking about pulling the plug tomorrow!

What about all the great and fly things that I was supposed to do? What about my dreams? What about my goals? Think, think! What the fuck happened? Everything was going so good. Wait, wait a second. I remember! Wait, I remember!! I was getting out of the game. How the fuck did I end up here? I was going to be one of the few that made it out. This wasn't supposed to happen to me. All that was left to do was tell Cash that the empire was his. I was done. The Tijuana Cartel connection was his, the blocks, all of it. I was supposed to be one of the few that made it out. This was some confusing shit.

It was time to do what grandma "ma" always said to do when things felt like they were too tough for you. Even though I didn't have much experience with it, it was time to pray. "God, if you're listening, give me one more chance. I won't fuck it off; I swear I won't. I know I made my mistakes. I know I made many mistakes God, but I was just making a change. I'm just asking for one more chance, God. Just one more chance. It's all I want. Well, you're the big G.O.D, so I can't lie to you. I want one more chance to make things right and the opportunity to erase my enemies and those who betrayed me from existence. Grant me the opportunity to see their blood flow through the streets. That's all I ask God if you're listening. Amen."

Chapter 1

CHILDHOOD TRAUMA

[Past]

"Get off my momma," I said as I beat my daddy across his back with my tiny fists. This is one of my earliest childhood memories, and I couldn't have been more than five years old. Too young to know what was going on or why but I did know that no one, including my father, would hurt my momma on my watch.

"It's ok, son, go to your room; your'e momma and me are just talking, that's all."

Now I've never considered myself to be exceptionally bright, but I've always been a "square" sharp on all four sides, so there's no need for you to be sitting on my momma while she's crying if you're just talking. I was relentlessly banging on my pops back until he finally got off my mom. I was standing there crying and remember my mom coming to me and holding me. Shortly after that, the front door slammed, and my mom was gone. I had no idea at the time how much and for how long this would affect my life.

A mother's love cannot be replaced, and it should not have to be.

Chapter 2

WHO I AM

[Present]

By the way, my name is King, and as far as the "game" goes, I've done it all, and I've done it quite successfully if I must say so myself. As we speak, I'm laying in bed with two bad bitches. I think it was Drake that said, "Girls like girl's where I'm from." That nigga ain't never lied on that one.

I'm living in a gated community in "white neighborhood" USA. I got four whips, all black on black foreigns, a pair of jet skis, and an off-road dirt bike. My jewel game will freeze an Eskimo's ass, and I don't punch no clock. I'm something like an Indian. I live off the land. What's "living off the land" mean? Could be selling dope, robbing, pimping, check scams, you name it. The specifics aren't what's important; what you need to know is that I'm self-made.

"Keisha, Keisha, get up and go cook some breakfast for Alisha and me." Keisha got up with her fat ass and booty shorts and made her way to the kitchen, where she posted her first Instagram pic of the day. She's a dancer, okay, okay, a stripper, and Alisha works at the DMV, but I'm getting ahead of myself. Back to moms.

Chapter 3

MOMMA ISSUES

[Past]

I didn't know it at the time, but that was the last time I would see my mom for about a year. Turns out that my mom was dead set on pursuing a singing career and my dad was dead set on turning her into the homemaker that he wanted. Both of them were passionate about what they wanted, and both were stubborn as shit, so clearly, something had to give. Unfortunately, my mom gave; she "gave up."

Understanding any of this was above the comprehension of a five-year-old but what I did understand was that things in my life changed pretty drastically. My dad, being only thirty years old, found himself more or less a single father. The stress got to him, and he began smoking cigarettes. We moved to a small one-bedroom apartment, and we didn't have a car. I remember him walking me to school. Sometimes he would carry me on his shoulders. Once while walking me to school, he flicked the last of one of his cigarettes, and I picked it up and smoked it. I damn near choked to death, and I got slapped in the back of my head, but I ain't smoked a cigarette since.

Times were tough, but when you're young, you don't know you're poor until you're old enough to have something to compare it to. If everyone in your hood lives in the same way as you, then to you it's normal. That being the case, it wasn't being "poor" that had a negative effect on me. What fucked me up was the fact that I felt abandoned by my mom. What fucked me up was not knowing where my mom was.

My dad had an explosive temper, and he wasn't keen on being asked or answering questions from a kid; not even his own, so it was never explained to me why he and my mom had separated. For all I knew, it was my fault.

Chapter 4

A DAY IN THE LIFE

[Present]

"What bitch?!"

"Baby, I'm going to be late for work; you're still taking me, right?" Alisha asked, rolling her sexy little neck and sucking her teeth as she did.

"Damn, it's almost eight already? Ok, let me get dressed, go tell Keisha to roll me a blunt, and we'll leave in about ten minutes!"

Alisha walked out of the room looking sexy and classy in a business suit with her long legs, long hair, and exotic face. Alisha was Portuguese and black with long curly hair. She had a tattoo of a dragon on her hip going down her thigh, and she was 5'10'' without heels. She's been wanting to start stripping because Keisha makes way more money than her. I have to tell her consistently that her job as a DMV manager is priceless because it gives her access to fake identifications and people's personal information. I love both of those bitches in my own way.

"Come on, Alisha, let's go; I got shit to do today," I yelled. Alisha and Keisha pecked on the lips, and Keisha slaps Alisha on her ass on the way out. Alisha hands me two freshly rolled backwoods stuffed with a delicious-smelling indica, and we walk to the garage. I opened her car door for her and watched her slide onto the soft black leather before getting in myself. The 750 BMW has remote start ignition, so the car is running, and the seats are already warm before we get in. Pulling out the garage, I spark the blunt and decide that this morning I'm not going to slap any music. I wanted to smoke and ride in silence while I thought about what needed to be done today. I had come a long way in the game, but it was time to make some life changes and moves. Don't nothing

come to a sleeper- but a dream.

Chapter 5

POPPA'S RAGE

[Past]

As I was saying, mom's split, and pops was on his own with a five-year-old son. Now I didn't know it at the time, but my pops never knew his pops. Supposedly he was killed in a liquor store robbery when my dad was five years old, but since I can't ever remember him talking about his dad, I could be completely wrong on that. My grandma "ma" did her best with him, God rest her soul, but as we all know, there's certain things a woman just can't teach a man, no matter how good her intentions.

For a few years, me and pops were alone, and I guess to me, it wasn't all that bad. Things are simple to you when you're that young. I didn't give a shit about material things back then, but that would change over time. You know how it is on the turf; nobody wants to be the nigga that ain't touching no guap. Quite often, especially in the hood, your value and self-worth are placed in the things you can obtain. You know what I mean, the cars, the jewels, the clothes. What you have is literally more important than the kind of person you are or in the way you go about getting that shit. Nigga's in the hood is known for misquoting Malcolm X's, "By any means necessary."

It had to be about when I was eight years old when my dad met my future stepmom. She's a remarkable woman, but you couldn't tell the eight-year-old me that. These are the first years I ever remember experiencing the emotion of anger. Who is this woman who is coming around more and more, and where the fuck is my mom at? Who are all these other "new" people in my life when it's just been my dad and me for so long? It felt like to me I was about to lose my dad too. Then they got married!!! Fuck! I was heated!

Yeah, at eight years old, and I've got the wedding photos with me wearing a classic gangsta mean mug to prove it. I understand now that it wasn't necessarily the situation I was pissed about. It was the fact that I felt like no one gave a shit about me. No one was even telling me what was going on. Little by little, slowly but surely over the years, I turned into the cold-hearted, go-getting mutha fucka I am today. However, it came at a heavy cost. You know what they say, "If you don't stand for something, you'll fall for anything."

Chapter 6

SLICK TALK

[Present]

"Baby, baby, we here!" Alisha was tapping my shoulder.

"Sup, mama?" I said as I snapped out of my daze.

"We here, are you good?" Alisha asked with a real look of concern on her face.

"I'm good babe; I was just in a zone caught up in my thoughts." Leaning over, I gave her a kiss and told her to have a good day. As she got out of the car, her shirt hiked up in the back. I couldn't help but notice how sexy her black laced thong looked, showing barely above her pants line. I must have been grinning cause she said, "Nigga, what you smirking at?"

"Huh, nothing ma, have a good day, ok?" I said lamely. I feel like I treat the women in my life good, but I learned a long time ago that it doesn't pay to be too predictable. Plus, when it comes to a bitch, actions run circles around words. I save my flattery for when they do something deserving of it.

"Are you going to pick me up on my lunch break? I didn't bring any money." Alisha asked.

Reaching in my pocket, I tore off a hundred dollars from a bankroll of about ten grand. This was just pocket money.

"Mama," I said, licking my lips in what I consider my sexy look. "I've got shit to do today. I'm on my way to pick up Tyreke; we've got business to tend to." I knew that when I said that name, she was going to cop an attitude. She can't stand Tyreke; said he's going to get me caught up one day and that I shouldn't trust him. She doesn't like the way he "eye fucks" her when he's around. She spared me that speech today though, smacked her lips, and said, "Be safe, please don't be late picking me up at five, it's supposed to rain today." I told her that she's too pretty to get wet in the rain and that all she needed to do was walk between the raindrops. That made her laugh, so she spun off and headed inside. I sat and watched her heart-shaped ass, long athlete legs, and black curly hair halfway down her back disappear between the double doors of the DMV. Not bad, I thought to myself, not bad King.

Exiting the parking lot, I made a right on Broadway and saw lightning and rain clouds in the distance. It was that time of the year in northern California. Actually, the capital of California, Sacramento. Late October through January was the "wet" season up this way, but that didn't mean that the hustle stopped. They say that if a shark stops swimming, it dies. Sacramento, especially the "Park", is an ocean full of sharks. I turn right onto the 99 freeway entrance; it was time to go pick this nigga Tyreke up, then get to the bag. Where were we though? Oh yeah!!

Chapter 7

THIRD-STRING QB

[Past]

At eleven years old, my first baby brother was born. I was both excited and angry at the same time. Excited to have someone around who wasn't grown that maybe I could teach shit to. At the same time, I was mad. My stepmom's family was showing more interest in this lil nigga than they had ever shown in me. He couldn't even talk yet. It didn't take long before I felt like my whole existence was in jeopardy. Moms was gone, and pops was starting a new family while here I am on the sideline like a third-string quarterback. You're there, but no one is paying attention to you. Just like a third-string quarterback, you only get recognized when some dramatic shit happens.

For the third-string quarterback, two other quarterbacks gotta go down or get injured before anyone notices you. Well, for the kid who feels like a "third stringer," he too soon realizes that some dramatic shit needs to happen before he gets recognized. Here's what I've come to understand. Every person desires and needs recognition, love, and appreciation. This is especially true for young nigga's. They are going to find or "force" a way to get this recognition. If it's not done in a positive manner, it's going to surely get done in a negative one.

I had this figured out by the age of thirteen. I'm not saying I had it figured out in the way I just described it, but the shit I started doing makes it clear that I knew this and that I was willing to deal with the consequences for my actions, so long as the attention I sought came with it. For those of you who can remember the age of thirteen, it seems like the age where you really start to shape your own identity. You start disagreeing, either verbally or in your head, to things your parents or teachers tell you if they don't sit well with your "new identity." It seems that it's about the age where you become "aware," but not necessarily in a good way.

For instance, I became "aware" that it was bullshit that my mom ran off and that my dad had started a new life. It's the age where the "concept" of what you do and don't "deserve" becomes ingrained. I did not "deserve" to be an outsider in my own family. I did not "deserve" to be a third-string quarterback. I did not "deserve" to feel invisible. This was also a dangerous time for me because it was the time I became aware of material things. The Payless shoes didn't cut it anymore. Neither did clothes with holes or wearing the same shit two or three times a week, even if it's clean. This seems to be the age where the ego begins to truly find its voice.

How do these issues express themselves when all these volatile ingredients are present? Shit, what do you think? In the ways that millions of young black and brown kids can relate to! Self-destructive ways!

This is the first age I remember stealing something that I didn't have the money for. It was basketball cards, and everyone at school had them. Shit, I didn't "deserve" not to. I'd be damned if I didn't too. I still remember like it was yesterday.

This white kid at school was showing off his collection of cards while having all the kids huddled up around him asking to see his card collection. That's the kind of attention I wanted. Thats the kind of attention I needed. That's the kind of attention I craved. A few days later, on a Saturday when I was supposed to be at the big park shooting hoops, I ran almost two miles to a comic and card shop where I pulled my first "heist." It would not be my last. On Monday, when I returned to school, I was "the man," showing off my new card collection.

Of course, I didn't tell anyone that the cards were stolen. I also began starting shit at home too. I'd talk shit to my stepmom until my dad would have to whoop my ass. I remember one time I told her that the tacos she made for dinner tasted like shit. She stared at me for about thirty seconds, started screaming, and then ran full speed from the kitchen to the living room, leaping over the living room couch as she did. She launched her one hundred and fifteen pounds at me, raining down punches as we rolled on the floor. The tacos were fire; they were actually my favorite meal. It was the attention I was after!

This type of situation started to put a strain on me and my pops, "Big Rich's" relationship. Progressively the ass whoopings with belts turned into full-out fist assaults. I was a skinny thirteen year-old kid, and "Big Rich" was 6'1" 230 pounds. Not exactly a fair fight!

Anyone in the psychology profession will tell you that if verbal abuse of a child is horrible, physical abuse can be catastrophic. There was a deep hate, rage, and anger that built up inside me. I learned that I could deal with physical pain. I never feared getting punched on. It fucked me up that it was my own pops that was doing it, but what really ate at me back then was the feeling of helplessness that came with it. I hated something that was hurting me, and I was unable to do anything about it.

I would go to great lengths in the future to ensure that no one ever made me feel like that again.

Chapter 8

THE PLAY

[Present]

...tap...tap..., tap...tap...tap... "Unlock the door nigga; it's raining out here."

I was parked in front of my nigga Tyreke's house, and he was tapping on my window with his .40 cal Heckler & Koch, which he never went anywhere without. Tyreke just got out of the pen from doing eight years, but he always said that he'd rather be judged by twelve than carried by six! He's dressed in all black. Black hoodie, black sweats, and black and white Air Max. His dreads are hanging out the back of his beanie down past his shoulders. He's got a gold grill with two carats of diamonds in it. He's a product of what you can find in every ghetto of America. He's young, black, uneducated, and "wit the shit." Today he was going to send a message for me to a nigga who needed to be taught a lesson.

"What's up bro, my bad!" I said as he slid into the car. Alisha left her scarf on the front seat, so Tyreke tossed it in the back.

"Damn you trying to give a nigga pneumonia, nah, I'm just fucking with you. Sup big bro, is everything set?" Tyreke asked as he opened a little duffle bag, pulling out zip ties, burner gloves, a mask, and some duct tape. He looked up, grinning at me as he held each item up.

"I told you it was good, we bout to get this fettuccini, now put on your seat belt, light that blunt in the ashtray so I can lace you on the play while we ride."

Tyreke got that cold, glowing look in his eyes. Unfeeling, unrepentant, and unapologetic. You know, like a shark!!

"Fasho, my nigga, you know I'm ready; I've been starving since I got out the pen. On the set, this is going to get a nigga right!" Tyreke was excited, caught up in his own thoughts.

"Alright," I said, "This is how it's going to go. You know I can't go in with you on this one!" I was really selective about how and when I got my hands dirty nowadays.

Tyreke responded with "fasho, fasho," while pulling on the blunt. This was his trademark response. So, I went on.

"We're going to switch cars, hop in the "g" ride, and I'm going to pull up right in front of the nigga's house. They got it booming over there, 24/7 with the pills and coke. I know for sure that he keeps a bag full of pills, a half-bird of soft, and most of his dough in shoe boxes in the bedroom. Get it all brodie! Knock on the front door, his baby momma is going to answer, they're super comfortable, because he never been robbed! When she opens the door, bo guard your way in past her and shut the door behind you. They got two little kids, but they usually be in their bedroom. The fat ass nigga is going to be sitting right there on the living room couch, probably playing Playstation or something. Drawdown on him immediately. He keeps a little .38 revolver under the couch cushion. Get that first, then do what you do. Don't shoot nobody, Tyreke! This is a robbery, not a murder." I was just sending a message to a nigga that was hustling on one of my blocks without paying his taxes. If he didn't understand this first message, the next one would leave him lifeless.

"I got you bro, don't trip," Tyreke said, but he was smiling at me as he said it.

"Ok, you got five minutes for everything, I'll be watching the clock. No more than five minutes because nigga's be coming over all the time to re-up. In and out, we split the cash and the dope fifty-fifty." I told him.

By the time I turn to get back on the freeway, Tyreke is already talking about the ways he's going to spend the money and how many bitches will be on his dick now that he's back, "up."

The rain is coming down hard now as Tyreke puts on that new Kodak Black Testimony. As the beat fills the car and the weed fills my lungs, my mind starts to drift off. Underneath it though is a feeling of uneasiness. It's not fear; this is just another day in my world. I push the feeling aside though, it's time to get back in my zone.

Chapter 9

A WAY OUT

[Past]

By high school, I was pretty much already fucked up. Plus, the emotional and physical violence I'd suffered over several years at the hands of my pops had made me aggressive with a quick temper. My mom was somewhat back in my life, but she was dealing with a crack addiction now. Don't ask me how it happened; it just did. It didn't diminish how much I loved my mom, but to say that it crushed my heart would be an understatement.

In my freshman and sophomore years in high school, I mastered the art of fucking up but not enough to be "officially" considered a "fuck up." I was stealing every weekend, mostly clothes from the department stores, and in the process, I was steadily building up my thug mentality. That mentality meant that I did what I want, when I want, to who I want. It meant that only my needs and my desires were important. It meant that I was placing myself in direct opposition to the rules that governed society. Not enough attention is paid to the childhood circumstances and conditions that lead to people's future life choices. Placing children in adverse environments with no mental or emotional tools to cope and no outlet is a recipe for disaster.

I got caught stealing a hat at the end of my sophomore year, so I decided that it was time to move on from that! My junior year, I got introduced to hustling. My nigga Rob was one of the few blacks at school with a whip!!! Not just any whip. He had a 1968 Chevy Camaro, pearl white with red rally stripes! It had Corvette Rally's, with beat. I knew him even though he was a senior, a year above me. I wouldn't say we were "friends," but that was about to change!

One day at lunch, I was in front of the soda machine when Rob slid up on me smelling like weed. He stepped in front of me in line without a second thought, then looked back at me, smiling.

"What you drinking lil nigga?" Rob said. Compared to him, I was a lil nigga in both physical and status stature. Rob was 6'2", and captain of the football team. I was 5'9" and ran long-distance track. I had just had my first piece of pussy the summer before, but it was well known that Rob got lots of pussy, usually older bitches that didn't go to our school.

"Pepsi," I said. Rob pulled out a wad of money that to me at that time, looked like a loaf of bread. He saw me staring at it then started laughing. He paid for our sodas, but before he left, he stopped, turned around, gave me twenty dollars, and told me to meet him right at this same spot at three thirty, after school.

"Don't be late, I've got football practice," he said as he walked off without waiting for a response. The rest of my day was a blur. It was amazing to me that a nigga in high school could just give out twenty dollars. Just buy another nigga's soda for him. Shit, twenty dollars would last me three days.

If I would have known then what I know now, I would have run straight fucking home. I would have run for the hills, but I didn't! I was curious, hungry, angry, and impressionable. Little did I know at the time, but I was about to let Rob set the course for my life for many years to come. I tell you this, addiction to money, especially "fast" money can be as addictive as crack. Strangely enough, it carries many of the same consequences. I met Rob at the soda machine that afternoon. I was there at 3:25 pm, five minutes early.

Chapter 10

STILL A RUSH

[Present]

"Come on nigga, drive, let's go!" Tyreke snapped me back to reality. I looked at my watch, four minutes and nine seconds. Tyreke was sweating but most importantly, I noticed that the duffle bag was full. I can't lie; a nigga still gets a rush out of shit like this. I put the car in drive and pulled off, careful not to speed. Can't risk getting pulled over in a stolen whip right after a lick. I stayed calm and composed even though my heart was beating out of my chest. After we were out of the neighborhood, and on to the main boulevard, Tyreke gave me a play-by-play.

"Nigga, it was just like you said brodie, except the fat ass nigga was sleeping on the couch!!! The kids wasn't there so that was cool. As soon as I pushed through the door, his bitch looked confused by what I had done, so I pulled out the banger and put my finger up to my lips, then told her "shhh". She did so I put her on the ground and zip-tied her. Then I duct-taped her mouth. Bro, the nigga was actually snoring the whole time."

At this, Tyreke couldn't help but to bust up laughing. When he finally stopped, with tears in his eyes, he said he needed to smoke. I felt the same way, but I told him not until we ditched the car and got somewhere safe. There's a lot of nigga's locked up for "celebrating" too early. Tyreke continued.

"So that nigga is on the couch snoring while I crept through the house just to make sure that no one else was there. I asked the bitch if anyone else was in the house, and she shook her head no, but I still had to check, ya feel me? When I got to the backroom, the coke, pills, and bread was all right there on the closet floor. Wasn't hidden or nothing. I had just started to scoop the shit up when I remembered what you said about him having a .38 revolver under the couch cushion. So, I went back to the living room and shook the nigga woke. When his eyes opened, he had this in his face." Tyreke pulled out his .40 and kissed it before putting it back in his waistband.

"When he realized what was going on, and saw his bitch zip-tied on the floor, the bitch ass nigga didn't give me no problems. I told him to cooperate so that him and his bitch would live. He couldn't even speak; he just nodded. He rolled his fat ass off the couch and onto his stomach, and then I tied him up!

"Here nigga!" Tyreke was handing me the .38 he took, but I knew that I wasn't going to keep it. It could be stolen or have a body on it!

Everything else went according to plan, but now I've got two things I need to do before I could relax. I had to get out of this stolen car, plus get Tyreke to part with his gun while we split the paper and the dope. I just didn't want Tyreke to get any bright ideas. You know what they say, "There's no honor amongst thieves."

Chapter 11

A WHOLE NEW WORLD

[Past]

At three twenty five on a Friday afternoon, two weeks before the end of my junior year, in front of the soda machine, my life changed. At that moment, I would have said that it was exactly what I'd prayed for and that I couldn't have asked for anything more. Today I know that just because we ask for something or want it, doesn't mean it's going to be good for us.

"Nigga, I saw you looking at my knot earlier," Rob was already half changed into his practice gear waiting for me. "And I notice that you've had that same pair of Nikes all year."

That was one of the most embarrassing moments of my life. I can still remember how I felt. I was ashamed. Rob stayed with the latest J's on his feet. He saw the hurt in my eyes.

"Don't trip lil nigga, I see something in you. Somebody had to put me on too, put me up on game. You smoke weed?" he asked.

I said, "Yeah, when I could afford it." As soon as I said it, I was embarrassed again. Rob reached into a little pocket in his football pants and pulled out more weed than I had ever seen. Looking back, it wasn't much, probably an eighth, but he handed it to me.

"This for you lil nigga. Meet me at the McDonalds across the street from the school tomorrow at one. It's Saturday tomorrow can you get there?" I wasn't going to be shamed a third time so I told him yeah of course. Even though I didn't live close to the school and had no way to get there on a Saturday, I'd have to find a way.

"Alright lil nigga, tomorrow I'll show you what's up; we'll find out if you got what it takes to be a hustler." I didn't know exactly what that meant but if it meant having a dope car, a fat bankroll, and fucking bad bitches, then that's exactly what I wanted to be. A hustler!! I couldn't sleep that night; my mind was racing like a Ducati. I was waiting at the McDonalds thirty minutes before Rob pulled up; his sound system had the whole car shaking. He was slumping. He had a bad little bitch in the front seat that fasho didn't go to our school. She had to be in her early twenties. Rob said, "Get in lil nigga, Samantha, get in the back seat."

Samantha opened the door. The passenger side window was already down. Then out stepped the baddest bitch I'd ever seen in my sixteen years. She was chewing gum. Her lips were juicy, shiny from Mack lip gloss. She smiled at me as she got out of the car, sliding into the backseat. I pulled the latch on the front seat so it would fold forward to give her room to get in. She bent over to get in the back seat, and I was stuck! She had the darkest, most flawless skin, plus the bottom half of her ass was hanging out of her designer shorts. The thing that I couldn't stop staring at was her pussy. Her pussy was so fat. When she put her first leg in the car, the shorts tightened up, forming a camel toe.

I had just never seen anything so beautiful. By the time I was done staring, Rob was busting up laughing. "Samantha," he said, "Say what's up to my nigga King."

She said, "Hi" and I mumbled something that probably sounded like Korean, but I felt twelve feet tall. I liked this feeling. I like the recognition. I loved the respect! I made up my mind right then, right there, that whatever the fuck it was going to take to live this lifestyle, I was going to do it. Whatever it takes!!!

Chapter 12

TWO MOVES AHEAD

[Present]

First stop was to get out of the whip occupied by two nigga's with guns. A recipe for disaster. I drove to a busy area around the basketball stadium and wiped the car down even though we were both wearing gloves. I grabbed the duffle bag and told Tyreke, "Come on bra."

"Where we going bro, to your crib?" Tyreke asked. I laughed inside but kept a poker face. I wish I would take a nigga like Tyreke to the place where I lay my head. It's good right now, but in six months when Tyreke's doing bad, he might get the idea that he could come rob me the way we just hit that sucka.

"Na nigga, my g-ma is visiting," I lied. "I don't want her in my business. We are going to catch a cab. I already have a suite reserved with a jacuzzi in it paid up for two days. After we handle our business, the room is yours."

I could tell Tyreke felt some kind of way about not going to my spot, but in the end, his vision of the good time he could have with a jacuzzi suite, plenty of paper and a few thousand pills got the best of him, just like I knew it would. This shit is chess, not checkers. The name of the game is to protect the King! Me!

We finally caught a cab. I told the cab driver to take us to the Green Store, which was bout two blocks from Tyreke's house. He looked at me, confused. I picked up my phone to text him so that the cab driver wouldn't hear what I was saying. The text read, "Nigga, I got you a room at the Embassy Suites on Arden and paid it up for two days. Security there is tight as fuck, and here come two nigga's pulling up. You with the dreads and gold teeth and me tatted from head to toe. Nothing good can come from carrying pistols right now, so we need to drop them off. You just call you a bitch or two, then get ready do it big for two days."

Tyreke liked the sound of that, and things went smooth from there. He ran to his house, dropping off both hamma's, and was back quick as fuck. He didn't even grab a change of clothes. He wouldn't say it, but he didn't want to be away from the duffle bag for long. I feel him on that! We went to the room, split five thousand pills, twenty ounces of raw coke, and thirty two thousand in cash. Not bad for four minutes and nine seconds of "work." Most importantly, a message had been sent to the nigga that thought he could hustle on one of my blocks without paying.

Chapter 13

PUT ON

[Past]

I rode with Rob all that day. He was serving dope sacks all over the city. Samantha sat in the back seat so quietly that after a while, I forgot she was there. Rob was lacin' me on the hustle. He was telling me how it was important not to trust no nigga, especially once you reach a certain status. He said nigga's is jealous, and jealousy caused Cain to kill his brother Abel. I just assumed that those were two nigga's that he knew.

Finally, Rob said, "So lil nigga you want to get money?" He didn't know that I had already committed my soul to it. I told him, yeah, but I didn't have no money to get started.

Rob laughed and said, "Lil nigga that's why I like you, your'e still honest! Don't trip, I'm going to put you on, but I got to see one more thing first." We rode in silence for about ten minutes before we pulled up in front of a dilapidated house with a broken-down wooden fence. The paint was peeling off the house like the make-up of a prostitute well past her prime. Four nigga's were sitting on the porch. Rob and I got out then walked into the yard. Rob introduced me to two of his brothers, a cousin, along with some friends he said he grew up with. I saw some of the nigga's around the neighborhood from time to time.

"Nigga's, this is King. I'm about to put him on, but ya'll know how we do it. No bitches in the circle."

My stomach bubbled because when he said that, everyone got up and walked down off the porch and to the front yard, which was half dead grass and half sand.

Rob looked at me, "You ain't no bitch, is you King?"

My mouth was so dry that all I could do is shake my head no. I was surrounded by the nigga's from the porch now.

"Well," Rob grinned. "These nigga's right here is standing between you and your'e scrilla. You ain't no bitch you say? What you gonna do?"

I shocked myself with how fast I lunged my hundred and forty five pounds at the first nigga catching him right below the eye. As I turned to swing on the next nigga I got fired on in the back of my head, but I didn't go down. Spinning, swinging with all my might, I got bounced from one nigga to the next. It wasn't my first fight, but it was the first time I'd been jumped. Finally Rob said, "thirty seconds," and everyone stopped. I was bloody, bruised, but not beaten.

Then something magnificent happened for the second time that day. The same nigga's that was just pounding on me lined up giving me hugs and dap saying shit like, "You a tuff lil nigga blood!", "You fasho ain't no bitch!"

If I felt twelve feet tall earlier when Rob first picked me up, now I was twenty feet tall if I was an inch. Rob called me to him, pulling me into his bulky frame. "Good shit," he said. "Come on, let's go get you cleaned up." Then and only then was I allowed in the house. My eyes couldn't believe what they saw once we walked in.

Chapter 14

DON'T JUDGE A BOOK

[Present]

Pulling back up to the gated community I called home, I finally let my mind and my body relax. One thing that many years of the game will teach you is that the moment you think your'e "good", you're not. It's a constant struggle of predator vs. prey. The thing about it, is that for the first half of the morning I was a predator. After that, I was potentially the prey. The police are sharks as well, so it's important for survival to always be aware of their whereabouts.

It was only eleven am when I got back to the house, so I sat in the car for about fifteen minutes, gathering my thoughts. Keisha was probably still in bed asleep, but she picks up on everything, so I like to keep my demeanor even keel so as to avoid a million questions. Sometimes it seems like the bitch was the police, the way she peeped everything.

I puffed on the half blunt that was left in the ashtray reflecting on a morning well spent. I didn't have any calls from the nigga we robbed, so that's a good sign. As I sit there, it trips me out how different white neighborhoods are from the hood. As long as you fit the ``image'' of what they expect visually and financially, they don't pay you no mind. With a Mercedes and Beemer in the driveway, the Brookes Brothers shirts and slacks I was fond of rocking, this white community has accepted me with open arms. I actually get regular smiles from my neighbors. I smile back, but I'm cracking up inside thinking, "if they only knew!"

As I walk in, the house is quiet. Keisha don't go to work until ten at night, so she usually sleeps till about one in the afternoon, but I smell weed in the air so at some point she got up and smoked. I walked down the hall, then peeked in the bedroom. I could see the silhouette of her full figure under the silk sheets. She was lying half on her side, and half on her stomach with her fat ass arched in the air. I felt my manhood throb; subconsciously, I grabbed my crotch.

I softly spoke her name, "Keisha," but got no response. I turned out the bedroom doorway, heading towards the spare bedroom where I keep my weights, my wardrobe, my arsenal, and my safe, along with all my financial records. I had the door reinforced with steel beams and had two deadlocks installed. I'm the only one with the keys. This led to a sort of argument with the girls, but I explained that it wasn't that I didn't trust them but that it was "safer" for them if they could say to the police or anyone else that they don't know what's in the room. That was partially true. The other part is that I trust no bitch! I know that what the bitch loves about me today; she could hate tomorrow!!! A woman has been the downfall of many great men.

I unlocked the door and walked in, locking it behind me. I went to the safe, punch in the code, and put the coke and pills at the bottom. I put the money at the top with my jewelry and watches. I didn't have to count it. I know that with today's take, I've got a little over fifty bands in the safe. It's not smart to keep too much cash on hand. My jewels are worth five times that. I strip down to my boxers, throw the clothes in the dirty hamper, and head to the bathroom for a shower. My day has just begun, I've still got shit to do, but I need to wash my ass before I officially get dressed for the day. After a quick shower complete with face and body grooming, I splash on some of that Versace Black cologne for men.

My underwear, socks, tee shirts, and shit are in the bedroom drawer where me and the girls sleep, so I head in there with only a towel wrapped around my waist. As I walked into the room, I see Keisha on her hands and knees at the edge of the king-sized bed. I started chuckling, "I knew your nosy ass wasn't sleeping, girl."

Keisha gave a throaty, deep sultry laugh. "I missed you, daddy. I felt you when you came in."

Smirking, I said. "You felt me huh?" By now, my cock was beginning to throb. The towel that was wrapped around my waist was pulsating up and down like it had a heartbeat. Keisha sat up with her legs folded behind her. She licked her lips as she half moaned, half growled. "Bring your sexy ass here nigga, so I can talk to you."

It's crazy how the mind works because at that moment, I looked in the full-sized mirrors on the closet doors and thought to myself, King, you really are a fine nigga. I was far removed from the 5'9" sophomore long-distance runner. Now I'm over six feet and weigh one hundred and ninety five pounds. I stayed ripped and toned from the habit of consistently exercising that I got while in prison. Short wavy hair, dark caramel skin, and a nice full set of white teeth gave me a clean and confident look. I'm also tatted from my neck to my calves. Like Nipsey Hussle (RIP) said, "Yeah, my body reads like a good book."

I dropped the towel. Without saying another word, Keisha took my dick in her hand, then started circling her wet tongue around the head in slow seductive motions. Almost as good as that feeling was the low moaning sound Keisha made while she teased my tip. In one motion, her hand dropped away while she took my growing thickness deep in her sloppy wet mouth. My dick grew inch by inch until the tip was deep in the back of her throat, making her gag and spit up more saliva.

Keisha knows what I like, so she turned over on her back at the edge of the bed with her face towards the ceiling and gently sucked my balls while she stroked my dick. "Fuck Keisha," I groaned. It's like she knows when I need this kind of treatment. Damn, this bitch is beautiful, I thought as she sucked my balls and jacked me off. I'm staring at how she opens and closes her legs at the knees to control the throbbing in her pussy. Keisha had beautifully sculpted thighs with pretty manicured feet. She really is a bad bitch.

Normally by now, Keisha would have been rubbing her tight smooth pussy with her fingers, but I could tell that this was all about me. That's one thing that I love about her; she knows when and how to let a nigga be a nigga. No doubt that I would have busted her lil pussy open if that was where this led, but there's something about a bad bitch just "serving" you while you relax and enjoy it that couldn't be beat.

With that, Keisha turned back over on her stomach, taking my dick in her mouth, stroking and sucking while she tightened the grip. "Damn, baby." I moaned.

"Mmmm, mmmm daddy, I want to taste all of you, cum in your bitch's pretty little mouth. Please fill my mouth up with your sweet cum."

As shit reached a climax, she did start playing with her pussy while moaning louder. This bitch is special!! I felt that first shake and shudder that lets you know you're about to bust. Keisha felt it too!

"That's it, daddy; fill me up so I can swallow every drop," Keisha pleaded seductively.

"Aaaagggh." My body convulsed as my abs clutched tight. I held the back of Keisha's head in place. She swallowed every drop. I just stood there for about two minutes; panting, looking down at her. She flopped back on the bed with the "cat that ate the canary" grin and said, "Tonight I'm going to cum all over that big dick, now have a good day. I'm going back to sleep before work."

Chapter 15

RESPECT

[Past]

I went home that night beat up but feeling more loved, respected, and appreciated than I ever had before in my life. Rob wasn't lying when he said he was going to put me on. When we went into the house after the fight, there were drugs, money, and several guns out in plain sight. We were only inside for about ten minutes, but I was hooked. This was power! This was freedom! The best part was that they weren't depending on no one but themselves to make it happen.

I left that evening with an ounce kush and a little chrome 25. My first gun! When I tell you that I distinctly remember the change in the way I felt about myself and my life leaving that day, I tell you because it was real. In my possession, I had "independence" in the form of finances from weed sales. I had power in the form of my .25 cal. I didn't even have bullets at the time.

From there would come respect! If a nigga wasn't going to give it, I was going to take it. I bagged up my first ounce that night in all twenty dollar sacks. Rob said it would bring about six hundred. To me at the time, six hundred might as well have been six million. In my mind, I became a "man" that day. I remember after everyone went to sleep that night, I went to the bathroom with my little chrome, slightly rusted .25 and cut on the bathroom light. Pointing the gun at myself in the mirror, I said shit like, "Nigga, I wish you would," "You got me fucked up," "You playing with my money punk?"

Self-fulfilling prophecy, I would use these phrases amongst others during my career in the streets.

Chapter 16

IF YOU WANT IT DONE RIGHT

[Present]

Having Keisha top me off was just what I needed. Now I was relaxed! I was focused! I hopped back in the shower real quick to rinse off, then I rolled a blunt. I went to the kitchen, poured some Captain Crunch, and sat on the couch in the living room, thinking about the rest of my day. I had to pick my nigga Jamille up at two so that we can meet this white boy at three. It's just a meet and greet, but the white boy is supposed to be interested in copping four birds. This will be the first time I've let Jamille set up a meet like this. They say that when you want something done right, do it yourself, but he's one of my three lieutenants, so I give him the opportunity. I'll just keep my antennas on high alert today. I've only been out of prison three years, but I supply ninety percent of the city's dope. Theres no way that I'm going to let a bad deal lined up by another nigga derail all that I've built. I've got bigger plans still!

The buyer is flying in from the East Coast. Some Jewish cat that I've never met. Jamille has screened him though and says he's legit, so we set up the meet. It's important to make your desired first impression when doing business, so today I'm rocking my grey Armani slacks, a long-sleeve charcoal grey silk shirt with some black and grey Louis loafers. No socks.

The only jewelry I'm wearing is my Rolex Oyster Perpetual. I learned long ago that attempting to be too flashy or flossy can attract the wrong kind of attention. I always tell my nigga's that you don't see Tom Cruise or Will Smith wearing a gang of chains and shit, do you? When a nigga is really at his money, his whole presence and his being says money. The buyer needs to know that we want you; but don't need you.

Today I'm going to leave my "baby" at home. No, not Keisha, my .357 snub nose revolver. This is just a meet and greet, plus Jamille will have his trademark "Bonnie and Clydes," two matching Sig Sauer nines that he wears in a fancy holster. The nigga runs around like the guns is legal and shit.

As I'm about to leave the house, Jamille calls, "King, what's good?" He asked.

"Shit about to be on my way." I knew he wanted to ask me something, and I was in a rush, so I just asked. "What's up nigga." Jamille hesitated momentarily before speaking.

"Hey, you think you can pick up ole' boy from the airport? He called saying he was having a problem with his rental car."

Now, this was a red flag for me. I don't even know this cat yet, and I'm a stickler for security. Especially my own. I don't want this mutha fucka knowing what kind of car I drive or anything else about me except the fact that I have some fish scales for sale.

Plus, what kind of mutha fucka comes all the way from the East Coast and then has trouble renting a car at the airport once he gets here? Especially someone who supposedly has over a quarter million to spend on dope. There are two things any hustler should learn to pay attention to if he wants to survive in these streets. One, is a woman's intuition. Not just any bitch, but the one that's really down for you. You know who she is, the one who puts up with all of your bullshit, and is still there for you. Two, is a hustler's instinct. In a sea of sharks, zagging left when you should have zigged right, can make the difference between incarceration, death, or success. Disregarding either of these rules, inevitably leads to a fall. I was about to violate one of my own rules.

Chapter 17

HUNGER FOR RICHES

[Past]

It didn't take long for me to commit myself to my new hustle just like it didn't take long for me to establish my clientele. I contacted everyone I knew who smoked weed, letting them know I had "fat" twenty sacks now. I kept a blunt rolled so they could taste the product, but I didn't have enough to be giving out no free samples. It only took me three days to get that first zip off, so I called Rob immediately to let him know I had his bread and that I wanted to cop another zip of my own.

Rob said, "Lil nigga, I knew it was in you; swing by the spot in about an hour, I'll hook you up."

I put the six hundred in my sock. By far, the most money I had ever had in my possession. I made a quick stop at the mall to look at some Jordan's that a week ago I wouldn't have a chance in hell in getting. Right there, I promised myself that I would buy them in two weeks. I made a commitment to get out and increase my hustle. I left the mall that day, making my way to Rob's house, feeling real good about my future.

"Sup lil nigga, come up the stairs and come in," Rob said as he waved me in. This time there wasn't any other nigga's on the porch or at the house. We talked for a minute while he asked me about how I got the kush off so quickly. I downplayed my hunger for riches while giving him the props. I was beginning to learn that there was an art to getting friends and influencing people. People tend to like to have people around them that make them feel good about themselves.

"You gave me the game; I just ran with it," I told him with a big smile on my face. He gleamed like a disco ball, smiling from ear to ear.

"Ok lil nigga, where the dough?" Rob asked. I reached down into my sock, and 1 pulled out a wad of money. A mixture of fives, tens and twenties. I handed it to him. Without counting it, Rob said. "That's six hundred, right?"

"Yeah," I acknowledged, nodding my head. I know it was because I counted it no less than ten times just for the joy of it. He threw the money in a shoebox on the floor by the table and pulled out two more zips, then tossed them to me. I was eager to go, but we talked for a few more minutes before I got up to leave. While standing on the porch with Rob inside the doorway, I turned to ask him a question that had been on my mind.

"Hey, can I ask you something?" I whispered.

"Sup lil nigga?" Rob smirked as he looked down on me from the porch.

"Remember when you told me to trust no nigga? Rob shook his head yes.

"Does that mean you too?" I asked. Rob turned deadly serious. Then he took the blunt he was smoking out of his mouth.

"Especially me lil nigga, especially me!" Rob said chuckling as he spun back in the house, shutting the door behind him.

For about a year, I tried to manage hustling with school. My grades dropped, but I didn't give a fuck; I was touching money in a way that I never knew possible. It only took me a week, not two, to get those Jordan's I wanted. Right after my seventeenth birthday, I bought my first car for three grand cash.. It wasn't my dream car, but I hustled for that shit so to me it could have been a Bentley. I started buying the clothes that were in style. I even got a few pieces of low-grade jewelry.

Here's the thing about the game, though. The thing about the streets is that enough is never enough. I had at that time acquired all the shit that I was sure would make me happy. I had a sort of a "reputation," and I had pulled my gun on a few nigga's but at that time, I hadn't shot anyone. That would change! I had a car and a pretty fly wardrobe for a young nigga. I had a consistent income from drug money. It took less than a year before it wasn't enough. My car wasn't as "fly" as it had first been. As I compared it to older and more advanced hustlers, it didn't cut it anymore. I wanted nicer clothes and flashier jewels too. All of that would cost more money. I hollered at Rob. He told me that he knew this would happen eventually. He proceeded to tell me that hustling weed is cool at first but that the real money was in coke. Crack really. The difference being he said that people who smoke weed "want" it, and people that smoke crack "needed" it. I had just been introduced to a whole other beast., but I jumped in with both feet!!

Chapter 18

TRICK BAG

[Present]

The white boy got in the car at the airport. I could tell that he's not impressed by the 2015 rental Impala I picked him up in, but I wasn't going to use one of my cars. This car is rented under a false name, so it can't come back to me. Plus, fuck what he thinks; this is business. He's wearing a nice dark blue double vested pinstripe suit with a pair of Versace dress shoes. He looks to be about forty and he's tanned with a square jaw. To me, he looks more Italian than Jewish, but all white boys look the same to me. He wastes no time attempting to start a conversation.

"So, you're the infamous King, huh? Jamille has told me a lot about you. Well, you guys, really, I'm glad we're finally getting together."

I nodded without saying a word. I always tell my nigga's, especially Jamille, that "lose lips sink ships." I could tell right away that Jamille has been trying to impress this cat. After about five minutes of attempting to make small talk with no success, he finally shut the fuck up so we rode in silence. For all I knew, this fool had a wire on. Ain't no way my voice is going to be on tape saying anything! Good or bad!!

We pulled up to the Ramada Inn, where I had told Jamille to rent a room. He was waiting in the parking lot, sitting on his motorcycle, a blue and gray Yamaha R1 with a matching helmet and jacket. I told him last year to stop riding that death trap after he crashed, breaking his leg and collar bone, but Jamille is a risk taker. He does what he feels. It's going to catch up with him one day.

I hopped out the car and told the white boy who I now knew was named Antonio, definitely a fucking Italian, to hold tight and that I'd be right back. I walked towards that hotel entrance, passing Jamille on the way.

"King, what's up nigga?" Jamille asked as I walked by. I kept walking without saying a word heading directly into the lobby. He followed behind me and finally caught up. I told him to give me the room key, which I saw was room 114.

"Come on nigga let's talk in the room real quick," I said as I headed that way with him following. As I slid the card key in to open the door, I couldn't help but think that this "Antonio" lied to Jamille about being "Jewish." I wonder what other lies he's fed the nigga Jamille, and why!!

Chapter 19

FAT LEON

[Past]

Money was coming fast now! Switching hustles from weed to crack was like going from a VW bug to a new Porsche. The fiends weren't patient enough to call you and then wait for you to bring them the rock, so a nigga had to be on the block if he was serious about a come up. Well, I lived on the block. You ain't hearing me! I literally got a little beat-up studio apartment downtown not five minutes from the dope track. Within six months, I had the block sowed. I made sure my dope was the best, I served it the fattest, and I was always available. This was a recipe for success but it was also when problems with other hustlers began. I wasn't mad, no one likes losing money, and I was getting other hustlers customers. Rob had warned me about jealous nigga's!!! I still remember what he had told me about Cain killing his brother over jealousy. I could feel in my gut that the time was fast approaching when I was going to have to make an example out of someone. I didn't know when or who it would be; circumstances would determine that.

By this time, I had upgraded from the rusted .25 cal to my first real gun. It was a Taurus 380. I got it fresh out of the box. I can't lie, I was itching to use it, and the way those nigga's was hating on the block, it seemed they wanted the same thing. In particular, there was one fat super black nigga named Fat Leon. He was older, probably twenty-five or so. He was known on the turf for beating nigga's up then robbing them for their dope sack.

When the clientele to the dope house would slow up, I'd hit the block to see if I could catch some new customers. In the downtown area, you never knew where you might find new business by just being out and available. When I turned the corner by the light rail station off E Street, I saw Fat Leon sitting at the bus stop. He normally posted at different bus stops in the area to slang his dope.

"King, my man, come here real quick, let me holla atcha." Fat Leon yelled out. His mouth was open and he was breathing hard even though he was just sitting there. I went over but stayed standing in front of him. "What's good?" I said.

"Shit, it's slow out here, I've only made a forty spot, and I've been out since seven this morning." What the fuck this got to do with me, I thought. This fat nigga and me have only nodded in passing on the block, and now he acting like we're best friends that ain't seen each other in a few days.

"That's what's up!" I scowled. At that moment, I became aware that I didn't have my banger on me. I never hit the dope track with it. The police could and did pull up on nigga's out the blue. There was no way to get rid of a gun if that happened.

"Sit down, King I want to chop it up with you for a second; I got some shit on my mind." Fat Leon gurgled as he spoke. I had stashed my bundle of rocks in the alley behind the track. If I got any new customers, I would just run and grab what they wanted. I only had about fifteen dollars in cash on me, so I saw no jeopardy in hearing what was on this nigga's mind. Keep your friends close, and your enemies closer is what I was told.

Fat Leon started. "So, you done made quite a name for yourself since you popped on my scene King." I noted Fat Leon's use of the word "my," but I didn't respond, just listened.

"I see you a real hustling young nigga, bout your dough, not like these part-time nigga's that be running around here. That's why I rob these nigga's and take their bundles." With that, I stood up.

"Nah." He continued, "Not you, King, but I've been on this block longer than anyone. I know you're eating right now;

some of my old knocks won't even fuck with me because of you."

Here we go I thought; here comes the attempted shake down. Wiping sweat off his greasy face, Fat Leon shifted on the bench so that we were facing each other, eye to eye. His expression changed; he was no longer looking like we were "best friends."

"This is what we can do, King," Fat Leon started. "I know you got that little studio apartment on E & 16ᵗʰ street booming. All the fiends are talking about it! I want to use it!!! You can hustle out of it one day; I'll use it the next day; like that." He said. "That way, we can avoid any future problems between us." Fat Leon took a deep gurgling breath as he finished talking. He stared at me with a long, hard, and calculating look.

I felt like I'd been kicked in the stomach by a mule. He said it so casually, so matter of factly, that I thought for a second that he knew something that I didn't or that there was more to what he was going to say; like what he would be bringing beneficial to the table. He just stared at me! I composed myself enough to say, "Let me get back to you," then I got up to walk off.

"King." Fat Leon said. "Don't take too long to get back to me; I get mad when I feel like someone is taking my kindness for weakness." I nodded while walking off. There was no mistaking that Fat Leon was threatening me. I knew that he was capable of enforcing the threat if given the opportunity. He wouldn't get it!

That night I replayed the scenario in my mind a thousand times, working myself into a frenzy. Who does he think he is? Who does he think I am? A punk? A bitch? This fat nigga thought he was going to threaten his way into my pockets? Everything I'd worked for, sacrificed, and given up was in jeopardy! Shit, I felt like my entire existence was in danger. For a split second, I felt like that vulnerable kid who's mom left when he was five. For a moment I felt like the angry thirteen year old who was helpless to stop his dad from beating his ass. I made up my mind on two things that day. First, I would never threaten a nigga. If I had to do something to a nigga, he wouldn't see it coming. Two, a nigga will never talk to me like that again. Fat Leon had sealed his fate that afternoon.

Chapter 20

FATAL MISTAKE

[Present]

We walked in the room and shut the door behind us. I walked to the window, looking down on the hotel parking lot. Without turning around, to look at Jamille, I said. "When he comes into the room, I want you to strip search him."

"What." Jamille huffed. "What are you talking about? Why are you tripping King? We trying to do business with this cat."

"Exactly Jamille, we want to do business, and I don't know who he is, but he seems to know all about me."

There was no need to go into detail about the shit the white boy had said on the way from the airport. I could tell by his facial expression that Jamille knew exactly what I was getting at. "Go get the buyer Jamille, bring him in, and make sure he's not wearing a wire. We can't talk about anything until then." I finished.

"You making me look bad King, I set this shit up," Jamille almost screamed. That's the problem I thought; you set this shit up. I watched Jamille go to the car to get the buyer. It looked like there was a heated discussion. I couldn't hear the words but assumed that Jamille had told him he'd have to get strip-searched. As Jamille and the buyer headed from the car back towards the hotel lobby, I got that old familiar feeling that I'd tried to keep buried deep down inside. My trigger finger was starting to itch. Once my bloodlust was let loose, it couldn't be satiated. Gone was that cool, logical, introspective King. Blood would spill! My jaw was clenching while my thoughts took me back to the things that I'd had to do to get where the fuck I am today. Kidnapping, murder, torture were old companions of mine. Fake friends and enemies alike had felt the wrath of my blood thirst. Then came

a knock at the door!

Chapter 21

BOOK 2 – FIRST KILL

[Past]

"Nephew, nephew, where you been? I been looking for you. These nigga's been running around with that bunk dope," said the smoker as he shifted from foot to foot in his tattered shoes.

"Yeah, I been out the way for a few days taking care of some personal business, what's good though, you trying to spend some bread or what? You know I don't like being out here in the open like this on the block." I shot back quickly.

One way to fasho get rolled up on by the police and get arrested was to be on the block dressed dope boy fresh, talking to a dope fiend who looks like he could be a zombie on the "Walking Dead."

"Na na youngster, I'm low on dough today," he responded.

I gave him that why the fuck you wasting my time look and was about to spin off when he said, "King! I got something better than money." He stopped talking, interrupted by a coughing fit that ended when he spit up the nastiest shit I had ever seen.

"Bitch ass nigga, you wasting my time. If you ain't got no bread, then get the fuck out my face!" The smoker grinned a toothless smile with nothing but black ass gums, scratched his ass, then went on. "Fat Leon been looking for you." He had my attention now. I looked him in the eyes. Now his eyes were smiling, he knew that he had something good to tell me.

"Come on let's walk around the corner so I can hear what you got to say. On my mama if you waste my time, I'm gonna beat yo ass in this alley."

"Come on King, come on youngsta," he groaned. "You gonna love me for this one, shit, you might give ole Fred your whole sack after this."

"Yeah okay we'll see, come on!" I said as I took off for the alley.

There were a few other hustlers out on the block, but no sign of Fat Leon. I found a spot in the back alley on the side of a dumpster next to an apartment building. It smelled like piss and old beer, but it was out of sight of any prying eyes. I had used this spot before to bust knocks.

"Talk nigga." I scowled.

Dope fiend Fred began to tell me how the day before he had been walking on a street past one of the bus stops that Fat Leon be hustling from. Dope fiend Fred said he was looking to spend his couple dolla's when one of the young hustla's, Marlon walked up. He said that Fat Leon and the young hustler started talking like he wasn't even there. Then it got good. "Black Leon asked Marlon if he had he seen your bitch ass?" The smoker got excited as he told me what was said.

I just stared, so he continued. "He told Marlon that a few days ago that he told you that he was going to start using your trap house. That you said OK and agreed to letting him use it." The smoker searched my eyes to see if it was true and now it was clear that this smoker had heard a conversation, there was no way for him to know this.

Fat Leon was already dead, he just didn't know it. The last two days had been spent planning the best time and way to down the nigga. The bus stops he sits at are in the open and have a lot of foot traffic from people getting off and on the light rail, so that wouldn't work. Then the dope fiend gave me the info that I really needed. He told me where that loud mouth bitch ass nigga Fat Leon parks his car in the morning when he comes to the block. My plan was set, I'd catch that nigga slipping early in the morning and tell his momma to pick out her best black dress.

"Take your clothes off." I barked at the smoker.

"What, what King, what did I say?" the smoker asked scared.

"You did good but strip down to your drawers, hurry the fuck up!" I yelled. He started stripping, slowly at first, until he saw me reach in my sock pulling out a plastic bundle with eight fat rocks in it. I waited until he was down to his dirty boxers, then tossed him the bundle. "Get the fuck out of here, you never saw me." He didn't say a word, just disappeared like a puff of smoke. I picked up his nasty ass clothes, rolled them in a ball then dipped off. At the age of seventeen, I was about to commit my first homicide.

It took me two days, waiting in the early morning cold, before I finally got my opportunity. I was dressed in dope fiend Fred's clothes, down to the shoes. A dark green beanie that looked brown now because I had soaked it in mud water the night before was covering my head. I wanted it to look like it belonged to someone who lived on the street. I also smeared mud on my face and arms. I hadn't washed my ass for two days. I couldn't recognize myself, so I knew no one else would. I grabbed a shopping cart from a nearby grocery store and filled it with a broom, blanket, some cans, and an empty Miller Lite box. I was ready to go. I was about to lite this nigga up like a Christmas tree.

Chapter 22

The Hit

Six thirty in the morning on a Wednesday was a typical day, for this time of year for the capital of California. It was October, two days before Halloween and it was overcast but not raining. It felt right! I was just about to curse dope fiend Fred with his "information", when I saw Fat Leon's Buick Lesabre turn the corner. He had a scraper with twenty-two's on it, clean as fuck with beat. I'm not going to lie, for a split second I had to admire his ass. He was a nigga that was used to taking what he wanted. Most days he was the first trapper on the block. Fat Leon's car, and the music shut off, then I turned on. I was surprisingly calm! It was the calm before a fucked-up storm.

Coming out from between two apartment buildings dressed in dope fiend Freds clothes I slowly pushed the shopping cart. I had on a pair of brown burner gloves. The empty twelve pack Miller Lite box was propped up on the part of the cart where bitches put their kids while grocery shopping. I made my way towards my prey as his car door slowly began to open, but his fat ass didn't hop right out, so I stopped with my head down and fucked with the cans that I had in the main part of the cart. Fat Leon's car door finally swung wide open. As Fat Leon shifted his weight to get out the car, the whole car leaned to the side.

Pushing the cart closer, I put my right hand in the Miller Lite box where the .380 Colt was waiting to bust a nut. Stepping out the car, Fat Leon immediately surveyed his surroundings, a hustler's instinct, I thought. He looked dead at me, at the "bum" walking his way and determined that there was no threat, so he turned sideways to lock his driver's side door. Ten more feet and the neighborhood was about to get woke up. Fat Leon put to sleep.

"You got any spare change, young blood?" I asked in my best homeless voice. Leon turned with a sneer on his face, reaching his hand in his right pocket. Before he could pull out a nickel, the .380 barked like a rabid pit bull. The first shot hit him right in his fat ass stomach. His shirt puffed up at the belly like a small gust of wind ran up under it, but the nigga didn't drop. He just looked confused and grabbed his stomach. I fired three more shots in succession. "Pop, pop, pop."

"Die mutha fucka die," I growled.

The next three shots hit his upper torso. His hand reached up to hold his chest like he was standing for the national anthem. He collapsed on the sidewalk with his car keys still in the door. Breathing heavily with a little blood trickling out his mouth and down his lip he looked up as I approached. He was trying to say something but no words were coming out. His mouth was just opening and closing like a fish out of water gulping for air. I reached in my pocket, pulled out a chess piece then threw it on the ground next to his fat ass body. It was the black King!

I stood over the nigga and had to wipe my mouth with the back of my gloved hand. I was salivating. Pointing the .380 right at the nigga's melon I pulled the trigger. Nothing! I pulled again but the trigger was hard, it was stuck in place. I looked down, fuck. There was a bullet jammed sideways in the chamber. I didn't have the experience yet to know how to unjam it. I didn't know what to do, but I didn't panic.

"What's going on down there? Hey you, what's going on?" A female voice rang out from an apartment window above me. I didn't look up, I just kept my head down, grabbed the cart, and went back the way I came between the apartment buildings.

I left the cart in the apartment building's small parking lot, and took the Miller Lite box with the four spent shell casings in it, then walked to a bicycle that I had stashed a few blocks away. I rode for about five minutes, hitting side streets and alleys to make sure that I wasn't followed. It was a clean getaway. At least I thought so.

Chapter 23

KING HEROIN

[Present]

Jamille walked in the room with the buyer following close behind. It was clear from the look on his face plus his posture, that he was salty. He felt like King treated him like a kid, never let him make decisions, and wouldn't let him shine the way that he deserved to. Shit, he'd put in work too. King wasn't the only one with bodies under his belt and he had never bitched up. He deserved respect. Plus, it had been three years since he'd been playing second man to King. The nigga King wouldn't negotiate, he was uncompromising with the way he wanted shit done, with the way, "it had to be".

On my momma, Jamille thought, I can do everything that bitch ass nigga can do if not better. It might be time for that pretty boy to get knocked down a few notches Jamille thought as he instinctively caressed his twin nines in their suede holsters.

The truth of the matter is that Jamille's dough was low. He was sick of the way King was so strict. So particular about who they dumped the dope to. Cash was fucking cash nigga and I'm tired of waiting, Jamille thought. Plus, the monkey was on his back heavy now. Ever since Jamille's motorcycle accident, he had been taking Oxycontin prescribed by the doctor. Once his prescription ran out, he started buying "scripts" from other people, but now even that was drying up, but the opiate was an oppressive master. The first day he decided that he would just quit cold turkey, he got kicked in his ass with a rude awakening. The opiate was in charge now. He was sick in bed for three days with the sweats, chills, stomach cramps and an indescribable back pain. He tore up his bedroom, and then his bathroom just hoping and praying that somehow, some way there was at least one pill to help ease the pain. When Jamille was on the brink of feeling that he would go crazy, literally crazy, God reached out to him in the form of a white boy neighbor knocking on the door to see if he had any weed for sale. By that time Jamille had been trying to sell whatever he could, to whoever he could for money to support his addiction. He also had to be sure that it didn't get back to King that he was using. "Never get high on your own supply," was an old school code but one that they had all sworn by. King would kill him if he found out he was getting high.

"Hey Jamille." The neighbor said as Jamille opened the front door. Jamille answered the door looking like death worked over. He was hunched over from the stomach cramps, and his face was dripping sweat. He had an agonizing and pathetic look on his face.

"Damn bro, you look sick, you got the flu or something." The skinny white boy asked suspiciously.

"I'm sick, what the fuck you want?" Jamille hissed.

The neighbor stood silent for a moment just staring at Jamille. "You're sick all right. I'll be right back." He left. Jamille stood in the doorway, using the frame to hold himself up while he watched his neighbor go back to his house. Jamille didn't have the energy to tell him not to come back. The white boy came right back grinning from ear to ear.

"What the fuck you go get, some fucking cold medicine or something? I'm good, that shit won't help me," Jamille grimaced.

"Nah," said the neighbor. "Trust me, let me in, I got what you need."

At this point Jamille was desperate so he stepped aside to let him in. The white boy went straight to the kitchen and started running the sink water. He pulled out what looked like a tootsie roll, and then a Visine bottle. Jamille was spent, he was exhausted, so at that moment he was willing to try anything to feel better. A few minutes later the white boy came out of the kitchen with the Visine bottle in one hand and a spoon in the other. He sat on the couch next to Jamille, then squirted a small amount of a brown liquid onto the spoon.

"Snort this." The white boy said as he held out the spoon. Jamille asked no questions. He snorted, then leaned back. Magic happened.

In sixty seconds, not only did every discomfort, and every bit of pain that he was just wrenching from go away, but a warm "spirit" came over him that told him everything would be alright from now on. The spirit told him not to worry about being in pain ever again. Jamille sat with the neighbor until the sun came up the next morning snorting heroin while watching reruns of "Good Times." He got nauseous and threw up once, but felt completely better as soon as he did. Jamille's neighbor became his dealer of the soft brown sticky candy after that. A month later, the same neighbor came over with a needle clutching a rubber hose and Jamille slammed heroin for the first time. You can't serve two masters!!! Jamille had a new

"King." King heroin.

Chapter 24

POPPING

[Past]

The next six months passed like a blur; I had shit popping. For my eighteenth birthday I bought a 1973 Oldsmobile Cutlass Fastback. It had swivel bucket seats, Flow Masters exhaust with a 350 Rocket engine, totally rebuilt. It was pearl grey, with burgundy rally stripes, and burgundy interior. It had two twelve-inch subwoofers, with four six by nines, plus mid's and lows for the beat.

I loved that car but my new real toy was a brand-new Glock 50. The next time I had to down a nigga, it wouldn't take four shots. The Glock 50 is a hand cannon. Nigga's know what happens to flesh when a hand cannon spits.

The block was different after Fat Leon's demise. It was clear by the way these soft ass nigga's on the block was acting that they had a good idea who did it. I walked the streets now with my balls dragging on the sidewalk. Nigga's crossed the street when they saw me coming, or they got real busy on their cell phones with their heads down as I passed. Nigga's knew that with me it was no words, only action. No one was trying to be the next one put on their ass, but I wasn't in the game to be a bully. I was in the game for success. I wanted to be rich, so as long as no one interfered with that mission, all would be good.

My nineteenth birthday came and passed. Shit was good. I was all over the city slumping. The Flow Masters on the Cutlass growled like a wolf and bitches came like rats to a cheese factory. I was turning down pussy now. Fucking was a past time, not a priority. My goal was to be a boss nigga; not a floss nigga. I stopped buying jewelry and instead I rented a legit apartment downtown. I got it fully furnished and then I set out to accomplish my next goal of buying my first brick. The streets had something else in store for me.

At the time, me and Rob had gotten pretty close. He introduced me to the game but now I was a hustler on an equal level as him. We'd ride back to back through the city in our cars smoking weed and knocking bitches. I was still buying my dope from Rob and I felt I owed him a lot.

One day Rob called and said, King. I was no longer, "lil nigga". "Can you ride with me real quick? I need you to make a run with me to watch my back." Rob asked.

He knew about Fat Leon and I felt honored that he wanted me to ride with him.

"Fasho my nigga, when you gonna swoop me up? I'm just at the house posted." I answered.

"I'll be there in an hour."

"Fasho, in a min." I said and hung up.

Rob picked me up telling me that the play wasn't a big deal. He was selling ten pounds of weed to some nigga's from Oakland but he'd dealt with them before.

I said, "Cool, don't trip, if it gets real the Glock will eat a nigga's face for dinner." I laughed at the thought. I'm not going to lie, that gun made me feel invincible.

We pulled up to Land Park, a big heavily wooded park that was especially dark at night. We pulled by the basketball courts. As we did, a set of car headlights blinked on and off.

"That's them." Rob whispered. We pulled alongside their car and parked. Two nigga's got out and both of them hopped in the backseat behind us. We had to turn sideways in the front seats to talk these nigga's. It gave me a bad vibe. It made me feel vulnerable. Rob seemed cool though and it was his move, so I relaxed a little bit.

Before I had time to think another thought, BOOM, Rob's brain and skull fragments were splattered on the front windshield, slumping him forward with the dead weight of his bulky frame. Then I felt it! Cold steel on the back of my neck. It wasn't hard to figure out that this was it; any second darkness. All I remember thinking though, is why did we let these nigga's sit behind us?

"You want to live young nigga?" One of the gunna's asked from the back seat. My mouth was so dry that I couldn't speak, so I just nodded. He kept talking.

"This was some personal shit with that nigga, it don't matter what," said the one that had just made Rob's head explode like a melon dropped from two stories up. As he did, he reached in the front seat and started feeling around until he found my banger in my waistband.

"I knew he wouldn't bring a nigga who wasn't strapped." He chuckled as he pulled the Glock from my waste. "Get out the car, walk, and don't look back or you get put in the black bag with this rat." I did as I was told and shortly after that I heard both cars start up and then drive away. They found Rob's body the next day in his burnt up car. He was charred to a crisp. Rob must have meant it when he said that he couldn't be trusted.

Chapter 25

RECKLESS AMBITION

[Present]

Jamille shut the door to the hotel room behind me, standing defiantly. I laughed inside but stared expressionlessly. This had always been the problem with Jamille, ever since we were young. He only thought one move ahead, so he never saw the full picture. In life, like in chess, you got to see three moves ahead or you get checkmated. Jamille has been getting high for about a year. My own momma was fiend, so I know the signs like I know every scratch on my cars. I've been preparing for what was to come since then. A dope fiend can't be trusted. Period!!

"He refuses to strip down King." Jamille bristled. "I don't think he should have to either. That's not how you start doing business with someone."

I just nodded my head. Jamille has that pasty look that addicts get when it gets close to time for their next fix. He's just made his first grave mistake though. He should have never questioned my decision. Jamille would have never acted like this before he started getting high.

"What do you propose Jamille?" I asked smirking.

"Let's just do business King, just get this shit over wit. He got da bread and I need da dough. Did you bring the dope?" Jamille asked.

I shook my head no! No words! The fact that Jamille just said the word dope out loud in front of a stranger confirmed what I'd been thinking, that he had become a liability. I began to grab my car keys off the bed to start heading for the door. Jamille jumped back to block the door while in one motion pulling a nine out of his right-side shoulder holster. The white boy's eyes were as big as some twenty-inch rims. Jamille didn't point the gun at me, but had it pointed at the ceiling. The white boy had both his hands raised in the air like he was in a stick up!

"Come on now fellas, there's no need for this amongst friends. Come on now, put the gun away." The white boy pleaded.

I just stared at my lifelong friend. Who I loved like a brother, who had turned into a drug addict. Who I would now have to put six feet deep.

I nodded, intent on not saying a word that could be played again in court then used against me; then I smiled, gesturing for Jamille to put his weapon up. He finally did, but had an ashamed look on his face like a nigga that had got caught in some under age pussy. I walked up to him, hugged him and whispered in his ear, "I love you, I got you, let's meet back here at ten in the morning tomorrow ok?"

"Ok King, ok, I'm sorry for that my nigga, I don't' know what came over me brah." Jamille explained stuttering. I just smiled and squeezed his shoulder, then began to exit the room. As I was leaving, I heard Jamille telling the white boy that everything was good and that we'd get down to business tomorrow morning.

Once in the car I made two quick calls. One to my nigga Rico, the other to my nigga Cash. I told them to meet me at the "spot" tonight at ten, we had things to discuss. When they weren't managing the legit businesses I owned, Rico and Cash enforced the blocks and trap houses I had under my control. I only dealt with my three lieutenants personally, face to face. They employed young hustlers to work the houses that they had under their control. It would be very hard for anyone to say that they did a deal with me. Once off the phone I couldn't help but think that I only had three people in the world that I trusted and it was about to be two!

Chapter 26

BOOT CAMP

[Past]

During the walk home four miles away I was numb. I couldn't put together two concurrent thoughts. This was a part of the game that I hadn't yet experienced. The pain. The loss! Rob's murder had me shook.

 No sooner than I got home, took a shower, and sat down to roll a blunt...BANG BANG BANG, came at the door. My stomach dropped!! Looking through the peep hole I saw a line of police officers a mile long and figured that it had something to do with Rob's murder at the park, but how could it get back to me so quick? At that instant the door busted, splintered and cracked in. Several police officer's swarmed into the tiny apartment.

"Get on the fucking ground, face down, don't move a fucking, muscle or your'e dead you got it!" One cop yelled. The rest of the op's stormed in and slapped a piece of paper down on the ground by my face. The cop that seemed to be in charge said, "This is a warrant for your apartment. We're looking for a .380-caliber firearm as well as certain clothes that we believe may be evidence in the murder of Leon Murdock aka Fat Leon. I was stunned. There was nothing to say! They tore up the apartment! When they were done my couch cushions were ripped, my closet and kitchen ransacked, but they didn't find shit.

With the selfish mind of a hustler I thought that if Rob wouldn't have got killed earlier tonight, and I hadn't had my gun taken, I would have got caught with my .50 cal and I'd be in jail right now. When the cops left, I sat there thinking and I finally determined that based on the day's events, it was time for a drastic change. Without telling a soul, I joined the Army.

I didn't give much thought of what my MOS (Military Job) would be because the point at that moment was to get the fuck out of town. Accepting a five thousand dollar signing bonus after basic training, I signed on as a Mortuary Affairs Specialist. It's exactly what it sounds like. Working with dead bodies. Now I had seen two dead bodies back home in Sacramento so it shouldn't have been an issue, but I wasn't prepared for what was in store.

Part of the training for the job required that all new soldiers in the company work several days a week at the morgue in the local big city! The idea was to get everyone used to working with dead bodies so that when it was time to do it in service of the Army, we would be prepared. I was the only black in my whole basic training platoon that signed up for that job. Yet another example of how my desire for wealth would betray me.

Everything started out well. I was stationed as a soldier in Virginia. I used the five grand signing bonus and I bought a

5.0 Mustang. It was fire red with black guts. Eventually I started taking my new whip off base and it didn't take long for me to see that these nigga's in Virginia were country and slow compared to what I was used to in California. There had to be an angle there and I was determined to find it.

There's a saying, "Wherever you go, there you are." What that meant was that my scenery had changed, but I hadn't. In the meantime, I had to start working at the morgue. Shit!! The first day was a nightmare. The smell of eight dead bodies laying, cut wide open with the "Y" shaped autopsy incision on morgue slabs fucked me up. This was not what I had expected.

The top of their domes were cut open with a mini buzz saw so that samples of their brains could be taken. It's actually indescribable. I just wasn't ready to jump right in and help with the autopsies. For a few weeks the chief medical examiner let me just sweep, mop and clean office windows in the building while I got used to the shit. It became a joke that the tough California kid was scared of a dead body. Not scared I told myself, just cautious.

After three weeks of janitorial duties at the morgue, it came time to shit or get off the pot. When I came in that day the medical examiner said, "So King, are you ready today to help with the autopsies today? We've got four bodies we need to do and could really use your help?" He was smiling broadly. All I could think about was how I could get by with one more weekend without helping with these damn autopsies.

"I tell you what Jason, it's a three-day weekend. I give you my word that I'll be ready when we come back Tuesday." I said hoping that got me out of the shit. Jason didn't press me, he just smiled like he knew a secret that I didn't.

"Well do your normal cleaning, but today the "cooler" needs to be swept, and then mopped." The medical examiner said as he spun off. Fuck!!! I thought to myself.

See, you're thinking "cooler", what's the big deal?! That's because you don't know what a "cooler" is like in a morgue. This ain't no ice chest or that freezer your grandma kept in the garage to put the cat fish your granddaddy caught in. This mutha fucka was as big as an apartment and it held up to thirty corpses at any time. It had a built-in air-conditioning unit that kept it misty and as cold as it had to be to keep the bodies from rotting while they waited to be cut open. The bodies were on "bunks" of three, like you see inmates on in overcrowded county jails.

On some you can see toes, arms or hands sticking out from under the sheets that are covering them. The "cooler" had dim lights like the setting you'd use for a romantic ambiance with your bitch. There was barely any light. Every kind of death imaginable is represented in the "cooler." You don't end up in the cooler if you die from natural causes. Gunshot victims, people who have been burnt to death, victims who are bloated and gassy from floating in water like rivers and lakes, babies and old people alike can all end up in the "cooler," and do. Not to mention, now this was the real bullshit, but a dead body could move after being "dead" for 48-72 hours. Don't ask me about the science behind it just know that I ain't no bitch, I keep it stitch, fuck one hundred, this one thousand, them bodies moved!!!

So, if I had to clean the cooler. I had to have a plan. This is how I was going to approach this. There were two doors that led into the cooler. One that opened into the hallway with all the offices in it. The hallway was clean but most importantly it was well lit.

The other door in the "cooler" led to the autopsy room, it was well-lit with eight tables for the unlucky people that were about to be dissected. The tables had dime sized holes in them so that the blood, bone, and body juice, with feces could fall through and drain. I opened both doors from the outside without stepping inside of the cooler. I put one of those industrial size grey trash cans in front of the doors to hold them open. That let a little more light into the cooler, and as far as I was concerned, the more light the better.

I got the mop bucket, mop, and broom ready. Here was the plan! I'd start from the lit-up hallway and make my way across the cooler sweeping in a strategic manner. I didn't give a fuck about sweeping under the bunks that the bodies were on. I would focus on the center, keeping my head on a swivel at all times. Once I made it across the cooler sweeping and to the other door, I'd take a break, wipe the sweat off my forehead, get some water, and then mop .

The first part of my plan went fine. My adrenaline was pumping and I was on high alert, but right while I was in the center of this big ass cooler mopping, the lights cut off and the doors slammed shut. I'll say this one time and one time only. If anyone ever brings it up again, I'll swear to God that I never said it, but I was scared as shit. I gave out a warrior's roar, really it was a scream, and then I picked up the mop and started swinging it because in my mind these dead bodies were up walking and they were closing in on me. I swung the mop once or twice and then slipped on a wet spot that had already been mopped. I hit the ground. When the doors finally swung open, bringing in a flood of light, I was curled in a ball on the floor. There was a crowd of soldiers busting up laughing when the door to the cooler finally opened.

After about a year of military service, my "opportunity" presented itself. As it turns out, weed on the east coast is a lot more expensive than it is on the west coast. After Rob's murder and my quick departure from California, I didn't really have the kind of connection that I would need to make this move. It only took a few days worth of calls before I found out that my cousin Natalie's baby daddy was selling weed back home. At the time he didn't have the quantity I would need, but that would change fast. I gave Natalie a call.

"Kuzzo, what's good military man! How's uncle Sam's racist ass treating you? I hear you cutting open corpses and shit." My cousin Nat answered on the first ring.

"Yea, you know how it go, sometimes a nigga gotta do what a nigga gotta do. It was the fastest ticket out of town. It ain't so bad though now that I'm used to the smell and shit."

"Nigga, you nasty, why you couldn't be a mechanic or something?" She asked.

I laughed! Natalie had always been one of my favorite cousins. She reminded me of my mom.

"Shit, they shot me a five-band signing bonus. That did it for me cousin!" Was my response.

"Oh well yeah cousin, I feel that. Makes sense, I know how your ass is about the bag." This was a perfect time to shoot my shot about the weed connection.

"Speaking of dough Nat, I hear your baby daddy is moving a few packs." I held my breath as I waited for a response.

"Nigga, I knew your ass wasn't just calling out the blue, you always got an angle, don't you?" Natalie chuckled.

"I really missed you though." I countered, "I just figured I could kill two birds with one stone since I'm calling long distance and shit."

"Mmmm, hmmmm, whatever nigga. Anyway, yeah, my baby daddy sorry ass doing his little weed thing. He grows his own plants. Shit, I wish he spent as much time with the kids as he did with them plants." I knew at that moment that I was going to be able to put this hustle together. I had only met Nat's dude once, he was five years older than me, but they had three kids together. I knew that the prospect of quadrupling his hustle would be too tempting to pass up. She gave me his number and shit was in motion.

It didn't take long to put things together. Shit started coming together shortly after that. I was getting packs of weed from California and selling them at prices in Virginia that you wouldn't believe. It began to be hard to stay focused on military things. I was making way more money selling weed.

Unfortunately, almost just as quickly as it started, somebody in my platoon snitched on me to the military police.

They started watching me, even following me when I left base. Three months after it started, and after only fifteen months of military service, it all came crashing down. They knew that I was hustling and the military police set up a sting operation in an attempt to bust me. The only thing that saved me was that I was planning on ripping the guy off that I was meeting so I didn't show up to the meet with the weed that I was supposed to. They pulled me over thinking that I had five pounds of good California fire on me but I had nothing, so there was little that they could do. It could have been worse, they could have tried me, and if convicted, I would have gone to military prison. Instead, they gave me the option of taking an "other than honorable discharge," and getting the fuck on. I got the fuck on!

There was one thing though; one thing that the military gave me that they could never take back. That was a military mind. This included discipline, and the attention to detail needed to conform to military practice. It gave me the confidence and knowledge to know that combining all of these qualities would make almost any plan possible, no matter how sinister. Fifteen months of failed military service would set the stage for the next phase in my adult life; as a serial heist man.

Chapter 27

THAT WILL BE THE DEATH OF HIM

[Present]

This has been a hell of a day and it wasn't yet four o'clock. I've got to pick up Alisha from work in a little over an hour but for now, I had more pressing matters to tend to. Jamille would be dead before I went to meet Rico and Cash at ten tonight. It just had to be. However, this was a situation that required some discretion. It was well known that Jamille was one of my lieutenant's and I don't want any heat on me. If that wasn't the case, Jamille would have just been gunned down pulling up to his apartment, another sad victim of black on black crime. Sometimes in the game of chess, you have to sacrifice a valuable piece in order to achieve your ultimate goal, which is to protect the King. Some may say it's cruel or cold, I say, who gives a fuck what another nigga says.

Jamille's white boy neighbor dope connect has been buying his heroin from me for almost nine months. I followed him one day and then I made sure that we bumped into each other in a "chance" encounter at Kmart. You could always count on a dope fiend to be a dope fiend and this white boy was about to be a pawn in my plan to murder Jamille.

"Oh, excuse me folks." I said in my best east coast accent . At the same time I dropped two aluminum foiled wrapped grams of black tar heroin. The white boy looked at me quickly before becoming transfixed on the dope that I'd bent down to pick up.

"No worries bro." He said, still staring at my hands and the packs of dope as I stood up. I had him. I needed him buying his heroin from me so that I could control the heroin that he gave to Jamille. Nobody feels bad for a heroin addict who overdoses on a bad batch of dope. After looking him over for a minute I hit him with the script that I had practiced and memorized long before today.

"Hey yo, my name is KP son, you think I could holla at ya real quick?" I asked. He bit like a big mouth bass on the Mississippi River. I gave him some dope that day and I've been selling him dope ever since. Today, he's going to be a casualty of war. I called his phone.

"Hey KP." The white boy answered excitedly calling me by the fake name I'd given him. "I was just about to call you bro. I've got some money lined up for later but I'm out of Bobby Brown."

He knew not to say heroin or dope on the phone with me. That was a sure way to get hung up on, and never dealt with again. The white boy already owes me over six hundred dollars, so the lie about having money lined up for later waiting was crap; it didn't matter. I didn't start supplying his dope to make money off of him. I started serving him because I'm King. I stay three moves ahead. I knew that this day would come eventually.

It had been almost a year since word first got back to me from one of the young trap boys on 65th Avenue that Jamille was on some shady shit. He overheard Jamille one day when he came to drop off some dope to the spot telling Capone, the little nigga I had in charge of the spot, that he was about to make a power move. He said he would need soldiers like Capone and asked the nigga was he with it, or was he loyal to King? Sometimes you gotta give a jealous nigga enough rope to hang himself. I knew then that Jamille would have to be killed. I didn't know when, but in "Rilla", disloyalty was a death sentence. So was getting high!!

"Ok yo, check it out, I got some new Bobby Brown, the "music" is going to knock your socks off." I told the white boy dope fiend in coded words that he surely understood.

"How soon can I meet you? I don't want to lose the customers." The white boy said quickly. He wanted the dope now and would say whatever he could to get it.

I chuckled; he was jonesing. I figured that by nine o'clock he'd be hard up, which meant that Jamille would be hard up too. They had become quite the dope fiend duo.

"Meet me at eight tonight in the Kmart parking lot on Stockton Blvd." I told him. I could hear the disappointment in his voice, but he had no choice. In his mind he was getting free dope. He never had any intention on paying me what he owed. To him I was just some lame from the East Coast that he was getting over on. I hung up!

It was almost time to pick Alisha up from work. I swung by the house to switch cars, and then stopped at Subway for a turkey sandwich, before pulling up in the parking lot at the DMV where Alisha was already waiting out front. Normally we'd greet each other with big goofy smiles, saying some slick shit to each another. Today she slid in the car and shut the door without saying a word. I could tell something was bothering her.

I was five minutes late and I thought that this was her issue so I said, "My bad babe, I stopped to get a sandwich. My stomach was touching my back, you good?" I turned down the music which I had on one of her favorites, Beyoncé's, Love on Top playing.

("Honey, honey, I can see the stars all the way from here, can't you see the glow on the window pane?") Came through the speakers.

"It's not that." Alisha said dryly. "I get tired of everybody and they momma coming to the DMV talking to me like they crazy. Like it's my fault that their license is suspended or that they tags are expired."

O.k., I thought for a second, she just needs to vent after a bad day at work. I put my hand on her thigh caressing it affectionately. Quickly I found out that there was more to it.

"Babe," she said, shifting in her seat so that her back was against the passenger's side door allowing her to look directly at me.

"What's up babe? What's on your mind? Spit that shit out girl, you know I don't like guessing games." I was smiling but I had that unsettling feeling in my gut, similar to the one I got this morning on my way to pick up Tyreke. It was just a mild sense of unease.

"Is everything alright King? I mean you would tell me if you were having problems wouldn't you?" Alisha asked.

She had my attention now, so I pulled over into a 7-Eleven parking lot.

"Alisha, bae, clearly something is on your mind, will you just ask what you want to ask, or tell me what's bothering you!"

I do my absolute best not to lie to my bitches, I feel that I'm too grown for that. Still, the fact is, that I wouldn't tell her if something was wrong unless it had to do specifically with her. If you're in the game it's a sound practice to keep bitches out of your business. It's bad enough that a nigga has to deal with bitch ass nigga's. Finally, Alisha started talking.

"Ok, you know I love you; I wouldn't have felt right if I didn't tell you." Alisha said meekly.

"Ok" I said, trying to gauge where this was going. Alisha had tears welling up in her eyes now.

"Well, I was doing driver's license re-newels today when this nigga name Denarius Williams comes to my counter. He gave me his driver's license and while I was typing in his information, he started commenting on how sexy and beautiful I was."

"Ok, keep going", I said. The name didn't ring a bell though. Alisha went on.

"I wasn't paying any attention, just another young nigga thinking he God's gift to a bitch when he says, "You don't remember me huh?"

I looked up then, giving him a professional smile. "No", I said, and I went back to typing up the necessary forms. Alisha looked me in the eyes to see if I was following her so far.

"Don't you fuck with that nigga King," he finally asked while I was typing, Alisha finally said. "My name Capone, I be on 65th Avenue."

I ignored him and handed him his receipt when I was done. He grabbed it but as he walked away, he said, "It's good, you'll be single soon enough, I'll be back then."

My blood began to boil but I had long mastered the "poker face." In the game, and in the streets, you never let your face tell what you're thinking. Being predictable in the field could get you murked.

Alisha broke out crying, "King are you unhappy with me? Are you leaving me? I told you I'd start dancing; you won't let me." She bawled.

Alisha was so sexy and beautiful when she cried. This is only the second time that I had seen her cry but it was something about how vulnerable she seemed that turned me on. It was clear that she hadn't picked up on the real meaning behind what Capone had said and there was no need to go into more details. She thought Capone meant that I was leaving her for another bitch. What he really meant was that I would somehow be getting erased or replaced soon! It was a threat and it was a mistake on Capone's part.

"Babe, come here!" I opened my arms as Alsiha slid across the plush leather. The beemer was as spacious as an airplane cockpit. I held her while she rested her head on my chest. Her tears began to soak my silk shirt. I told her, "I'm not going anywhere and neither are you. Look at me." She lifted her head, looking at me with beautiful brown, almond shaped eyes. "Have I ever lied to you?" Alisha sniffled and shook her head no. "We're a family! A team! That was just a young nigga with some wishful thinking." I pulled her back down to my chest, kissed her forehead while rubbing her back. As I glared out of the window, I clenched my jaw and wondered how deep in my organization this treachery went. One thing for sure, the homicide department was about to earn their pay. Bodies were going to pile up, no matter who had to get it, anything to protect the King.

Chapter 28

BACK TO CALI

[Past]

Getting back to California after being away for a while was exciting. I didn't realize how much I'd missed it. The thing was, I didn't want to go back to selling dope on the block so I was looking for a new hustle. My patna Jboy was a pimp and had moved to Las Vegas. Driving through Sac town it was clear that not much had changed. A few new nigga's had come up, and some nigga's that used to be up, had fallen off or gotten knocked off. I had been talking to Jboy over the last few weeks and he convinced me to come visit him in Vegas. Without much going on in Sac at the moment, the decision was made to take the trip.

"Ok nigga I'm gonna slide out there but I'm not trying to be paying for no hotel room night after night," I said. I was clowning but my dough was low at the moment.

"That's how you get at me?" Jboy asked. "I forgot your ass been gone for a minute or you would have heard that I'm up like a meth addict. Nigga, I got a four-bedroom house with a pool and jacuzzi. I got three bitches, all snow, as white as the Republican Party Convention and they all bring me chips every night, and I'm not talking Doritos." Damn I thought to myself. Jboy even talks different now. He talks like a whole new person. I was intrigued.

I had to bust up laughing at that. Jboy had never been known for having such a slick tongue but the nigga had figured something out over the last year. I was eager to learn more.

"Give me a couple of days bra and I'll be on my way," I said smiling, picturing my nigga's new found success.

"Hey King," Jboy said before I hung up. "Bring me a few zips of that Cali Kush, these nigga's smoke bullshit out here!"

"Fasho," I said before hanging up.

Two days later I was in Vegas. It didn't take long before I was hooked. It was my first experience in a twenty-four hour city. Shit, the 24-hour city. Life was popping out here at all hours of the day and night, and to my young hungry mind, nothing could be better. Jboy picked me up from the airport. He was in a black on black Cadillac CTS V, with the Corvette engine. That mutha fucka was beautiful and it sounded like it had a rocket under the hood. Jboy read my expression, "All on a bitch King," he said smiling.

We rolled the windows down and headed towards the strip. Riding down the strip, I saw more activity than I had ever seen before. People were walking; lights were everywhere. There were Lamborghini rentals, towering casinos, hookers, homeless people, and shops and stores of all kinds as far as the eye could see. Money!! This town was the fattest sweetest pussy and I was desperate to fuck.

We went to Jboy's house and that nigga wasn't lying, he was living lavish. His house had hardwood floors, a fat ass kitchen with marble countertops and a plush living room with money green suede sofas. His house was two stories and had a backyard so dope that he hosted pool parties. When you're proud of someone you should tell them.

"My nigga, you made good! I'm proud of you," I told him. When I left you was living with your'e mama nigga." Jboy laughed.

"How did you end up out here anyway?" I asked. I was curious.

Jboy told me the story.

"Nigga, about nine months ago I went to the cannabis club down off Florin Road to buy an eighth of weed when I met this pretty ass white bitch named Sara. She was visiting her family for the week but said that she lived and worked in Vegas. I'm not gonna lie King, at first all I was thinking about was fucking the bitch. Shit, you know I wasn't no pimp. So, I shot my shot, and asked if she wanted to smoke later and kick it. She said yeah, gave me her number, then left. When I called that night, she didn't answer or call back so I said fuck it. On my momma a month later she called me out of the blue, telling me to come see her in Vegas. I told the bitch that she faked on me once and that it better not happen again."

"For some reason bra, the bitch liked me calling her a bitch. She liked a nigga going hard on her. She sent me a ticket and I ain't been back to Sacramento since. Come to find out, the bitch was an escort. I didn't give a fuck, I still wanted to kick it, smoke and fuck. One night after about a week of being with her in Vegas, she came to the hotel we was staying in and dropped two bands on the bed. She said, "Here daddy!" The rest is in the books." His story was finished so he sat there looking at me.

"Damn nigga that's a come up," I said. I was bewildered. "Where did you get the game on what to do next? Who laced you?" I asked. Jboy laughed until he doubled over.

"You wouldn't believe it if I told you nigga."

"Tell me nigga, this shit is crazy," I said.

"I watched "Bossin Up" with Snoop Dog." His black face was beaming with satisfaction. Now I had never been one to rely on a bitch for my money but this shit was fascinating. Then I realized that I hadn't seen no bitches yet. He said he had three. "Where yo bitches at now?" I asked skeptically.

"That's the best part bra, out here in Nevada they got brothels where prostitution is legal. My bitches live there while they work and only come home once a month for a week.

They spend three weeks at work, and one week at home, which means that I don't even have time to get tired of the bitches."

Damn, I thought, I don't need to ask how much money he makes because it's clear that it's more than enough! He was living lavishly. I didn't know many young nigga's living as good as he was. The cold part was that Jboy was always the nigga that hustled but never made any real progress. When the homies was flipping old schools; he was the passenger. He wasn't broke, he was just never balling. That had changed.

That night Jboy took me out on the town. First we went to a club inside the Mandalay Bay. Jboy was well known! We got a VIP booth with a bottle of 1800, and they let us smoke weed inside the club. Bitches stayed making their way to us, but Jboy said that he didn't have time for square bitches, no matter how fine they was. If the bitch wasn't selling pussy or stripping, Jboy said that he wasn't interested.

Then we went to a strip club called Cheetahs, where Jboy was in his element. Damn this nigga had changed in the year and a half that I was gone. The quiet passenger was now a confident pimp. Some bitches at the strip club wouldn't come anywhere near him and some seemed to thrive off his attention. He did a lit tipping but only in small amounts. I watched him give his number to at least five bitches. He said that if just one bitch called, it was a night well spent. He told me that the bitches that wouldn't talk to him were "in pocket," that they already had pimps. We got back to his house at five in the morning and I slept till noon.

"Get up nigga, we got a run to make," Jboy said waking me up out of my sleep.

Chapter 29

Who's Who?

[Present]

After consoling Alisha, I took her home. While there I changed real quick into more comfortable clothes. I threw on some jogger's and a hoodie with black Adidas. I grabbed my banger. I'd grown to prefer revolvers because I didn't have to worry about picking up spent shell casings or the gun jamming. Plus, the 357 snub nose would knock a nigga off they feet. After grabbing a few other things I would need for the night, I was ready to bounce.

"King?" It was Keisha calling me from the bedroom.

"Yeah babe, what's good?" I said while popping my head in the door.

"You know I work at ten?" Keisha whispered. I just stared at her. Alisha was in the shower.

"Yea I know, look, don't worry bout going to work tonight. I got some other shit I gotta handle. I'm not sure what time I'll be home."

Keisha smiled.

"That's cool daddy, but what about that long thick dick I've been thinking about since this morning?" She got a sexy-sad look on her face while biting down on her finger seductively.

"I'm going to have to give you a rain check." I told her. I had more pressing matters to deal with. Keisha flopped back on the bed in mock anger. On the fly I said, "Don't' trip, I got something planned for all of us this weekend. I promise you'll love it." Keisha perked up at this, lighting up like a schoolgirl.

"What is it? Give me a hint," she begged. I started laughing.

"It's only Wednesday daddy," she pleaded.

"If I tell you it won't be as special, just be patient ma!"

I didn't have shit planned, but I had three or four days to put something together so it wouldn't be a problem!

Keisha was horny, but I also knew that she would lose respect for me if I told her that I had important business to handle and then dove into some pussy. Whether they say it or not, a bitch respects a man that has his priorities straight; a man who handles his business. I walked into the room, and went into the top drawer pulling out her and Alisha's little dildo with the vibrator.

"You and Alisha enjoy yourselves," I said tossing it to her. "There's wine in the fridge and plenty of weed. Put on

Netflix and do what y'all do!" I tongue kissed her deeply while squeezing her fat ass. Keisha purred.

They'll be fine. Both of them were bi-sexual, they wanted me but didn't need me for their nut. It was almost six-thirty and I had to go.

My first stop was one of my spots on MLK Blvd. When I pulled up, the two young thugs working the spot weren't expecting me so they seemed on edge.

"King, what's good big bro," said Bj, the skinny one. He was twisting his shirt in his fingers nervously. "You know Rico came by earlier to grab the trap money right? It was all there!" He asked not looking me in the eyes.

"It's good, I'm not here for that." I told him to put him at ease. They know of my violent past. They were clearly uncomfortable. "Go chill in the living room. I'll be out of here in ten minutes," I commanded.

"Ok King, fasho big bro, we got you!" They agreed, rapidly walking from the kitchen to the living room.

"Hey, turn the porch light off, and don't bust no knocks while I'm here," I said. They did as told. When they were seated in the living room I went to work.

I pulled out two grams of black tar heroin and dropped it on a plate. It was soft and sticky from being in my sock. After that I took out a ball of aluminum foil with about two tablespoons of battery acid on it. Carefully, I added the battery acid to the heroin and mixed it with a wooden spoon. As the battery acid changed the color of the heroin, I added chocolate Nestles Quick powder to give it it's natural color again. Then I put it in the freezer for five minutes to harden it back up. It was time to go meet Jamille's white boy connect with my deadly concoction. Before I left, I looked long and hard at the young hustler's that were working one of my spots. I didn't sense any animosity or jealousy, only admiration, but there was still something that I needed to tell them.

"Look lil nigga's, y'all been holding it down over here for a while now. The trap ain't never short and you nigga's control the block like you was taught. There are bright things in y'alls future if you stick to the script." They both beamed, but not for long. "But if you ever, and I mean just one time, think that you can cross me or play me, you'll suffer the most excruciating pain, and then death that you can imagine. I love you lil nigga's; y'all my family, but nothing pains me more than a disloyal family member." They both nodded in agreement. I stared at both of them with coal black eyes; the eyes of the shark. As I reached in my back pocket, they both flinched.

"Relax, relax, I told y'all we good! This is for y'all, spend it wisely," I said throwing a few thousand on the couch between them. "Cut the porch light back on," I said as I left. "Get back to work.

As I pulled up to the K-Mart I saw the white boy looking around like he was waiting on the messiah. He was dope sick.

I parked the car amongst the other shoppers and then walked up to him. "Are you waiting on somebody?" I asked sarcastically.

"Oh hey, hey KP man I thought you forgot about me." The white boy was anxious and jumpy.

"Na man, you one of my best customers, just had to make a quick stop," I said lying.

"Ok, ok, cool, I know I owe you a lil money but that should be taken care of tonight when…" I cut him off!

"Don't worry about that, I know you're good for it." I gave him a dollar, and told him to go buy a soda from the Coke machine in front of the store. He looked at me confused; he didn't want a soda, he wanted dope. Then he caught on! No hand to hand transactions with King. Possession is nine-tenths of the law. If he found heroin in a soda machine it can't be linked to me. He went to the soda machine and grabbed the heroin I'd left for him.

Within the hour, the person who could tie the dope to me, the white boy, plus the nigga I loved like a brother, Jamille, would be dead. From here on, I would exterminate all those who opposed me, and anyone whose loyalty was in question. The King must be protected. Blood was about to spill!!!

Chapter 30

THE MEETING

[Present]

Rico and Cash knew that when I wanted to meet at the safe house, it was serious, so when I got there, they were already sitting in the kitchen smoking. I gave both of them hugs and then hopped on the kitchen counter to sit myself. I got straight to it.

"Y'all are my family!" I stared at both of them individually, looking for signs of discomfort or unease. They both sat calmly so I continued.

"Several things have taken place over the last couple of days that are going to affect us all both individually, as well as an organization." They were looking more concerned now. Rico passed me the blunt. I hit it twice, then went on.

"There's treachery and disloyalty amongst the ranks," I said as I pulled the snub nose from the small of my back, setting it in my lap. If they had nothing to hide, it shouldn't concern them. It didn't seem to; they just kept smoking.

Cash and Rico were street nigga's through and through. Our bond was sealed in blood. You can't have pussy nigga's running a drug organization. We had seen it all in these streets so I wasn't surprised at their nonchalant reactions so far.

"Jamille is a dope fiend!" I said. Neither Rico or Cash looked surprised.

I could have said, "was" a dope fiend but I was choosing my words carefully. They didn't need to know what had been done to Jamille yet. This was about seeing where they stood. To see if they were loyal or if they somehow played a roll in all this shit.

"I am sure that both y'all knew this!" I wasn't looking for a response.

"We don't get high on our own supply. You both know this, this is a rule, but since he is our brother, I exercised restraint." Rico was looking down in his lap and he'd known me the longest so he probably knew where this was headed, but he knew better than to interrupt me.

"Earlier today, Jamille's addiction got the best of him. He questioned my authority in front of an outsider, and then pulled his strap on me but didn't bust it," I said stretching the truth. Only then did Cash speak up in his slow drawl.

"On bloods King, I'll body the nigga, just give me the word bra. After all you did for that bitch ass nigga. He was a bum when you brought the nigga in." I was searching Cash's eyes for sincerity. It seemed to be there!

"Jamille's also been running his mouth about a takeover. Actually, he's trying to recruit some young nigga's to ride with him." I left out Capone's name for now, but I was paying close attention to both of their reactions. The less info I give out right now the better. I didn't know who I could trust.

"Sheesshhh," whistled Cash as he got up to head to the fridge. It was beginning to bother me that Rico hadn't uttered a word yet. I knew him and Jamille had an especially close bond, but he also knew that it was blood in and blood out! I stared at him intently and cocked my head to the side then threw up my hands, "Nigga you got something say?" I asked.

Finally, Rico said, "So what you wanna do?" But there was no conviction behind it. No anger and fury like what was coming from Cash. I decided to keep my cards close. No need to tell him that I had murdered Jamille earlier tonight.

"I'm thinking on it," I said as I smirked. I was also thinking what role Rico might play in all of this. I'd deal with that later, for now it was time to slide over to 65th Ave. Recent events had ignited my desire for blood. For the truth! There was only one way to get the truth. By force!! With

ruthlessness! By murder!

Chapter 31

PIMPIN

[Past]

"Aight, aight, nigga damn. Why you shaking a nigga like the police?" I said, getting the sleep from my eyes as I focused on Jboy. It was clear he had been up for a while. The nigga was used to the twenty four hour Vegas lifestyle. He was also cleaner than the board of health. He had on Gucci from head to toe. He was wearing a black Gucci hat with the red and green stripes, matching Gucci shirt, and a clean ass black Gucci watch with matching black Gucci shoes. The whole fit had to run at least three grand.

"Get up and shower blood. We gotta run out to the Chicken Ranch so I can pick up this trap from my bitches," Jboy said.

I was fully showered and dressed in twenty minutes. I was excited! I put on my best fit and said. "Let's go, I got to see this." Jboy chuckled.

It was about a forty-five-minute drive to the brothel. Nevada has legal prostitution for bitches over eighteen years old in some counties. I had heard about it but now it was time to witness it with my own eyes. We smoked a few blunts on the way, and chopped it up about old times. We was there in no time. Pulling up, I wasn't initially super impressed. Maybe I was expecting something different. It just looked like a big one story house with a blinking "World Famous Chicken Ranch," sign outside. It was surrounded by an iron gate. You had to be buzzed in at the gate to get in and you couldn't see inside from the outside. The windows were frosted over with white paint; it was that shit that you see on all the department store windows around Christmas time.

"This is it?" I asked. Jboy didn't respond, he just grinned, then hit the buzzer. We were buzzed in almost immediately. Just as quickly, my impression changed. We walked in the door and there were bitches of every age, nationality and body type rushing to line up like I used to do in the mornings in the Army. Most were running out from their rooms in the back. They were all wearing lingerie. They were all wearing six inch stiletto heels. They were running from the hallway out to the main area where there were couches, a full bar, and a small stage with a stripper pole in the center. Jboy had a look on his face like there was no place on earth that he'd rather be. It would be hard to argue with him. It was definitely something to see.

Once the bitches came out of the hallway and saw that it was Jboy, they stopped hurrying, "girl it's just Jboy," "bitch stop running, it's J," they all huffed. They knew he wasn't there to buy any pussy.

"Sara, yo nigga here!" One older black bitch said. Most of the bitches were heading back down the hallway to their rooms. A few stayed and sat at the bar and a few others lounged on the couches. We sat at the bar even though I was just shy of twenty-one. Jboy ordered Hennessey for us both. I'm not too big on alcohol, but this was an exception; a special occasion. Five minutes later a tall, thick, blond with green eyes came out from the back.

"Hey daddy," she said pulling up a stool next to Jboy.

"Sup bitch, where's Jen and Tabatha?" Jboy replied smugly.

"They're on dates right now, they probably won't be done for at least an hour." Jboy nodded and looked around. Without being asked, Sara casually slipped Jboy a purple Crown Royal bag that looked stuffed. He just as casually slipped the bag into his pocket.

"Daddy did you bring any weed, we haven't had smoke for two days?" Jboy's bitch asked. Jboy looked at me. Before we left the house, he told me to bring an ounce. I was glad to be part of the situation. I wasn't a pimp but at least I had something these bitches wanted.

"My nigga King got some weed. Find out all who want some and how much they spending, so he can go to the car to bag it up," Jboy commanded.

"Ok daddy," Sara said bubbly, hopping up. She came back quickly with the amounts. Five bitches was spending a hundred dollar's each. I got up to go to the car, but Jboy stopped me.

"Nigga, this ain't California, give each of them bitches about an eighth. Plus, that's dro, these bitches are used to smoking dirt. You'll fuck around and kill one of them bitches," Jboy said. I laughed. In the car I handled my business quickly. I went back in and Jboy gave the weed to his bitch. She returned shortly after with four hundred dollars in cash.

"Bitch this is four hundred, supposed to be five." Jboy snapped.

"I know, I know daddy but Juju said that she wanted to give him the money herself." She was nodding at me. JBoy beamed.

"Nigga go get your dough." He said looking at me as he tilted his head in the direction of Juju.

"Which one is Juju bra?" I asked. There were a few old bitches in there. Hopefully it wasn't one of them. Jboy pointed her out. "On bloods," I said, squeezing his shoulder excitedly. I liked what I'd seen so far.

Juju was about 5'1", long brunette hair, and she was thick as a Snickers with hazel eyes. Now pimping had never been my thing but I'd never had a problem getting bitches. On top of that, while I was in the Army, I put on ten pounds of muscle. I wasn't arrogant but I was confident. I was about to get a crash course in pimping.

After walking to the couch, I shook Juju's hand then asked her if it was cool to sit down. She just smiled and nodded.

"So, your name is Juju, right?" I asked. I was sitting next to her, thigh to thigh.

"Yea, that's what my friends call me." Juju blushed as she answered.

"Well that's my goal before I leave this couch," I shot back.

"What?" she asked. She had missed it.

"To be able to call you Juju," I responded while smiling my sexiest smile. This got her. It was on from there. I would glance up from time to time and Jboy would be watching me like a proud father.

"Are you living in Vegas now or are you just visiting King?" Juju asked. Her eyes searched mine while probing them deeply.

"That depends," I answered. This was the moment that would determine if this bitch would be mine.

"On what?" Juju asked shyly. She tilted her head down towards her lap while looking up at me with her eyes.

"On how many f-r-i-e-n-d-s, I have here?" I spelled out each letter for her. She didn't miss it this time. She threw her leg over mine flirtatiously.

"Call me Juju, daddy," she said finally.

At that moment the buzzer from the front gate went off again. All the bitches lined up introducing themselves in front of an old white dude. He looked the bitches over for a minute before picking Juju. As she was walking him to the back room, she passed me and mouthed, "you better not leave." Coolly, I shook my head ok. What I really wanted to say was, "Bitch, eight gorillas couldn't drag me out of here right now." Jboy waved me back over to him when Juju went in the back.

"What she talking bout bra?" Jboy asked. He already knew a little about her past from his bitches. Juju had recently moved to Vegas to get away from an abusive pimp in Waikiki, Hawaii. He used to whoop her ass regularly.

"Shit, just gettin to know her, I asked about her past and shit." I told him.

"Did she give you the money for the weed yet?" Jboy asked.

"Nah, why, should I press her?" I didn't want to fuck this up. So, I was listening closely to what Jboy was saying. He was the one with the experience.

"No, no, I'm not saying that. I'm just trying to figure out her play. She's a real ho, so if she wasn't feeling you, she wouldn't be sitting there chopping it up with you. When she comes off of her date, ask her for the money she owes you for the weed and tell her that we're about to leave. If she wants you, she not going to let you go without making it clear." That was all the help that Jboy could give me. It was up to me now.

"Order me another shot of Hennessey," I said.

Jboy laughed, then ordered the drink. Thirty minutes later, me and Juju were back on the couch. She had changed into sweats but she was still sexy. She had a small purse with her now.

"Hey gorgeous, you good?" I asked.

"Yeah, yeah, just another day at this camp." Juju was smiling, but there was sadness in her eyes.

"So look, can we exchange numbers? I'd like to kick it with you some time." I wanted to see where her head was. She stared at me for a long moment before answering.

"Yeah we can do that, but don't take my number if your not going to call King."

Bitch I'm calling tonight, I thought to myself, but said, "stop it," like I wasn't tripping instead. I pulled out my phone and she typed her number into my iPhone. Jboy was nodding his head up and down rapidly, smiling. I was just about to ask her about the money for the weed when she casually rubbed my thigh, then slid her hand in my pocket. I could feel that she had put something in there. Juju and I hugged and then me and Jboy left.

When we got to the car, I was floating. She was actually a cool bitch who had her own income. I wasn't thinking about pimping. We pulled out of the parking lot of the Chicken Ranch headed for the freeway but needed blunts so we stopped at 7-Eleven. I pulled the cash out of my pocket to pay for the blunts and my stomach dropped. Juju owed me a hundred dollars for the weed but had given me a thousand instead.

I ran back to the car with the cash in my hand and held it up to Jboy. Shit, I was still thinking that it might have been a mistake.

"You just knocked your first ho King." Jboy seemed genuinely happy for me. He was also genuinely proud of himself. On the way back to Vegas he laced me on the pimp game and how to play it when I called her. Jboy had introduced me to a whole new hustle.

Chapter 32

CAST THE FIRST STONE

[Present]

"There is no one righteous, not even one…there is no one who does good, not even one" (Author: Unknown)

Pulling up on 65th Ave. at a little after midnight I parked across the street and down the block a ways. My mind was already made up. There was no going back or any other options! Out of habit, I sat there for about an hour getting the feel for the street. I wanted to know how many cars passed? Did the police ride by? How many dope fiends were coming over? This was a solo mission because sometimes you couldn't let the left hand know what the right hand was doing. I got out of the car, with my "truth kit" and I headed towards the house. A smoker hit the corner obviously going to the trap house to buy dope. Perfect I thought, this was about timing now.

The element of surprise is a powerful weapon of its own. The smoker knocked at the door and the curtains moved to the side as Capone peeked out. Capone had made a vital mistake by telling Alisha that I wouldn't be around for long. A lesson that I had learned many years ago was to never threaten a nigga. The ego wants you to think that your'e scaring another nigga, but all your'e really doing is giving an enemy the opportunity to strike first.

The front door started to open. As it did, I walked up behind the dope fiend and I shot him in the back of the head with a Smith & Wesson 9mm, equipped with a suppression muzzle. His own momentum pushed him forward and through the door. His brain matter splattered half on the door; half in Capone's face. The element of surprise! I walked in and calmly shut the door behind me.

"What the fuck, what the fuck King! Nigga, what the fuck is going on." Capone cried out loud confused. He had a look of terror and shock on his face.

"Nigga sit down and shut the fuck up, I'll ask the questions. You got it lil nigga?" I barked. Capone started to say something so I shot him in the thigh right above his knee. He collapsed quickly. "Who else is here besides you and this little ugly black bitch?" I asked, pointing to the bitch on the couch.

"No one King, no one. It's just us, what is this…"

"Woooomph!" The banger spit. It hardly made a sound as I shot him in his other leg. The suppression muzzle made a gunshot sound like a slap on the back.

"What part of I'll ask the questions don't yo pussy ass understand?!" I growled. Capone was curled up on the floor in front of the couch clutching his legs. The girl was on the couch. She hadn't made a sound. Probably in shock. It didn't matter, everyone in this bitch had to die. I was committed to murking everything. No witnesses period!

"Hey lil ma," I said with a sympathetic smile. "Grab that blanket from the couch and bend down so that you can put pressure on those bullet wounds for him."

She did as she was told and while her head was bent down, "Woooomph." I fired a single shot to the back of her head. She slumped forward like a drunk bitch stumbling out the club doing a face plant. Capone flinched as his chest was splattered with baby's brain matter. He shoved her off of his lap. It was just me and him now. I turned the porch light off and turned to Capone, staring at him intently.

"You're going to die tonight," I said. He dropped his head and then started crying.

"Bitch ass nigga, lift your head up and pay attention." After several more sobs, he slowly lifted his head.

"Now, you do have some control in the matter!" I spit. He looked up hopeful at my words, but only briefly. "You can decide how fast or slow you die tonight. You can also decide whether your daughter Tiffany lives to see her sixth birthday – Do you understand?" His hope faded just as quickly as it came so his head dropped.

"Ok nigga, I see your hard of hearing, I said pick yo head up!"

I reached in my "truth kit" and pulled out the duct tape and zip ties, then snatched him up and forced him to his stomach. I took the zip ties and locked his hands behind his back. The duct tape would muffle his screams. I sat him in a chair so that we could continue.

"Now, since you can't talk, you'll just nod yes or no. Do you understand?" I whispered close to his face. Tears were streaming down his cheeks but he nodded, yes. "Ok good, good! First question. Are you a loyal nigga?" Hope again appeared in his eyes! He must have thought that the question meant that I wasn't sure if he was loyal or not yet. He nodded up and down violently, trying to convince me that he was loyal. "My bad," I chuckled. "I forgot to tell you that every time I catch you in a lie, there's a penalty." This nigga was about to learn what real pain was! I bent down into my "kit," never taking my eyes off my prey and pulled out a shiny, sharp, metal potato peeler. Capone's eyes were about to pop out of his head. Without saying a word, I took up position behind this pussy nigga while grabbing him in a choke hold with my left arm to hold him in place.

He was breathing heavily. The duct tape was pushing out in a bubble because he was panting so hard. From the base of his neck I began to slowly peel a fine layer of skin down the middle of his back. Muffled screams ensued. His eyes rolled up into his head as I bent down to whisper in his ear. "You had plans on going up against King huh? This right here is the cost to be the boss nigga." Once his screams died down, I went on.

"This can last all night litlle nigga. No more fucking lies." I growled. "Let's try this again! Are you a loyal nigga?" Capone shook his head no this time. "Good, good! Now we're making progress! Next question, was Jamille talking about taking over my organization?" Capone took a moment before nodding yes.

"See, this ain't so hard! Now, last and most important question nigga. Was it just you two pussy nigga's plotting against me?" He shook his head no. My anger built so I peeled another long strip of skin away along his side and under his armpits. Tissue and muscle were showing under the skin. Blood began rushing to the surface and dripping down his side in thick long streams. I gave him a minute to catch his breath. I knew the shit hurt, I'd been through worse.

"You need to listen real carefully nigga. I'm going to take this tape off your mouth, if you scream, we start over! Feel me?" Capone nodded. Snatching the tape from his mouth allowed him to breathe better but he was still panting heavily. Sweat and spit were pooled around his mouth. I wiped sweat off his face and forehead while reaching back to grab the 9mm.

"You did good, you did good! I give you my word that your daughter will live. Now who else was in on this plot? No lies nigga, no lies!" He was having trouble catching his breath. The pain must have been immense. He swallowed over and over like something was caught in his throat. I put my ear down by his mouth to hear better, "R, R, R," he stammered.

"Spit it out!" I growled.

"R, R, Ri, Rico," he stuttered, finally getting it out.

My world felt like it was caving in around me. A week ago, shit seemed perfect. I didn't have a care in the world and now my closest associates, my family, Jamille, my brothers, were conniving and plotting on my down fall. Real talk, who can predict the hearts of men?

I eased the banger from my side, and put the barrel of the suppressor under Capone's chin.

"Don't worry little bra," I whispered, "You'll have plenty of company in disloyal nigga hell coming right behind you." With that, the top of Capone's melon exploded as the round from the nine catapulted up from under his chin. The blowback sprinkled droplets of his blood all across my face like tiny raindrops.

Chapter 33

CAN'T LEAVE WELL ENOUGH ALONE

[Past]

There's something about Vegas, about "Sin City", that will grab a hold of you if you're down for a "sin" here and there. Jboy had come for a visit but never left. It was looking like I wouldn't be leaving anytime soon either. It felt like to me that Vegas would be the place I made my mark. Shit started out good enough. So, I didn't have any complaints.

"Daddy," Juju said. "I'm so glad to be out of that place. I've been there for almost two months straight. It's not so bad but it's nothing like being with you. Them tricks get on my fucking nerves." I was picking Juju up from the brothel.

"I know ma, don't trip, we going to get set up and established now." At the moment we were staying in a motel room. I was also renting a car weekly. That shit was hitting my pockets. It was hard to stack your money when you were living like this. Shelling out money on a daily basis to survive gets old fast and makes it almost impossible to save money.

"Go ahead, get dressed Juju, we're going to look at apartments today. After that we gonna go get lunch, then go look at cars so we can get out of this expensive rental."

"Ok daddy," Juju said bubbly. When I picked her up the night before she handed me almost ten bands. It was a decent amount of money but that was for two months worth of work. My plans would bring that much in two minutes, but Juju didn't need to know that.

We hit Vegas that day and went to different neighborhoods until we found an apartment in a good neighborhood that we both liked. After that we went down on the strip to a restaurant in Caesars Palace for lunch. It was dope. Juju was great company. We talked a lot but it would be hard for me to say about what. My mind was really on one the thing. Surveilling the city for licks. Even though I had a good bitch making good money, who was really down for me, I just couldn't leave well enough alone. That same day we put a deposit on our new apartment and I bought a 1979 Pontiac Trans AM; Smokey the Bandit with the gold bird on the hood. It had a .455 with posi rear end. All that was left to do was tint the windows and I'd have the perfect car for my robberies. Next, I called my nigga Bheef from Bounty Hunter Watts.

"What's good my nigga?" I said excitedly when Bheef answered the phone.

"Well, well, if it isn't' the King. Me and Tanya was just talking bout you. On my momma, your ears musta been burning. What's hood bra! Where you at, this is a "702" area code number you calling from." Bheef was a factor in his hood. He was also a known gunner.

"I'm out here in Vegas nigga. You know me, trying to stay down for my come up. What you got going on out that way right now?" I asked. He knew where I was headed.

"Shit King, I'm laying low out here. Ya boy got two warrants right now and I'm looking at nine years in the pen." Malik ass is my co-defendant. They already booked that nigga for thirteen years. Why what's up?" It seemed like Bheef was going to jump at the opportunity to get out of town and to get some money. It was one thing to go to the pen, but it was another thing entirely to go to the pen broke and have to depend on others to take care of you while you were there.

"There's some good opportunities out here," I said. "You down to go on some job interviews?" I asked. We always talked in this type of code on the phone. Technology was a bitch and you could never be certain that no one was listening.

"Hell, yea blood, I been unemployed for a minute." Bheef caught on immediately. We clicked because his gangsta was undeniable but the nigga was sharp too. Most nigga's would have missed that "job" meant robbery. For what I had in store I needed more than a hired gun. This would be our first time doing dirt together though, so I needed to make sure that he was on his game.

"You know I'm wit da shit, King, on da set, how soon do you need me?"

"Tomorrow night your flight leaves out of LAX, flight 1269 United, the ticket will be waiting for you."

"That's why I fucks with you King. You bout yo shit, on Bounty Hunters! Oh yeah, you got "interview" clothes for me?" Bheef asked.

"Don't trip." I chuckled. "You'll be the cleanest nigga in the building." It had been surprisingly easy in Vegas to find a plug on pistols, ammunition and vests! What can you say, "Sin City".

With that settled it was time to finish my homework on the licks. Vegas is full of check cashing places, casinos and mini casinos inside grocery stores that boasted twenty thousand dollar jackpot payouts. They had to have that money on site in case someone hit the jackpot. I found one that seemed to be in the perfect location.

I headed to the spot that I'd decided would be the first to get hit. Out of habit I parked down the block next to a lingerie store that gave me a clear view of the location that I planned on robbing. Settling in to watch, I sparked a blunt. The limo tint on the car windows ensured that I couldn't be seen. After sitting there for about three hours, the lights in the lingerie store I was parked in front of were cut off. Instinctively I sat lower in my seat. This is why I was there; to get the pulse of the area. To see who came around, why, and when.

Then out walked a bitch so bad that my mouth dropped open. She was about 5'7", caramel brown skin with her hair pulled back in a long ponytail showing off a slim sexy neck. Once she turned around to lock the front of the store up, her plump but firm ass brought me back to reality. I hopped out of the car momentarily forgetting what I was there for.

"Hey, hey excuse me miss," I said. Baby jumped startled.

"Oh, hell no! You scared the shit outta me. Where did you just pop up from any ways?" She asked. Even though she was startled her voice was calm, smooth and sweet.

"I apologize, sweetheart, but I guess that makes us even," I said sliding up on her. She put her hand on her hip tilting her head to one side.

"And how does that make us even? I just came out of the store to lock up and you scared the shit out of me!" Her eyes stared into mine as she waited for an answer.

"Exactly!" I shot right back. "I was just sitting here minding my own business and your fine ass came out and startled the shit outta me." This made her laugh.

"I'm going to keep it real, if I wouldn't have at least introduced myself to you tonight, I would have never been able to forgive myself." I extended my hand. "I'm King, it's a pleasure to startle you." I was smiling genuinely as I cracked the little joke.

"King? Like Martin Luther King?" she asked, chuckling at her own joke.

"No ma, like King, looking for a queen." That did it. She put her head down blushing, and when she looked back up, her eyes were different, they were softer. "I'm not tryin to hold you up, you probably got a nigga at home waiting for you," I said, probing further.

"Nah, I don't have that problem. Where are you from, you're not from out here?!" she asked.

"That's right, but why do you say that?" At first, I didn't understand what she meant.

"Cause nigga's out here is dusty and they don't know how to approach a female." She got momentarily irritated. I had to keep her in the moment. Baby was beautiful!

"Oh well shit, I'ma be rich then!" I shot back.

"Huh!?" She was curious again.

"I'm going to charge these nigga's, and teach them how to startle beautiful woman." At this she busted up laughing again. "Can I walk you to your car?" I asked.

"Yea, I guess so," she said mockingly. "You made me laugh and you ain't bad to look at."

"That's what up!" I responded, downplaying the compliment. I didn't want to seem arrogant. "Look gorgeous, you done got me so twisted that I forget to ask your name."

"Faith," she replied sheepishly.

"Oh shit, you the one my grandma used to talk about." Faith gave me a disbelieving look. I continued. "You think I'm playing huh?" I said teasing her. She was curious so I went on.

"When I'd ask my grandma how come you're so positive no matter how bad things seem grandma?" She would always look me dead in the eyes and say, "Cause baby, I got Faith!" Faith punched me in the chest affectionately but it was clear that my wit made her curious.

It's important to remember that you won't ever be the flyest. You won't ever have the biggest dick or be the richest, but if you can do two things, you will have a woman's heart! If you can make her laugh and stimulate her mind, you can get any woman. Faith and I exchanged numbers, hugged, and then parted ways for the moment. I was grateful that she never asked what the fuck I was doing there sitting in my car at two in the morning. We both drove off but I doubled back. There was still surveillance that needed to be done. Little did I know at the time, but Faith was soon to become a permanent fixture in my life.

Chapter 34

BETRAYAL

[Present]

"Hello," Keisha answered gruffly. She looked over and saw that King was already out of the bed. She walked through the house real quick calling his name. No answer. She opened the door that led to the garage. The AMG Mercedes was gone. He probably went to run errands after he dropped Alisha off at work, Keisha thought.

"Yes, I'm calling to confirm a pizza order before delivery," came a voice over the phone. Fuck, Keisha thought, this was her supervisor at the DEA. Antonio Vargas, no other than the white boy Jamille introduced to King, who was supposedly looking to buy two keys of dope. This phone call was how the DEA made sure that Keisha was alone. If King was there or if she was unable to talk, she would say that she hadn't ordered a pizza, then hang up. If King wasn't around, she would confirm the order.

"Yes, medium pepperoni," Keisha replied. She was already irritated.

"One moment Special Agent Johnson, I'll patch you through," said the dispatcher from the other end. Keisha took a second to wipe the sleep from her eyes.

"Agent Johnson, are you there?" the voice of Keisha's supervisor cracked through the phone.

"Yea, I'm here," said Keisha.

"I'm calling to get a report of where the investigation on King stands. The higher ups are getting antsy. You've been deep undercover for nine months now, with little results."

Keisha sat on the edge of the bed, she knew that this white asshole was going to try and push her buttons. He must have forgotten that the DEA had sent her undercover because those little dick fucks had their eyes set on bringing down King for three years, and had gotten nowhere.

"I would think that you of all people, Agent Vargas, would know that it's easier said than done. King runs a tight ship. He doesn't say incriminating things. I've never seen him make any kind of narcotic transactions. Not to mention, if I push too hard for information, I'll blow my cover. King is suspicious of everyone and everything. Let's not forget that I put you on to his boy Jamille. Where have you gotten with that?" Agent Vargas breathed heavily into the phone. He knew she was going to ask this.

"That's the other reason I was calling. Jamille set up a meeting for me with King to buy several keys. I was so fucking close," Agent Vargas momentarily lost his cool. "This shit happens every time I get close to that mother fucker."

"And?" Keisha was getting impatient.

"I had a wire on, but King wanted me strip searched. He wouldn't say a single word before I was." Keisha smiled on the other end of the phone.

"Ok?" Keisha replied dryly.

"Well things quickly got out of hand because Jamille was anxious to make the deal. We knew that he had a drug problem, that's why we went after him in the first place. Anyway, he pulled a gun out and blocked the door preventing King from leaving." Keisha had a feeling where this was going. Although she had never personally witnessed King's violent side, she was briefed before she went undercover as a "stripper", and she had been shown pictures of people the DEA believed had been tortured and murdered by King.

"So, what about the meeting? How did it end?" Keisha asked.

"That's the thing, we were supposed to meet this morning. Neither King or Jamille showed up. We had surveillance on Jamille's apartment, so we knew that he hadn't left his apartment since the previous night. He had one visitor at about nine in the evening. It was his heroin dealer from next door, but after that no one came or went. We would have rather had Jamille at home getting high, instead of risking King getting a hold of him before we could," Agent Vargas sighed as he finished.

"Did you guys do a knock and talk?" Keisha asked. This was a tactic that law enforcement used when they didn't have enough evidence for a search warrant. They would just knock to see if someone would answer the door and they could rattle some cages.

"We did," said Agent Vargas. There was no response so we finally got the building's maintenance man to unlock the door! We told him that we needed to do a welfare check on the tenant. Once inside I can't say that I was surprised at what we found. Jamille and his dealer were both sitting on the couch with needles still sticking out of their arms; dead! Their mouths were fixed in an agonizing grimace. They had white foam around their mouths and their heroin was still sitting on the plate between them. We sent the dope to the lab but either way we can't connect it to King," Agent Vargas finished, sounding defeated now.

"And yet?" Keisha knew that there was more.

"And yet I knew that he was behind it." Agent Vargas sounded like a man under a lot of stress. "If you could have seen the controlled fury in King's eyes at the meeting. If Jamille wasn't so high he would have known that death was staring at him. King was smart though, he didn't say anything. He just sat there, smiled and whispered something in Jamille's ear as he left."

"That's why I had agents posted on Jamille all night, I didn't want to lose him before our next meeting, but I was only worried about King having him killed, fuck!" He yelled. "Every time it seems I'm one step closer, I end up moving three steps back."

Don't feel bad Keisha thought, King is smarter than you!

"Hello, hello, Agent Johnson are you there?" Agent Vargas was getting irritated now.

"Yeah I'm here," Keisha snapped back from her thoughts.

"Ok listen, the chief of the department has decided that the King indictment is now the top priority. He said if you can't close the book on this thing in ninety days, we're pulling the plug and taking a different route." Keisha knew that a "different route", meant some shady shit. Planting dope or getting a "witness" to lie on King would be their next tactic in an attempt to bust King. Keisha had never been involved with anything like that personally, but she had heard the stories told by older agents. She knew for a fact that it happened in the

DEA. The line between the good guys and bad was hard to see sometime's. The DEA had done its fair share of dirt.

"Ok I'm on it!" Keisha replied halfheartedly.

"Are you Agent Johnson?" Vargas asked sarcastically.

"What the fuck is that supposed to mean?" Keisha snapped. There was a long silence.

"Just don't forget whose side you're on! We're the good guys," Agent Vargas chastised. Keisha laughed out loud and hung up.

Sitting on the bed, "Keisha's," Agent Johnson's head was reeling. She came into this believing in fact that they were the good guys. Now she wasn't so sure. The picture that the DEA had painted of King was that of a monster. This was not the King that she had fallen in love with. She knew a man who would help anyone he could, even strangers. She knew a man who bought the whole Sacramento Vikings pop warner football team cleats and uniforms when they were in jeopardy of not having a season because they didn't have them. They didn't know the man who was intelligent and who could stay up all night talking religion, politics, or philosophy. They didn't know the King who went to get me cold medicine at three in the morning when I was sick, or lifted my spirits with motivating talks when I was feeling depressed.

Plus, Keisha thought, who is the DEA to want to put King away for life? What about the prescription pill epidemic that they knew about for years before it became an issue? Hundreds of thousands of addicts created with Uncle Sam's consent because the big pill companies were paying millions in taxes and bribes to government officials. Where's the justice there? Keisha sighed, she knew that if the DEA got its hooks into King, there would be no justice. She better than anyone knew that. The courts would go through the motions but his fate would be sealed.

Then Agent Johnson reached for her vibrator as her thoughts shifted to the way King made love to her. After they met at the club it didn't take long for them to make a genuine connection. Still, it took a month after she had moved in with him before he laid a hand on her. Even then it came as a total shock and surprise.

(Memory) Keisha thought she was dreaming since she'd been sexually frustrated recently but it felt so real. She felt the covers move like someone had slid under the cover from the foot of the bed. Strong hands began to gently caress the inside of her thighs. She felt soft gentle tickles at first, and then full strong rubbing and gripping of her inner thighs. Her juices began to flow, soaking her laced Victoria Secret panties. Suddenly the hands stopped and Keisha thought that the "dream" would end. Keisha rotated her hips sensually, then realized that this was no dream. King had placed his hands on the inside of Keisha's thighs at the knees and gently but firmly pushed them down, and open!

King was going to take her pussy and she had been waiting for it and wanting it. King put his mouth on Keisha's honey pot while her panties were still in place. His hands still clenched her thighs at the knee's. Licking slowly at first, right through the lace of the panties, he seemed to be taking in the very essence of her being.

King slipped a single thumb inside Keisha's skimpy panties moving them to the side and began tracing his tongue along the outside of her beautifully sculpted and shaved pussy lips. This was not a dream! Keisha thrust her hips forward wanting to feed his hungry mouth. She reached out, gripping his back, as his muscles flexed, and then released with each lick. Keisha could tell that King was getting hungrier but he was patient. King pulled her panties up, right between the lips of her juicy mound, stimulating her swollen clit. Keisha groaned! Then her panties slid off, almost magically.

"King, I need you!" She moaned before she realized what she'd said.

"Relax, feed me that sweet pussy!" King said as he reached up tracing her firm nipple with his finger. Before she could speak, he had a finger inside of her tight wet pussy while massaging her clit with his tongue. King could feel Keisha's walls gripping his finger. He didn't know that she had only had sex with one other person, and that was while she was in college. So, when he curled his finger inside of her pussy, pushing up from underneath her clit while gently sucking on it from the outside, Keisha could barely contain herself.

"Fuck King, oh my God! What are you doing to me?" Keisha asked. Seeing her so outside of herself had Kings dick on throb. "I'm going to cum King, I'm going to cum!" Keisha reached down and grabbed his long hard steel in her hand "Holy shit," she half moaned and cried. "Fuck, my God I want that dick inside me please!" She screamed.

In one motion King slid up, placing the head of his monster between her pussy lips but not inside of her yet. He guided it up between her lips stopping to let the head gently rub her erotic center. King grabbed her hands in his, holding her hands down over her head and on the bed. At the same time, her tight little wet pussy hungrily swallowed the tip of his shaft. Keisha opened her mouth but nothing came out. She felt her body shudder.

Slowly, King slid inside her and was shocked at how tight she was. His hard flat stomach was pressed against hers. His thrusts were massaging her clit while he was filling her up in a way that she never knew possible. Keisha was flat out screaming.

"Ahh, ahh, ahh, please don't stop, King! Ahh, ahh, oh shit! Yes, oh fuck ahh, ahh! I'm going to cum on your fat black dick King! Oh God, don't stop!" The second King took her tongue in his mouth in a passionate kiss, Keisha's body shuddered like the exorcist. She gripped his ass, and arched her back to give him the perfect angle to pound on her pussy.

"Don't stop Keisha, I'm about to cum!" King groaned. This violated every rule of undercover work, but it was too late. Keisha was caught up.

"Right there ma, look at me!" King commanded. When she looked at him, he reached underneath her grabbing her fat ass, and pulled her over his long rod that was dripping with her sweet juices. She could feel him explode inside her. While he came inside her, he gently sucked and kissed her neck, and then her mouth. They lay there for minutes. Neither one talking. For Agent Johnson, it was an out of body experience.

Keisha worked the vibrator in slow circular motions while reliving these memories. It didn't take long before her thighs locked and her back arched in orgasm. That's the thing she thought, they don't know that there are, "Two Kings".

Chapter 35

GRAB THE BAG

[Past]

Me and Bheef sat in the whip talking and smoking. He flew in the day before, so we spent the time going over details and inspecting our equipment. For him, a Mac II with a soft suppressor. He also had a twelve pound kevlar vest and a sawed off twelve-gauge Mossberg pistol grip pump. For me, the same vest and a Cz75B 9mm.

Lastly was the masks, zip ties, ear pieces and burner gloves. It may seem like a lot for a lick when the purpose is to be in and out, but this ain't no fucking movie and in the real world, what can go wrong, usually does. You just better be ready for it.

"So, like I was saying," I said as I passed the blunt to Bheef. "I've already been in the store twice, so I know the whole layout." Bheef nodded. "At this time of night there will only be four employees inside. Two regular cashiers, an unarmed security guard and a white boy in his twenties that sits at the little desk inside the mini casino." Bheef didn't ask any questions, so I continued.

"The name of the game is control! Ya feel me!?"

"Fasho blood, just lay it out for me one more time," Bheef said, blowing a cloud of kush smoke out.

"Ok, check game! We're going to pull up on bicycles right to the front door. I'm going to walk in first. Make sure that you're right behind me! After I walk in the front doors, I'm gonna bust a quick right, to head to the mini casino. I'll contain the white boy there and get the cash. Right when we walk in to the left will be the security guard. Draw down on him first, put him face down and then zip tie him."

"Ok, ok King, got it!" Bheef nodded.

"I'm gonna have to walk my guy to the safe, so while I'm doing that, you go to the two women at the cash register and put them face down and then zip tie them. Don't say anything more than what's necessary."

The police would try to use anything in court, even the sound of a voice to try to identify a suspect.

"Ok what about after that King!?" Bheef wanted to be sure that he understood everything. Ever since King got back from the Army, there was something about him that made Bheef not want to disappoint him. The way that King carried himself now was different. He was more confident. He also had a violent side that made Bheef cautious.

"Go back to the front doors, pull the security guard by his feet to the side and out the way so that no one can see him from outside. When you tie up the two cashiers, make sure that they can't be seen from the front doors. Then just post on the side and out of the way while you wait for me. All of this shouldn't take more than two to three minutes. With these ear pieces you'll be able to hear everything I'm saying and doing but don't talk into it unless it's an emergency."

"Ok King, on da dead homies, I got you!" Bheef exclaimed.

"One last thing Bheef!"

"Sup my nigga!" Beef turned his head to look at me. I looked him straight into the eyes.

"This is a robbery, not a murder. The pistols are for emergencies only, ya feel me! A last resort!" Some nigga's you had to say that to.

We sat for a few more minutes in silence finishing the blunt. At first butterflies and nerves are racing inside of me but right before it's time for action, a surreal calm comes over me. I'm not sure if this is true for Bheef. I started the car and then headed to where the bikes were stashed, which was about a half mile away, on the side of a canal. There was nothing else that needed to be said!

We got on the bikes and headed to the lick. "Can you hear me?" I asked Bheef over the ear pieces. I wanted to make sure that the ear pieces were working.

"Yea nigga, it's like you in my head." Bheef replied. Good I thought, then this will go smooth.

Before we pedaled into the parking lot, we pulled our masks down. No part of our skin or face was showing. Long sleeve under armor shirts with ninja style masks made sure of this. Only the slits of our eyes could be seen. Bheef had the Mac II hanging around his neck from shoelaces. The Mossberg was strapped on his back in a tennis racket holder. My .9mm was in my waste.

"Let's grab the bag my nigga," I whispered before I hopped off of the bike and through the double doors.

"On you blood, I'm right here," Bheef whispered.

Thing's looked just the way it did when I cased it out days before. Everyone was in their places like it was the set of a movie stage or some shit. Within ten steps of entering the store I was drawing down on the clerk. He looked up to see who this late-night slot player was but it wasn't what he expected. His mouth dropped open and his eyes bulged out of their sockets when he saw who stood before him.

"Listen please sir and listen carefully cause I'll only say it once ok?" I said as I leveled the .9mm at him for effect. He shook his head vigorously. "First I want you to open that cash drawer with those keys on that hook." I pointed at the keys and it clearly unsettled him that I already knew where the keys were located.

"Then I want you to open that cupboard where the safe is and...." He looked like he was about to speak so I cut him off by putting my finger to my mouth, "shhhh!" I whispered. I saw that he had a wedding ring on so I kept talking.

"If you tell me you can't, or won't open the safe, you'll die tonight sir. What will that do to your wife?" He unconsciously looked down at his left hand to his wedding ring. When he looked back up, he said, "Ok."

"Get to it, hurry up!" I demanded as politely as possible. It's hard for people to think when they're under this kind of stress and pressure, so calm but direct words work best. He did as he was told and within two minutes the dough was stuffed in my small backpack. "Get on your stomach and put your hands behind your back!" I ordered once he was done.

"No please, you promised," he pleaded.

"You're gonna be fine sir, I'm gonna just tie you up so that you don't hop up and do nothing stupid while I'm still here!" He was consoled and relieved a little by this.

"O-o-ok!" He finally got out. After tying him up, Bheef and I calmly walked out and hopped on the bikes. We pedaled the half mile to the whip, threw the bikes over the fence into the canal and drove away at a leisurely pace.

When interviewed later, that witness told the police that no, he could not identify the suspects. In fact, no one could describe anything about the suspects except for their clothes. He also said that he had never been robbed before, that he was scared, but that if he had to be robbed again he'd want it to be the same guy. The detective asked, "Why?" with a curious look on his face.

"Cause he was just so damn polite," the witness responded.

As the number of heists increased to about nine, the LVPD dubbed me the "Polite Prowler." It was funny at the time but in reality, this was the way detectives formed MO's (Method of Operations). With little else to go on they tied a string of armed robberies to the same one or two suspects based on these similarities in the way that the robberies are done. It wouldn't be funny to me for long. It's like I said earlier, in the game, enough is never enough. Entering the game without an exit plan is where most hustlers go wrong.

Chapter 36

TREACHERY

[Present]

I needed time to think. It seemed like my whole world was caving in. What the fuck else could go wrong? This shit was overwhelming! First Jamille, and now Rico? I wasn't even sure if I should believe that bitch ass nigga Capone? Was Rico really a part of this shit or was Capone just trying to fuck Rico over since he knew that he was about to die?

Rico's been down with me from the beginning! Since I first got back from Tijuana Rico has been there! We've shed blood and tears together. He'd gotten rich off of the organization that I'd built, but at the end of the day, what the fuck does any of that shit mean? What is loyalty except a concept bitch ass nigga's hide behind? It's easy to say that you're loyal when your'e loyalty ain't tested. One thing for sure, I had to get to the bottom of this treachery. There will be no rest for me, or anyone else until I root out all of the infected parts in my organization. I don't give a fuck if I have to kill everyone in the circle and then start fresh. If my nigga's have they mind set on being King, I'll bring in my out of town killa's to put in the work. The personal shit I'll handle personally. It's time to play chess!

"Hello." Keisha answered.

"Sup baby girl, watcha got going on right now?" I was driving on the freeway when I called her.

"Nothin, jus sitting here flipping thru the channels, trippin off this Love & Hip-Hop shit! Why what's up?" She suddenly said more seriously.

"I'm on my way home, I'll be back in like thirty minutes. I want you to pack me a bag with my boxers, t-shirts, socks and my toiletries."

"O-o-kay," Keisha sounded it out, looking for more info.

"Ha, yo ass is so nosey" I chuckled, masking my unease.

"I told you the other day that I had something planned for you," I said.

Deciding that I needed time to think, I'd sent Alisha to her mom's and planned a trip out of town for me and Keisha, since I'd promised her a surprise anyway.

"Just pack us some light bags, we're gonna be gone for a few days. Don't trip off packing a bunch of clothes Keisha, we're gonna shop while we there." I knew that saying that would get her excited.

"Ok, ok, yee, I'm so happy! Where are we going?" she asked.

"You just don't quit huh?" I said while shaking my head over the phone laughing. "Just ride wit me love; you know I got you. Just be ready in thirty minutes ok, I want to pull up and be gone."

"Im going to start packing right now King, yeeee, I'm so excited, see you in a minute babe," Keisha almost screamed with delight.

"Ok, bye." I was about to hang up.

"Wait, King?" Keisha said softly.

"Sup!"

"King, I love you!"

That was the first time that she had ever said that shit and it caught me off guard; I didn't know exactly how to respond. With everything that's been going on, I just didn't know who I could trust.

"Okay baby girl I'll see you in a little while," I answered. It sounded weak when it came out, but I'm just not sure that I know what "love" is, or if it's real! For sure I care for her strongly but I don't know what real sacrifices I would make for her, or her for me. Right now, I need to focus, not be thinking about love.

It was going to take about two hours to get to the cabin in Lake Tahoe from Sacramento. I called the maid service to have it cleaned, the refrigerator stocked, the linen changed and some flowers with candles waiting. The cabin had a beautiful view of Lake Tahoe from both the bedroom and living room balconies. Keisha would get her "special" time and I would get time to walk on the beach alone and think. I had to go back with a plan that would expose the treacherous nigga's in my organization. No one else knew of this cabin so I could relax my mind and think clearly for a few days. I was taught many years ago that you had to keep a spot that absolutely no one knew about. I'd never realized how important it was until now.

"Keisha, lean the seat all the way back, I don't want your nosy ass tryna figure out where we going the whole way," I told her.

"King, you playin, come on babe. I won't look I promise," Keisha lied weakly.

"Ok," I laughed sarcastically. "You can't help it, on everything, I swear once you stop dancing your ass needs to apply to the Police Department with your detective ass."

Keisha looked at me with an almost guilty look. I just figured that she didn't like being called nosy. She started to recline her seat back again. I wanted to let her know that I was just teasing.

"Babe, it's just the woman in you, I ain't mad atcha," I said harmonizing with 2Pac's song. She smiled a forced smile and we hit the highway. The BMW 750 floated on the freeway, smooth as a newborn baby's butt; Keisha dozed off and I began thinking.

Nigga's see a muthafucka's success and they want what he's got. They think that he got to where he's at easily. They don't know the sacrifices, the pain, and the loss that he went through! They just see the results. I'd sacrificed too much, endured too much pain, and suffered more loss than anyone knows. I don't dwell on the past, but that don't stop the memories from being painful. It still hurts when I think about it.

Chapter 38

PAINFUL MEMORIES

[Past]

"Cell 248 lockdown," the officer screamed. Clark County Jail was run by a bunch of racist white Sheriffs. The nigga's that were there were all throw off members of gangs that originated in L.A., like Rollin 40's, Backstreet and shit like that. I needed to bail out asap. I was working on that.

"Man fuck you, I'm trying bail out, y'all not given me time to handle my business," I said as I turned my back to the officer and started dialing my next number. The slider door to the mod slid open and in came ten steroid using sheriffs, excited to have someone who bucked back. They worked me over real good. I was tased, busted in the head with a nightstick and thrown in the hole. My hand swole up to the size of a balloon. They broke two of my fingers in the tussle.

I was only in jail at the time because I got pulled over and Juju's ass had left one single loose valium pill in the center console. The charge was possession of a level IV-controlled substance. It was a felony, but barely. They called it a "wobbler". The pill wasn't mine, but that didn't change the fact that I was the one in jail.

Finally, I got a hold of a bail's bondsman. My bail was ten thousand, I only needed ten percent, which was a thousand dollars to post bond. That's official, I could swing that.

"Ok, look Mikey," I said to the bondsman. I could hear him typing over the phone. "I'll have the thousand dollars to you in thirty minutes. How long after that will I be out?" I asked excitedly. Shit, I was thinking that I might have a lawsuit or some shit. The way that they had whooped my ass had to be illegal.

"Hold on King, I'm trying to figure something out," the bondsmen replied.

Fuck!! I mouthed silently. It was always something. I tried to stay calm, "Ok, what you mean, figure out what?" I asked in my most composed voice.

"Well, it says that your bail is ten thousand, but when I tried to initiate the bond process it says that you have a seventy-two-hour hold, and in red it says, "Contact Jail Facility". This is new to me; I've never seen this. Can you call back in five minutes King? Let me see what I can find out." The bondsmen sounded genuinely perplexed.

Looking at the clock, I saw that I had about twenty more minutes before I had to lockdown for the night. It was weird that they had me on high level security, 23-hour lockdown, and I just had a bullshit possession charge.

"Ok Mikey. I'll call back in five, I need outa here ASAP!"

We hung up. It was the longest five minutes in history. A hustler's instincts sniff out bullshit. There was some bullshit brewing. I called back five minutes later.

"Well Mikey, what did you find out?" I asked nervously.

"They got you on seventy-two hour hold while they investigate you for other crimes. They wouldn't say what." But I knew what! Fuck I thought!

"I can post your bond now though; you just won't be released until the seventy-two hours is up." I was sick in the stomach, but I kept it cool. We can't choose what happens to us, but we can choose how we react to what happens to us.

"Let me check on something Mikey and I'll hit you back. If not tonight, then tomorrow for sure."

"Ok King, no worries, good luck." He sounded genuine but the fact that he thought I needed good luck unsettled me. Did he know more than he was telling me?

I hung up and tried to call Faith who I had been seeing since the night in front of the lingerie store. She had been my "square" bitch for the last six months. I still had Juju, but while she was at the brothel I was booed up with Faith. I even got a side spot with her. That's where I kept my pistol, masks, gloves and everything else I used during the robberies. She didn't answer the phone the first time I called. Fuck!

"King, hang it up, your'e time's up!" The deputy yelled.

This punk ass officer was smirking at me. They knew that I had a lot going on and they couldn't wait to lock me down. I didn't want him to see me sweat, so I played it smooth.

"Yep," I said as I locked it up – sleep would not come that night.

Early in the morning the next day right after breakfast, "King, get dressed, you got an official visit," came over the cell intercom. A little part of me hoped that it was a lawyer or bail bondsman, but since I hadn't paid for one, the odds of that were really low. I got dressed and they escorted me to an "interview" room. Really, it was an interrogation room. When I walked in, there were already two plain clothes detectives seated with a tape recorder on the table.

"King, nice to meet you, I'm detective Walters, this is my partner, detective Jennings," the short clean-cut detective announced. "I'm going to keep this brief; we're investigating you for a string of armed robberies here in Clark County." I looked shocked and shook my head no. "Well we were hoping that you could clear a few things up for us." He tried to continue. I shook my head no again. Again, no words.

"You won't talk to us?" The other fat sloppy detective chimed in. Another head shake no was all that he got in response. "Ok, well right now we're getting a search warrant for your house." He barked. I looked unconcerned. Really, my heart was pounding so hard that I swore they could hear it.

"You think I'm bullshitting you little fuck!" He slammed his hand on the table and flipped over a picture of the apartment that me and Juju shared. I threw my hands up like I didn't know what to say. I still didn't speak though. I learned early in the game that the police would literally use anything that you said against you. When they read you your rights while placing you under arrest, they tell you that, "Anything you say, can and will be used against you." They mean that shit.

Sleep didn't come that night. I was stressed. The good news was that I didn't have shit at the spot that me and Juju shared. The bad news was that once they got to that spot, they would find the paperwork that I had hidden in the closet for the rental of the apartment that I had with Faith. It would take them a little time to get another search warrant for that apartment but they would get it. If I didn't get Faith to get that shit out of the apartment, it would be bad for me. That next morning, I was blowing Faith's phone up but I knew that she was at work. These county jail phone calls are also recorded, so I had to choose my words carefully once I did finally get through.

"Hello!!" Faith finally answered the phone. She sounded irritated.

"Babe it's me!" I knew that she could hear the relief in my voice.

"Nigga, this been you calling? What happened? What's going on?"

Faith was a good girl. I hoped that she could catch my message without me having to say too much.

"Faith, listen, they locked me up on some bullshit, it's no big deal, I'm not worried," I lied. "They'll figure out that I didn't do shit." Faith told me to hold on so she could help a customer. I was getting impatient. I was working on borrowed time. When she came back on the line I started talking again.

"Look Faith, I left the house really messy, you know I hate that! You need to go home and clean up now," I tried to lead her.

"King, I'll do that when I get off!" Faith definitely wasn't catching on yet. She was more confused by why I was worried about that when I was sitting in jail.

"No Faith, you need to do it now! Listen to me!" I'd never really been demanding with her before; she went silent.

"Go home, clean the vacuum bag out because it's full of dirt and dust from all the house work I've done! Dump out all of the crap in the bag so that the vacuum will work better." That was as far as I could go over the phone. I was sure that the detectives were listening to my calls.. If I said something that even hinted at my guilt, they would use it to fuck me.

"King, the only other person here is new, she can't run the store alone!"

"Faith, fuck that goddamn job, fa real, do what the fuck I tell you!" This shook her. I'd never cursed or raised my voice at her either, but this was life and death. One armed robbery in Nevada could get you thirty years.

"Ok ok! It's eleven I'll leave at noon on my break, ok?" She replied meekly.

"Listen Faith, once we get off the phone, I won't be able to call till tomorrow. Do you understand exactly what I need you to do?" I shot back sharply, but I was pressing my luck by even saying that much.

"Yes King, why are you talking to me like this?" Faith said in a hurt voice.

I wanted to explain to her but couldn't, she'd find out when she got home. She had no idea what was in the bag of the Hoover Vacuum but if the police got to it first, I would never get out of prison. They would have all they needed to give me a life sentence.

"I'll call you tomorrow. Make sure you throw everything away in the bag too. I don't want that dust and shit to come out on the carpet." This would definitely show me how down she was. In that bag was a Glock, mask, zip ties, and over twenty thousand in cash. There was nothing that I could do now but wait. There was no telling what she would do once she saw what was in the bag.

I had another restless night followed by a long day, but before I got a chance to call Faith, the officer told me that I had a visit. It was Faith! When I got seated behind the glass in the visiting booth, I grabbed the phone. Faith stared at me for a minute. She finally picked up the phone on her side of the thick glass that separated us.

"Soooo," she started. "I cleaned the house, King." I looked up saying thank you with my eyes. She went on. "About an hour after that, a shitload of police officers came banging on the front door."

I just stared at her. This is not what I needed to hear.

"They had a warrant and started tearing shit up." Faith was about to start talking again.

Before she went on, I set the phone in the booth down to mouth to her that she needed to be careful of what she said. She nodded her head letting me know that she understood. "I told them that there wasn't shit there," she said proudly. I smiled at her.

"But before they left, they took two pairs of your shoes and your dark grey Jordan hoodie." She looked at me closely to see if that worried me.

Ok, I thought, I know what that means, but every piece of clothing that I did dirt in, I burned. Shoe prints could be matched like fingerprints, so even my shoes had been destroyed. As long as the other shit was gone, I would be ok.

"King, we need to talk." Faith gave me a serious look but I gave her a look that let her know that she needed to be careful of what she said. Eyes and ears were on us, for sure!

"I'm pregnant, King," Faith finally said.

Definitely not what I expected to hear. I wasn't ready for a baby but Faith was a good female. Plus, the hustler in me thought, I fasho got her locked in now. No telling where all this legal shit was headed. I would need support from somewhere, especially if I went to prison.

"I'm not mad at that at all, are you good? You know I don't have no kids and I've been wanting a son." I wanted her to feel good about being pregnant, even though I wasn't sure how I felt.

"Yea I'm good King, but I need you home, not in jail." When she said that, I let out a sigh of relief. I had her, I thought to myself. As long as she wasn't considering having an abortion, she wasn't going anywhere, no matter what happened.

"Babe, this bullshit will be over in no time. Just take care of my baby and be there for me."

I don't' give a fuck what anyone tell's you, a real street nigga is concerned with himself first. His own needs! His own desires! A good bitch can't change that. A baby won't change that. His very existence is one of control over his environment and the people in it.

Faith drove home from the jail that day asking herself what she had gotten into. No doubt that she loved King, but she wasn't raised like this. The things that she found in the vacuum bag had taken her breath away. Who was this man who could be so funny, witty, and romantic? Who could be so supportive and nurturing? Who was so intelligent and kind? There were obviously two Kings, she had no idea he even had a gun before now. Hopefully it would all be over soon like King said, Faith thought to herself.

It wasn't meant to be. In addition to the possession charge, that night I got booked on eight counts of armed robbery.

(Prison) After four months in county jail fighting the possession charges, I ended up taking a plea for one year in Nevada State prison. The robberies were still pending but those would take longer to deal with. I'd be lying if I said that I wasn't scared. No matter how much dirt a hustler is doing, prison is one of those things that happens to other nigga's who was slipping, not you!! Turns out; that's not the case either.

I was on my way to ESP (Ely State Prison) a Maximum-Security Facility. It was designed to break you're spirit, and it often did. I'd already decided that it wouldn't do that to me.

When the prison bus pulled up to the prison, the bus had to go through a mountain that looked like a hole had been blown through it barely big enough for the bus to drive through. Once you drove through the crater in the mountain, the prison was surrounded on all sides by the same mountain. Basically, the prison was inside a mountain crater. There were four feet of snow on the ground when I got there.

"King, AJ2619," the officer yelled as I began to step off the bus.

"Right here," I answered dryly.

"Right here?" The officer shot back with anger in his voice. He put the clipboard down in the snow and stared at me.

Right here?" The correctional officer mocked my tone again. "You sound off with your name, number and sir when you speak to me do you understand!!?" There were about eight other officers lined up outside watching this all play out. This punk knew that they were watching to see how he'd handle the new nigger.

"You just said my name and number and I don't even call my pops sir, so that's not gonna fucking happen," I said calmly.

With that the other officers jumped into action. I was slammed to the ground and handcuffed.

"You little smart mouthed nigger, you think this is a fucking game? You're going to do what the fuck we tell you to do period?" There was a lot I didn't know about prison, especially this one. Needless to say, this was hands down the toughest and most violent prison in the state of Nevada. The officers participated in much of the violence.

"Now, you smart mouth monkey , lay the fuck down, face down," the officer yelled! He turned pink in the face as he did.

Damn, is this how the people that I robbed felt? It didn't matter, this cracker wasn't about to humiliate me. All the convicts on the bus were watching too, I couldn't go out like no bitch.

My memory from there over the next two days was blurry. Much of what I know came from the white convict who brought my food to me in solitary confinement. He was the only person I'd have contact with for the next ninety days.

"Hey, you're King, right?" The white convict asked as he slid the tray through the tiny slot in the door of my cell in the hole.

"Yeah why?" I asked.

"I'm a trustee, I saw what happened to you last week when your bus pulled up. That shit was fucked up, they didn't have to do that to you."

I didn't want to tell him that I couldn't really remember what had happened. Ever since the beating, my memory had been foggy. All I knew was that my head was heavily bandaged. I had a loose tooth and my back was shooting painful spasms.

"Oh yea, why do you say that?" I wanted to see if he would tell me.

"Man, you don't remember do you? You were probably knocked out which was good, but when you took your last step off the bus and into the snow, officer Roberson hit you in the back of your head with his nightstick. Roberson's a real son of a bitch and I just wanted to warn you to be careful King. We've had eight murders here this year and there's only a small black inmate population. The Aryan Brothers run this place. I'm from Oregon, so I'm not with that mess but I'm white and even I have to be careful. Anyway, I got to go, just wanted to put that bug in your ear."

"Thanks for that my man," I said as he pushed the food cart down the bleak corridor.

Over the next eighty-five days I went through hell. I wasn't allowed to use the phone. The officers would always say that the phones were broken. In the middle of the night several days a week two or three officers would storm in my cell at three or four in the morning screaming "stop resisting," as they beat me with padded clubs. Padded clubs didn't split you open but they damaged your insides. For about two weeks I had blood in my urine, but I was denied medical attention.

Nigger, coon, monkey, spade, jig-a-boo were the constant names that I was belittled with. I'd try to stay up all night to avoid getting caught slipping and beat up but that only lasted so long. I had to sleep. My food would come on the food trays clearly tampered with, so I started eating only fruit and unopened peanut butter packs. Through it all though I never begged these mutha fuckas for mercy. They were tryna break me but the only way that would happen, is if they killed me. That attempt was coming next. With five days left in my solitary confinement sentence, officer Roberson's steroid using racist ass came by my cell and kicked the door.

"King." He yelled, startling me out of my sleep. "You think you're a tough little monkey, don't you?"

I didn't respond, just stared at him.

"Well, let me tell you something you lil punk, you came with a year sentence, but you really got a death sentence. You see you fuck, what me and my boys can't do, I have the convicts do for me. It may be best for your fucking health if you do all of your time right here in solitary," he whispered while clenching his teeth and grinning. He left laughing loudly.

Two days before I was scheduled to get out of solitary, Officer Roberson came back with a sergeant. The sergeant did the talking this time and he was holding several papers.

"King, we have reliable info that your life may be in danger if you hit the main line. The only way that I can let you out of solitary is if you sign this release form acknowledging that we told you of the danger, and that we're not responsible for any harm that may come to you as a result of your release from solitary."

I signed the forms without delay or questions. They were shocked! For a second officer Roberson's face expressed something like admiration.

It didn't take long after my release from solitary to see that this place was in fact run by the Aryan Brotherhood just like the white boy had said. In a unit of eighty convicts, only thirteen were black. Of those thirteen blacks, only five were nigga's. Almost immediately, I clicked with a stocky nigga with dreads from Kansa City, Missouri. As soon as I walked in the mod, he walked up to me and introduced himself. After that, he gave me the lay of the land.

"Sup King, my name is KC my nigga." He kept his head on a swivel, looking around from left to right as he talked.

"What's good black?" I shot back. It was good to see a black face in "klanland".

"Come on brudda, I'll show you where ya cell is." Everyone was watching us. Some looked curious and others had hate in their eyes, but everyone had their eyes on us.

"Damn KC, what's all these bitches staring at?" I asked.

KC chuckled.

"Mutha fuckas been hearing about you King. Most the blacks here suck these white mutha fuckas dicks. They got no nuts, they've been castrated. Some probably feel that you're bad for the status quo. Here's your cell."

We stopped at cell 212 on the upper tier. It was written above the door in rusty yellow paint. We were standing outside the door.

"Them fools is harmless tho, it's that white boy Skinner and his Nazi crew dats deadin mutha fuckas around here. Eight murders this year, six of them blacks," he said, shaking his head.

"God damn," I said. By the numbers alone it looked like a bad situation. Shit, it was a bad situation. My door racked open with an electric buzz. I walked in and sat my laundry bag on the bed. At least I had a cell by myself for now. KC slid in behind me and shut the door a little.

"Here my nigga," he said as he handed me a prison made knife, a shank. "Don't go nowhere without this. If the officers catch you wit it, you go back to solitary. If Skinner and his boys do, you go home in a body bag." KC paused, then continued. "They open the doors at 5:30 am for breakfast and at 4:30 pm for dinner. When they do, wait for me! Don't leave your cell yet, don't walk nowhere alone. I've been here the longest of the blacks and I got a few white boys, not Nazis, that feed me info. Let's play it close until we figure out what these white boys is up to." It wasn't a question. He was letting me know that if I didn't listen to what he was telling me, it would cost me my life.

"I appreciate that KC, Roberson has it out for me, he threatened me directly."

"You have to take his threat serious King; he helps these white convicts do they dirt. He helps cover for them." KC looked concerned!

"Ok KC, good looking my nigga." We gave each other a lil dap, and I went in and shut the cell. There was a lot on my mind that night. Faith; my child in her stomach; and whether or not I'd make it out of here alive. What was it about me that would cause me to risk my life before I went out like a bitch? I could have stayed in solitary confinement where I would have been relatively safe. How the fuck did I end up here in the middle of this mountain with a bunch of racist violent white crackers? Fuck it, I could worry about that shit later, for now I had to stay alive.

For two weeks everything was smooth even though you could cut the tension with a knife. Anyone who's ever been to prison will tell you that before something big pops off it's like the air freezes. Time momentarily stops before it erupts! Things seem to be moving in slow motion.

Every morning me and KC would walk to chow together. Both of us were strapped down with shanks. We had to walk down a long corridor of about fifty yards before passing through a sally port with two sliding doors that opened and closed but that were controlled by the officers in the control room. They could lock whoever in or out as they saw fit. I was in front of KC as we approached the double doors. The three convicts in front of me were white boys.

"King, watch out my nigga!" KC screamed.

As I looked back, two white boys grabbed KC from behind, holding him, preventing him from coming into the sally port behind me. At the same time, the doors began closing, locking me in. Everything was happening so fast but it seemed like slow motion. As I reached for my knife, I had a split second to notice that it was officer Roberson at the controls in the control booth. He had set this up and he had a smug look on his face. There wasn't even enough time to be scared. My survival instincts took over.

The first sharp pain that I felt came in my right side, right above my hip. I yelled out in pain but just as quickly my knife got to slashing and striking back. All the rage and frustration that had built up over the last months had finally found a release. It was three on one, but if I was going to die today, I would go out banging.

I rushed the white boy that stabbed me first, driving him into the wall with my left forearm. I stabbed him three times under his left armpit. He shrieked out in pain, and he had an agonizing look on his face. I could smell the tobacco on his breath as he screamed. All the while the other two white boys were sticking me in the upper back, ass and legs.

Turning in a fury I could see the blood beginning to soak through my shirt. I took a quick glance to the right through the sliding doors at KC and I could see that the white boys were holding him down on the ground, but not stabbing him. This was a hit on me. I was on my own.

I switched my full attention back to my attackers. The buzzer and alarm finally started sounding that was supposed to bring officers rushing in to break this shit up. They did rush in but they weren't rushing to rescue me, and six seconds in this kind of situation might as well be six days.

Since Skinner was their shot caller, I focused the last of my strength on him. I rushed him in a football tackle wrapping both of my arms around his waist and then in a move instinctive from my military training, I trip slammed him. We both hit the ground with a thud, but I landed on top. His shank slid from his hand and into the wall. I pinned him to the ground and my shank violently entered and exited his side at the rib cage. The other white boy had a hold of my shirt collar and was attempting to pull me off with one hand while stabbing me in the back and head with the other. It didn't matter, I was latched onto this mutha fucka, locked like a pitbull. I was determined that someone was going to share my pain.

In a rage, while sticking him like a pig I said, "You wanna kill King you faggot mutha fucka?" I bent closer to his face and bit down over his eye, into his cheek and forehead. He screamed louder than before as the salty taste of this honkeys blood filled my mouth. My hand and knife were soaked with blood but I could feel my strength draining. The sliding doors finally began to open.

"Down, down, drop the fucking knife, drop it," the officers yelled as they stormed in. You would think that since I was the one getting assaulted by three people, they would go after them first. Wrong!! I was snatched off of Skinner and a boot was placed on the back of my neck. This was it, I was about to die today, in my early twenties with a baby on the way, at the hand of some racist convicts and correctional officers.

"Medics, medics, code ten, code ten priority." Another officer yelled into his radio. I lay there with a boot on the back of my neck pinning me to the ground and my life blood draining from my body. The medics rushed in. They went straight to the two Nazis that I had stabbed, assisting them while I bled out. Not only did I not get immediate medical attention but my arms were yanked behind my back, then handcuffed. Roberson intended for me to bleed to death. I passed out!

Chapter 39

The Trip

[Present]

"Baby, baby!" Keisha was calling my name. I was zoned out!

"Yeah, what's good!" Keisha snapped me out of my thoughts and back to reality.

"How much longer till we get there? I gotta use the bathroom." Keisha asked. She was still half asleep.

"We still got about an hour; I'll pull over at the next exit wit' a gas station."

"Ok," she said as she reached over and rubbed my thigh affectionately before shifting sideways in the plush leather of the BMW and dozing back off to sleep.

Chapter 40

Past Memories

[Past]

Once I regained consciousness, I was in a helicopter being airlifted to a hospital one hundred miles away. Ely State Prison was in the fucking boon docks. My shirt and pants had been cut and ripped off of my body. The medics were still trying to locate and stop the bleeding of the most serious wounds. At last count I had been stabbed eighteen times. Strangely enough the most serious wound was in my leg next to my femoral artery. Every time my heart beat, a little squirt of blood would shoot out. It was serious. The medics were frantic. It was clear that I wasn't out of danger yet. I was on the brink of death. They put something in the IV that took me back into a slumber.

The next three weeks were spent in a hospital room handcuffed to the bed, but it was still way better than what I had been through in the last nine months. As it turned out, with my county jail credits and my time in prison, it was about to be my release date. The problem was that I was supposed to have a "hold" that would make sure that I got sent back to Clark County jail to deal with the robbery charges. I was only being paroled on the drug charge, but for some reason that "hold" didn't show up, and they "accidentally" released me. I think they did it because I didn't die and Ely State prison was worried about being exposed for the criminal activities of their officers. Either way, I wasn't about to voluntarily go back to fucking jail; to "klanland". The day before my release I called Faith.

"Sup ma!" She wasn't expecting the call. The baby was almost due. "Oh my God King, I've been so worried about you! I'd call up there but they wouldn't tell me shit about what was going on with you!" Faith started crying.

"I know babe, these mutha fuckas is shady." Faith didn't even know all that I had been through while locked up.

"So, what's going on now? Your times supposed to be almost up isn't it?" Faith asked, sounding so hopeful that I couldn't' stand to break her heart again, not yet anyways!

"I get out tomorrow Faith." I couldn't even finish my sentence before she broke in excitedly.

"Oh my God, thank God, I'm so happy, I need you here so bad." I had to take my ear away from the phone. I knew that tomorrow I would have to break her heart yet again.

"I know, I know, me too babe. Look ma, I need you to be up here at eight tomorrow morning, don't be late ok!"

"Are you crazy? I won't be a second late", she screamed. Now came the tricky part, I asked, "Babe how much money do you have saved up?" She paused trying to figure out where I was going with this.

"Um, about $1,500 I think," Faith answered hesitantly.

"Ok look, I need you to bring all of that with you when you pick me up." I shot back quickly.

"Ooooh-kaaay." Faith was looking for more answers.

"I'll explain tomorrow, don't trip. I'll get the bread right back to you." It was a lie, but her excitement about me coming home overshadowed her logic.

"Ok King, oh my God I can't wait to see you." Faith got excited all over again.

"I know babe I'm so excited too." For the first time ever, I said, "I love you."

"I love you too, King." Faith replied as we hung up.

I didn't know if I loved her or not yet, but I needed her to do what I needed her to do. What she didn't know and what I couldn't tell her was that if that "hold" didn't show up in the next eighteen hours, I was going on the run. No way in hell was I going to give these crackers the chance to give me over a hundred years, or worse, kill me.

———————————

That Tuesday on the evening news in Las Vegas, the top story was, "Serial Armed Robber Tagged, The Polite Prowler Accidentally Released". The news went on to say that they believe he went on the run. They were right, but what they couldn't have known is just now far on the run I was going.

The next evening, I was crossing the border into Mexico through the SanYisidro border crossing in San Diego with fifteen hundred dollars to my name. That same day Faith lay devastated on the living room floor having awakened to a short letter trying to explain why I had to go. There was no explanation as to where I'd gone or when I'd be back, or back in contact. For now, I'd just as soon be considered dead to those who knew me, even those who loved me. The life of a hustler is often cold and lonely.

Chapter 41

PITSTOP

[Present]

"King, daddy, here comes an exit with a bathroom. Can we stop, please?"

"Oh shit," I had completely forgotten Keisha had to use the bathroom. "Yea Keisha, fasho, I'm a pull off right now."

"Are you ok, King? What's wrong?" Keisha asked lovingly.

"Nothing Keisha, I'm just in my thoughts." I wanted to change the subject. "Look, get some Swishers, Peanut M&M's, and a Kiwi Strawberry Snapple for me. If you want anything, get it, but we'll be there in thirty minutes."

"Ok, I'll be right back; I'll hurry!" Keisha exited the car. Now she had an idea of where they were going. Either Tahoe or Reno because they were at Donner's Summit. She'd been skiing there once before in high school. She pulled out her phone and was about to call her supervisor agent Vargas to let him know where she was. She dialed the first three numbers, then changed her mind and hung up. Keisha still had a few things that she needed to figure out for herself first. After using the bathroom, she got Kings' snacks and then went back to the car.

"Thanks, Keisha. Put your seat belt on, love."

Keisha smiled as she handed King his drink. This "monster" treated her better than any other man that she'd had in her life before now. Keisha and King were in tune. They vibed. When she was in one of her "moods," he didn't press her, but he was the best listener she'd ever known. His advice was always sound and based on concern for her. More and more, she wondered if she'd be able to betray him. Not to mention, she loved the lifestyle that he provided for them. The little money that she made dancing was nothing compared to the money he spent on her and them.

"Can I put the music on, King?" Keisha asked.

"Yea ma go ahead, do what you do!"

Keisha could tell King wasn't in a talking mood yet, so she put her shit on. That old-school Usher album, Confessions. She knew every word by heart. Keisha skipped the first song, "Yea, Yea," with Lil John, and the Harman Kardon system filled the car with beautiful clarity.

Keisha leaned back and was drifting off by the time they were back on the highway.

Chapter 42

TIJUANA CARTEL

[Past]

Crossing into Tijuana from San Diego, I might as well have stepped foot onto another planet. The looks alone were enough to shake me to my soul. I can't lie; it was scary. It was overwhelming to the senses. There was a multitude of bright colors on everything. There were storefronts in hand-painted bright red, blue, and yellow signs everywhere. Street vendors were selling everything from tacos to leather coats on the street corners. Cars were honking, speeding, and cutting each other off like there were no rules of the road. Then there was the graffiti!! Graffiti was on everything. Even though I couldn't read or speak Spanish yet, the graffiti sent an ominous message. It said, "All this shit belongs to someone or something."

Prostitution was legal, or at least it looked that way, and hookers lined an area by the border called Kohila in the hundreds. There wasn't an officer in sight to fuck with them. Mostly, it was the stench of poverty that couldn't be avoided. Poverty was everywhere. Many people still lived off unpaved roads, on dirt mountains, and in houses made of aluminum siding. That's what garage doors are made of in the United States.

On top of all this, I had nowhere to stay, and I didn't know a single soul that could help me. Dogs ran in packs on the streets like hyenas. I saw a fucking donkey pulling a cart on the highway, and I didn't see anyone with it. Once again, I was completely on my own. I started walking towards a group of taxis parked on boulevard Revolución.

"Amigo, amigo, morenito, ven acá," one of the taxi drivers called out, pointing at me. I looked behind me to be sure that he wasn't pointing at someone else, then I pointed at my own chest and said, "Me?"

"Si, si amigo," the taxi driver waved me over. "A dónde vas moreno?" he asked.

I didn't speak Spanish. He smiled brightly. I think he was proud that he spoke a little bit of English.

"W-h-at are you going?" the taxi driver asked in broken English. I put my folded hands to the side of my head like a pillow and said, "Sleep?" I was really tired. "Dormido? Tiénes sueño?" He followed what I was trying to say. He'd made the same gesture for sleep that I had. I nodded my head yes.

"You come; I take you good sleep." The taxi driver was smiling from ear to ear and seemed genuine. Shit, I was going to have to trust somebody at some time out here. No way I could pull this off on my own. Sometimes in life, all your choices are flat-out shitty. That's when you just have to choose the least shitty one.

"Ok," I said, getting into the taxi.

We drove for about ten minutes, before pulling up to a mom-and-pop's Mexican store. In the neighborhood back home, it reminded me of how the homies mom would sell candy, sodas, hot dogs, and chips out of her garage to us after school. There were no more than twenty items in the store but it was what we looked forward to most after school. The taxi driver hopped out of the car first, running around the front of the car to the passenger's side door to open it for me.

"Ven aca, ven aca. Todo está bien amigo! Está es mi familia. Todo es bien" He exclaimed. I was looking around. We were in an actual Mexican neighborhood now, not down by the border where you could still see the impact of American culture. The "houses" here were all packed together or stacked on top of each other. The streets were barely big enough for two cars to pass simultaneously side by side. The streets were littered with trash. Almost all of the houses had rudely constructed bars on the windows or gates around them. Then the dogs! The dogs were everywhere. I hopped out of the car as an older Mexican lady came out of the store. My taxi driver spoke rapid Spanish to the woman while she probed me over with curious but kind eyes.

Shortly after that, she waved me along to a gate; she unlocked the gate with a key that she had tied around her neck. Once she opened the gate, I saw that it led up some stairs. There were three small "apartments" above her "store." The apartment was no bigger than two prison cells. It had a toilet and sink, a two-burner stove that ran off propane and one window with no glass in it. This would be my home for the next ninety days.

The lady was the taxi cab driver's grandmother. Their whole family lived in the house below my apartment. They turned out to be kind and very family-oriented. Most important though, they weren't nosy. My rent was sixty dollars a month. They never once seemed to give a shit about why a heavily tattooed black man showed up on their front porch with a duffle bag and moved in. The grandmother even began teaching me Spanish. This would come in very handy; necessary even. I bought a bed, a small television set from Electra, our version of Best Buy, and settled in. After the initial fear left, I finally started venturing outside. I started by taking short walks in my new neighborhood, which was called Solér.

It may seem strange, but after about two weeks of being in Mexico, I was more at peace than I had been in a long damn time. Soon I figured out that although many Mexicans were poor, they were clearly happier and had better family relationships and values than do most families in America.

The streets in Solér were active. There were taco stand's, gymnásios, and tiéndas everywhere. Niños con chicles were being sold on all corners. Kids were playing soccer barefoot in the streets. Neighborhood swap meets were everywhere.

Banda music was bumping from houses or from live bands on the streets.

The best thing for me at that moment was that the police cars didn't have computers in them! At least I didn't have to worry about getting stopped and having my name ran by a Mexican cop one day. I didn't think I was the first mutha fucka to go on the run to Mexico, but I knew that I had the best chance of staying free if I was smart about how I moved. I knew that the moment I lost focus, I'd make a mistake. I had no plan as of yet except not to be in fucking prison, and for now, that was good enough for me.

I had about a grand left, and Mexico was pretty cheap, but I'd still have to figure out my next moves before I got too low on money. Sometimes life chooses for you. I was coming out of my "apartment" in Tijuana one day after I'd been living there for a month and heard.

"Hey, my boy, what's up?" I looked around but didn't see anyone. "Up here, my boy." The voice said again.

I looked up across the street and saw a tattooed face poking out of a window with a little curtain in it. He was pretty high up.

"Hey," I replied. He spoke perfect English, so I was excited.

"Where you goin my boy?" He asked.

Why was he worried about where I was going? I looked up at him suspiciously. He caught my hesitancy.

"Na man, it's not like that. I just been seeing you for a minute, my guy. You don't see too many blacks out here, especially ones that move in furniture and shit." He started chuckling to himself, and I thought that he really had been watching me. From where he was on top of a two-story house in a shed, he could look down on my apartment perfectly, so it wasn't hard to figure out how he had been keeping an eye on me.

"Hold on my boy, I'm coming down." He finally said.

It took so long for him to get down to me that I thought that he was bullshitting and wasn't coming at all. After I got to know him and went to his crib, I understood why. He had ladders, two sets of stairs, and a rope to climb down to get to me. Only in Mexico!! He finally made it down, then popped out of his gate grinning, and pushed his hand towards me.

"My boy, what's good? My name is Luni; I'm from 18th Street Los Angeles. That's my Aunty's crib I'm living in up there." He looked up towards the sky at his window. Luni was only about 5'4". He was powerfully built though and tattoo's covered almost every portion of his body, even his face.

"That's what's up," I said. "It's good to meet someone who speaks English. How long have you been living out here?" I asked.

"Shit, what month is it right now?" He asked me. I started laughing while he used his fingers to count. "Eighteen months now." He finally said.

"Damn," I said. "That's a minute; my name is King, by the way."

"Nice to meet you, King. What you doing right now, my boy?" he asked.

"Shit, I'm bored, mostly just tryna figure out the neighborhood," I responded.

"Well, come on, let's walk. I'll show you around," Luni said excitedly.

"Ok cool, let me go put some tennis shoes on real quick and take these sandals off."

I did change shoes, but I also tucked my money. I didn't know this cat, and to say that I was a fish outta water was an understatement. Turns out that the last thing that I needed to worry about with Luni was something like that; he was solid.

That day Luni walked me around the neighborhood almost a mile in every direction. He showed me where everything was. The best places to eat. The dope houses. The laundromat and where to buy my drinking water. We also went to several houses that belonged to his friends and family. Sometimes he'd knock on a door, and sometimes he'd just yell up to a window.

"Carlos, Carlos, es mi amigo King. Todo está bien con él." He'd yell up to a window.

"Bien, bien, mucho gusto King." They would waive out to us answering. I would nod. Luni told me later that that mucho gusto means nice to meet you. I didn't know it at the moment, but Luni had done a lot more than introduce me to the barrio. He had taken me around and, by doing so, he had given me the stamp of approval. He had let everyone in the neighborhood know that the new black kid was o.k.

When I walked around after that, it was all smiles, waves, and "hola amigo, como estás", from my neighbor's! I finally felt like I belonged. Luni and I were inseparable over the next six weeks. Every day we linked up. Sometimes we just chilled and smoked that Mexican brick weed or walked the neighborhood. He even took me to where all the nightclubs are at, down near the border. That was dope. Don't let nobody tell you differently; Mexicans know how to party.

After about two months in my jail cell sized apartment, I woke up to a shock. I had just opened up my eyes and was about to open the wooden shutter to let some fresh air in when I saw something that made my stomach drop. Federáles (Mexican Feds) lined the street in front of my spot, but they were all looking up towards Luni's shed on top of his aunty's two-story house. I could tell that his window was open because the sheet that he used as a curtain was flapping in the wind. Fuck I thought. I wanted to scream out to him, but I couldn't.

By that time, I knew that Luni was living with his aunty because he was on the run for a murder in Los Angeles. On several occasions, he had said that he wouldn't be taken back alive. He also had a six-shot .38 revolver with four bullets. I was there sitting there on the floor with my back against my front door, thinking and trying to figure out what I should do next. Shit, I was on the run myself. My thoughts were interrupted by a single shot. The sound made me jump.

"Pop!!" I could tell that the shot came from above me. Luni had fired a single shot at the Federáles. Then no more than three seconds later, a one-sided war broke out. The Federáles returned fire. Semi-automatic rifle fire filled the morning air. So many shots were fired that I was wincing and flinching behind my door. It sounded like a thunder storm. I was shaking like a leaf. The Mexican police clearly operated under different rules of engagement than in the US. After thirty seconds, all was quiet again. I felt bad for Luni, but I hoped that he didn't rat me out if he wasn't dead.

I found out the next day from his aunt that Luni had been shot, but that he didn't die. That hit too close to home for me. I needed to find somewhere else to live! I wouldn't feel safe there anymore. It only took two days to find it, and I moved to my new house a week later. I never found out what happened to Luni after that, but I don't think he ratted me out. The police would have found me pretty quickly if he had; there weren't too many blacks running around Tijuana.

Chapter 43

LAKE TAHOE

[Present]

"Oh my God King, this is so beautiful." Keisha shrieked.

"Huh?" My mind was still in a jumble. When I had important decisions to make, it was hard for me to give anything or anyone my full attention. My empire had been threatened, but these bitch ass nigga's didn't know what it took for me to get here. They don't know what I'll do to keep it either.

"Yeah, ma, I told you I had something special planned."

The maid service I'd hired to get the cabin ready did everything just as I had asked. It was beautiful. The fire was burning, champagne was on ice, and the candles were burning on the tables with Keisha's favorite roasted lamb warm in the oven. Upstairs in the jacuzzi tub, two dozen red rose petals were floating in the bubble bath.

"Mr. King, will you need our services any more this evening?" One of the assistants asked.

"No, that's all, thank you, everything looks wonderful."

I'd paid five hundred already for the service, and I tipped her two hundred as she left.

"That's very kind, Mr. King."

I smiled softly and nodded as I shut the cabin door behind her. Keisha was in front of the fire warming her hands. She'd already kicked her shoes off. I went to the kitchen and poured her a glass of champagne.

"Keisha, come here babe."

Keisha walked into the kitchen. I set the glass of champagne on the table and waved her to me. As she walked to me, I opened my arms, and she hugged me, wrapping her arms around my waist. Hugging her, holding her close, I put the side of my face to the side of hers and whispered.

"I want you to know how much I appreciate you. You've only added to my life and happiness; you've taken nothing away." Keisha moaned softly. "I want you to go upstairs; your bag is in the bathroom. Take a relaxing, slow bubble bath. Here's your champagne." I handed her the glass. "When you're done, come down in front of the fire so that I can give you a massage." Keisha just nodded. She damn near had tears in her eyes. While Keisha took her bath, I was going to walk on the Lake Tahoe shore to clear my head. By the time I got back to the cabin, I'd have all my important decisions made.

Chapter 44

CHANGE OF FORTUNE

[Past]

My next spot in Mexico was a little bigger. It was a brick house with an iron gate around it and it was on top of a dirt mountain. It was also more out of the way, so I only had two neighbors. The bad part was that now I was paying two hundred dollars a month, almost a hundred and fifty more than my last spot. The time would come fast when I would need to make money, but Mexico wasn't really booming with jobs.

After another month of paying my rent, my money was getting low and I was getting stressed. There were no jobs, especially if you didn't speak good Spanish. This wasn't a place to be selling dope or hitting licks, because that was a sure way to find yourself stuffed in a barrel with your hands and feet cut off. Overcoming this situation would be difficult, but I was determined to turn it into my greatest success!

Walking around Tijuana looking for a job started to get depressing. I also became very aware that my only "skill set" was hustling; selling dope, robbing, and pimping. Then it hit me, I was certified as a mortuary affairs specialist also. The military had to be good for something. I went to the three morgues in Tijuana, but there was no work to be had. Fuck! I was getting desperate. My feet were swollen. My spirit was on the brink of collapse. What the fuck was I thinking coming way out here anyway? In one more month, I'd be broke and homeless in Mexico. I would have been be better off locked up in the United States.

I sat down at a bus stop not far from my house and didn't know that I was sitting on my destiny. When I finally got up to walk home and looked down at the bus stop bench, I saw a faded advertisement for Carlos Medina and Family Funeral

Home. I walked the two miles to the funeral home. My life would never be the same.

"Buenos dias, ¿Cómo estas?" The middle-aged Mexican man said as I walked in. By then, I spoke a little Spanish, so I answered, "Bien gracias." But my Spanish was limited, so I just stared at him after that.

"Necessito ayúdar?" he asked. I nodded because I knew that he had asked if he could help me, but I couldn't explain more in Spanish. After he looked me over for about a minute, he continued talking in perfect English.

"How may I help you, sir?" he said. I wouldn't have looked more surprised if it was God talking to me. Once I picked my mouth up off the floor, I said.

"Yes sir, my name is King, and I really need a job."

He looked at me like, "What the fuck?"

It's not everyday that a black American walks into a Mexican funeral home looking for a job. He leaned back in his chair like a man holding all the cards. It was then that I noticed how well dressed he was. He had on clothes by Italian designers. The funeral home did not have the same look of money that he did. Except for the sign out front, it could have been any other shabby building or house in Mexico.

"I'm confused," he said. "Why would you come here looking for a job?" Now he seemed suspicious. I had to be quick on my feet, so I mixed the truth with a lie.

"Sir, I was living in San Diego and I was down to a thousand dollars to my name. I have no family, no friends, and nowhere to go, so I moved to Tijuana. I thought that my money would last longer out here. I've been looking for work, but I'm not qualified for anything! Anything except this!"

"And why are you qualified for this work?" he asked curiously.

"I served in the US Army as a Mortuary Affairs Specialist," I answered, leaving it simple.

"So why are you not in the Army doing that now, King?" There was something about the way he asked that question that momentarily shook me. He was probing to see if I would be truthful.

"I got kicked out," I said dryly.

"For what?" he asked, placing his knees on his elbows with his chin resting in his palms.

I paused, weighing my options! Fuck it, what have I got to lose, I thought.

"For selling weed," I answered quickly. Either he'd kick me out, or he'd have understanding. He followed up with more questions, and he was more serious while asking them.

"So, you say that you moved out here, King? You live here and are not just visiting?" He shifted forward in his chair as he asked the question.

"Yes sir." I said. I could barely answer; my throat was so dry. This felt like something deeper than a job interview.

"Where do you live?" He asked next. I explained, and he knew exactly where I was talking about. He knew exactly where my house was.

"You say that you have no family or friends?" He shot another question in as soon as I answered the last one.

"No sir." I partly lied. Then he became deathly serious.

"King, are you an American law enforcement officer?" That question caught me completely off guard. Subconsciously I looked around and cleared my throat. No one had ever asked me no shit like that before.

"No sir, I don't know what you mean!" I answered. At that same moment two more guys walked in, and these mutha fuckas wasn't funeral directors. They was gangstas, period!"

"King, if I consider helping you, and I find out that you've lied to me, you'll suffer more pain than you ever knew possible." All three of them stared at me. It seemed that they were trying to gauge whether or not I was being truthful. I didn't waver. I had nothing to lose. There was a coffin that could be seen in another room through an open door. He looked in its direction for effect.

I was scared as shit, but I was more desperate than scared. I nodded my head. The guys in the doorway stared at me with a different kind of shark eye. These were great whites. They were real killers. Then the older one who had asked me the questions, and who was clearly in charge stood up. He was smiling broadly now. He reached out and shook my hand.

"I think that we may have a use for you around here. Be back here tomorrow at ten in the morning. We'll see if you qualify. If you do, I'll start you out at a thousand a month, ok?" Now I was the one smiling. Fuck the bullshit; I wouldn't be homeless in Mexico now.

"Yes sir, yes sir, thank you so much! What do I call you sir?" I asked.

"Señor is fine for now King. You'll learn more on a need-to-know basis."

I nodded and walked out, heading home. There were three Cadillacs parked in the front lot of the funeral home, but he did not offer me a ride home. His goons made no effort to hide the fact that they were following me there though. There were no sidewalks, so I walked on the side of the road. They drove the Cadillac slowly right behind me all the way home, making all other cars go around them in the process.

The one time I looked back at the car, there were no smiles or nods from these killers. This was business, and it was serious. They followed me until I walked up to my front door. They watched me unlock my front gate and my front door before they slowly pulled off. I didn't know it, but I had just met the head of the violent Tijuana Cartel, "El Señor."

The "work" was simple enough. All I was doing was cremating bodies. Putting them in cardboard "coffins" and feeding them through the incendiary. This was an oven that burns at four thousand degrees turning the human body; including all bones and teeth, into ash. What I noticed right away though, was that the bodies that they gave me were always fully clothed. Often the bodies were riddled with bullets. It was also strange that there were never any family members around or funerals following the arrival of the bodies. It was after about a month of working that the boss came in as I was finishing up one day.

"King, buenos diás!" He said smiling brightly.

"Buenos días Señor." I answered

"Come to my office, King." He said as he walked off.

"Yes sir," I said as I followed him. When I got to his office he gestured for me to sit down and then he began talking.

"This week, we're going to do something a little different." He paused to see if I would ask questions. I didn't and just nodded, so he went on. "The bodies we get this week, I want you to open up as you described doing for the military. I want the bodies hollowed out." He knew that this wasn't a common request, so he watched me closely to gauge my reaction. He was still trying to figure out if I could be trusted or not.

I didn't know exactly what I was dealing with yet when it came to this man, but I'd seen enough in thirty days to know not to ask questions. He was the boss of whatever was going on around here.

"Ok Señor," I responded. His eyes probed me for a few more moments.

Then, he said, "Good King, very good." He shook his head up and down. "That will be all." He was finished, so I walked out.

The Army really did teach me all that I needed to know about dissecting a body. Señor's goons brought me the tools that I'd said I'd need to do the work, and after my second body, I could have a body hollow in fifteen minutes.

I would start with the Y-shaped incision that ran from each shoulder to the sternum, that's the bone right in the middle of your chest. From the sternum, you cut right down the center of the chest and stomach to the crotch. After that, pull the skin and muscle from the breast bone and rib cage. All that's left from there is to crack the ribs with some hedge clippers and then yank down the esophagus from the throat. It's not pretty, but it's effective. El Señor came in later that afternoon.

"¿Cuántas más personas tienes King? El Señor asked.

"Tengo tres El Señor. ¿Cuántos necesitan?" I responded.

"Dos más King, muy buen trabajo." He was pleased with my efficiency, but he wanted two more bodies done before I left for the day.

"Gracias El Señor." I answered since my Spanish was improving daily. I could understand Spanish better than I could speak it.

I gutted two more bodies, placing them in empty caskets before walking to Señor's office door and knocking.

"Es abre." El Señor answered, so I walked in.

"The bodies are all done, El Señor. Anything else before I go home?" I asked. I stood in the doorway waiting for his response.

"No King, very good." He opened his desk drawer and tossed me a wad of cash.

"Qué es eso Señor." I tried to use the Spanish I knew. Plus, I'd already been paid for the month. I didn't understand why he was giving me more money.

"It's for you, King, for all of your hard work." I didn't know it at that moment, but El Señor already knew my whole story. The real story about why I was in Mexico. He sat there looking at me stone-faced as I looked down at the money, turning it over in my hand.

"With all due respect Señor, you've helped me when I had nothing. I was down and out. I was desperate. You've been like a father to me. You have my loyalty. I'm not here for more money; I'm here to prove my worth."

El Señor wasn't one for small talk. He knew that by now, I understood that this wasn't a "funeral home." It was a front for his cartel. A way to send thousands of kilos of cocaine, heroin, and weed across the border weekly. I could only figure that these latest bodies needed to be hollowed out so that Señor could stuff them with dope and somehow have them shipped across the border.

"You understand what you ask me, King?" Señor inquired. I nodded and stared at Señor intently. "My enemies will be yours!" He said. I nodded. "There is no room for emotion, you must become ruthless, dispassionate, and logical." I nodded again. "There must never be any question of where your loyalty is, King! If you become a part of my family, there is only one way out. No exceptions."

"I'd die before I disrespected or betrayed you, Señor." I whispered as I leaned forward, staring at Señor in his eyes. Señor seemed to like the fact that I was firm in my decision.

"One last thing King, you have certain legal matters that need fixing before I can place you in the best position for the both of us." I was stunned. I shouldn't have been surprised, though; this was Señor. He dismissed it with the wave of his hand like he was swatting a fly.

"Tranqúilla King, it will take a little time, but I have connections everywhere. We'll get it taken care of. I have big plans for you!" He was done talking, so I got up to leave. When I got to the door, Señor called my name, "King!" I turned around. "Call me El Señor."

For the next few months, El Señor took me under his wing. He was ruthless and calculating with his business, and he used to tell me that "Savagery in the quest for power is older than the Bible itself." He said that to maintain power, all signs of individual weakness must be removed. In the event of disloyalty or rival transgressions, you must act swiftly and harshly.

El Señor told me a story of a town in central Mexico where an informant once lived. There were twelve hundred residents in the town, but he didn't know exactly who the informant was. Without hesitation, El Señor said that he had the whole town slaughtered. Men, women, and children alike. He didn't seem happy about it, it was just business, he said.

The United States government was after El Señor, and so was his rival cartel, the Baja Syndicate. Murders and tortures were as common as breakfast in the cartel's battle for power. El Señor had an entourage of enforcers with him wherever he went. He also had over sixteen safe houses in Tijuana, and they weren't shacks. They were fortresses. As he groomed me, I got to see how he moved; how he carried himself; and how he acted. He wasn't a boss; he was "the Boss." After about six months of being under his wing and being with him almost daily, conversations were being had about the "négro" who was regularly seen with El Señor. El Señor knew that once that happened, I'd be in danger. It was about then that Paulo, El Señor's top goon, gave me a compact Mac 11 submachine gun, a vest, and a Ruger 9mm. It couldn't stop what was about to happen to me.

El Señor had moved me to a small villa in La Playa de Tijuana, not far from the beach. On Sundays, I would go on a two-mile run along the beach before having breakfast in a little café not far from the villa. As I was seated and digging into my eggs and chorizo, a van crept up and out hopped three masked cartel foot soldier's. I was snatched up. A hood was thrown over my head, and I was forced into the van. Then I was handcuffed. I'd been caught slipping. When the hood came off, I was in a torture house. I knew what it was because I'd been to others with El Señor and one torture house was just like another, which meant that I was somewhere that no matter how loud I screamed, it wouldn't be heard. I also knew that people didn't leave torture houses alive. Once inside, my hands were chained above my head to the iron rings that were hanging from the ceiling.

A very well-dressed latino in his mid-thirties, clean-cut, walked in casually with his hands in his pockets, smiling. He could have just been an average guy going out for an afternoon stroll. His English was perfect.

"We know that you are not with the FBI or DEA." He said, it wasn't a question. "We know that over the last months, you have spent considerable time with El Señor. Do you deny this?" He questioned, smiling.

In my most innocent voice, I said, "Sir, you must have the wrong person. I work at a funeral home in Calle Cúenta. There must be some mistake," I pleaded weakly. He shook his head, frowning.

"I was hoping that we could be gentlemen here. Be truthful as men of honor. I see that you are going to make me be most un-hospitable. My name is Mano," he said, introducing himself like this was a business meeting, and I wasn't chained to the ceiling. Fuck I thought, he was the second in command of the Baja Syndicate. El Señor had told me about him. El Señor said that he was an educated psychopath, and for El Señor to call someone a psychopath meant something. It was like Michael Jordan saying, "That boy can ball."

Mano means hands in Spanish. He was known for chopping mutha fuckas hands off at the wrist before torturing them to death. He always made sure people saw what he did to his enemies. He would place their bodies in front of churches on a Sunday morning or hang them from a light pole on a busy street for everyone to see. He had a reputation like the boogeyman.

"You have heard of me maybe?" Mano asked. He smiled like a child and he gauged my reaction to see if his name meant anything to me. I tried to keep my wits about me.

"No, sir." I lied. "There must be a mistake." I tried to sound convincing.

"Ok, very well." He clapped his hands fast like an excited kid. "Get comfortable negro; you will soon give the answers that I am after one way or another." With that, he walked out.

A million things were running through my mind. Juju! My child with Faith! My hands! However, no thought could have prepared me for what was coming. Mano walked back into the bare room about five minutes later and stripped me down to my boxer briefs. I tried to tell him that this was a mistake, but he paid me no attention. He whistled as he began pulling items out of a black bag. At the position I was hanging from, I couldn't see the items that he was pulling out clearly, but it wasn't hard to figure that the items were tools of torture. As I finished the thought, Mano walked back in front of me, grabbed the top of my head, and yanked it head back violently. Two other sets of hands held me still as a mouthpiece was shoved in my mouth. The mouthpiece was held in place by a black strap that snapped on in the back of my head with something like a belt buckle.

"This will stop you from biting off your own tongue negro." Mano said.

Mano's eyes twinkled as he slid a small metal table in front of me, placing his items for torture on it. He looked at me calmly and then back down at the table and tray.

"Negro, you can prevent all of this. All I want you to do is give me the locations of El Señor's safe houses." Mano put on black latex gloves as he talked. "If not, within the hour, you'll be begging me to kill you negro, but I won't. I've made a science of this. You see this?" He said, holding up a syringe. "When you're begging God for death or praying that you can pass out; I'll inject you with one hundred milligrams of pure adrenaline; it will keep you awake negro. You will feel every single thing that I do to you." His calmness was unsettling. He looked at me to see if I would try to talk, "No?" He said finally. "Ok negro, now we begin." He lifted up something that reminded me of what people used to carve Thanksgiving turkeys. Mano then walked to me so that we were face to face. My eyes were wide, and I was scared, but I did not beg. If I was going to die today, I'd die as a man.

"This negro." He said as he hit the button, bringing the little chain saw to life. "Will cut layers of skin and meat off of you so thin that I could place it on a sandwich." He laughed heartily at his own joke. "I think in America they call it deli slices, yes?" With that, he spun me around, so that I was facing the concrete wall behind me. Two different sets of hands gripped my ankles, holding my legs in place. The small machine popped to life with a soft buzzing sound.

"Aahaaagh, aaaahghhhh, aaahgggggaa, aaagh!!" I screamed as the saw sliced into my flesh. My screams were muffled by the gag that was in my mouth as the back of my thighs exploded in an indescribable pain. I tried to twist, flip, flop, and wiggle, but my hands remained chained above me to the ceiling, and the two goons held my legs. My head snapped back and forth with a force that I never knew was possible. Mano spun me back around so that we were facing each other again. In his hand was a thinly sliced piece of the back of my thigh. The hairs were still attached to the skin. Mano was enjoying himself. He held up my flesh in his hand.

"Dark meat, no?" He asked as he giggled.

Not being able to breathe out of my mouth had me thinking that I'd suffocate. Warm blood was dripping down my thigh and onto my calves. I didn't have any hope of getting out of there alive.

"You wish to talk to me now negro?" Mano asked. I leaned my head back onto my shoulders. The pain was shooting from my thigh up into my chest. "I'll take you down and clean you up. All you have to do is point out El Señor's safe houses as we ride, no?" He unstrapped the buckle holding the mouthpiece in my mouth so that I could breathe. I gulped for air and breathed in heavily.

"Who, who, who, is El Señor?" I finally said with a dry mouth.

Mano clapped his hands like an excited kid waiting for a rollercoaster, "Ok negro!" He smiled. This time Mano took the turkey carver and picked a spot right below my belly button. I watched as the flesh from my stomach was slowly carved away down to my crotch. A flap of flesh the size of a pancake was hanging down by a thin piece of skin from my stomach. Mano stared at me, gripped my hanging flesh in his hand, and slowly tore the meat off of my stomach like a piece of paper in a notebook. He had a maniacal look on his face the whole time.

This time I didn't have the mouthpiece in my mouth, so I let out a blood-curdling cry. My head slammed back against the cinderblock wall, and my teeth rattled, causing me to bite a deep gash in my tongue. Mano was pleased with his handiwork.

"Negro, I will give you a little time to reconsider your situation. I'm in no rush. I will go have a nice dinner with a beautiful señorita and then I will return. We will pick up where we left off."

I was barely holding on to consciousness. Memories were blurring, and I'd been here since this morning. I'd been snatched at breakfast, and now Mano was talking about going to dinner. My head drooped forward. I heard a door slam. Thankfully my mind shut down as I passed out. I was dreaming about my mom; she was knocking on the door to my house, "Bang, bang, bang! Pop, pop, pop."

"Come in, mom," I whispered. "Pop, pop, pop." The knock came faster, louder, and harder this time.

"Come in mom," I said again as the heavy metal door to my torture chamber flew open. In the doorway stood one of Mano's hitters looking around frantically. First he looked at me and then back down the corridor.

"Pop, pop. pop, pop, pop." The sound was getting louder and closer. Mano's hitter raised his arm to aim his banger at me when his head exploded like a busted piñata; splashing his brains on the doorframe. It looked like someone threw a plate of spaghetti against the wall. His body collapsed where he stood just seconds ago. A tear made its way down my cheek. I was barely able to lift my head. In walked El Señor and Paulo, his head henchman.

"Cut him down, Paulo." El Señor commanded. Paulo cut me down and caught me before I hit the floor. I couldn't stand on my own. The only thing holding me up was the chains that I was hooked to. El Señor walked up to me.

"Tu eres mi familia ahora King." El Señor said as we walked out. I saw that the compound was littered with dead bodies as we left to get in the SUV.

Chapter 45

MY KING

[Present]

In an instant, it all became clear, that there was only one way to deal with this situation. Ruthlessness! It was my time to slaughter the whole "village" as El Señor had done so many years ago. Killing everyone was the only way to make sure that every disloyal mutha fucka disappeared. All other pieces could be sacrificed. Only the K-I-N-G was irreplaceable. This would require me to tap into some old resources. Killers from outside the circle. That would not be a problem. For now, I'd enjoy my time with Keisha. In two days, Sacramento would start to resemble the set of a horror flick. There was about to be a gruesome cleansing of pussy ass nigga's who wanted to checkmate a King, but who weren't three moves ahead. I placed the necessary phone calls to set things in motion and then headed back to the cabin. I immediately felt better once my decision was made. Keisha was out of the bath but she was still in the bathroom, so I took a quick shower in the guest bathroom and then went down to the plush rug that lay in front of the fireplace. I was asshole naked.

BOOK 2

"Keisha, bring the massage oil down with you," King yelled up to Keisha.

"Ok baby, I'll be right down," Keisha responded. When she came down the stairs, she had a silk sheet wrapped around her waist. After seeing King asshole naked, his six-pack bulging, arms and chest sculpted like an African God, Keisha dropped the sheet that covered her naked body. She walked to him, nestling up against his warm hard body so that her back was up against his chest. Her plump ass arched back against his already growing thickness.

"Ohh." Keisha moaned as King wrapped his arms around her from the back, gently kissing the back of her neck, and then her ears. Keisha's body erupted with goosebumps.

As King intensified his nibbling and sucking on Keisha's ear, she found herself grinding her ass over King's constantly growing shaft. Her honey pot was beginning to drip. It was dripping down along the inside of her milky soft thighs. She wanted King inside her, but King was patient.

King continued to gently suck, kiss, and lick Keisha's neck while pouring edible coconut oil on both of their bodies. With strong hands, he rubbed it over and down her thighs and on her perky breasts and hard nipples. Then he made his way to her ass and down her ass crack, making them both smooth and slippery. Suddenly, King pulled her even closer and began to slide his long dick up the crack of her slippery ass, but he did not enter her.

"What are you doing to me, King?" Keisha moaned. She felt her body shake in ecstasy. King didn't answer; he just shoved two manicured figures into Keisha's mouth. She immediately began to suck on them hungrily. She gripped his wrist as she gobbled his fingers passionately. All the while, the full length of King's throbbing dick was sliding between Keisha's slippery ass cheeks. Then King pushed his full weight on Keisha from behind, forcing her face down to the floor on her stomach. His chest was flat against her back. He worked his hands from her lower back to her shoulders, massaging her deeply. Once at her shoulders, he paused, placing gentle kisses on her neck, as his manhood thumped down on her glistening ass cheeks.

"Please, King, please fuck me!" Keisha pleaded as she cocked her ass in the air. Without saying a word, King grabbed Keisha's arms and pinned them to the floor out in front of her. In the same motion, King entered her tight pussy from the back.

"Oh fuck!" Keisha moaned as King began to find his rhythm slowly. It felt like he went deeper with every stroke. Keisha wanted it all. His hands on top of hers, Keisha gripped the plush rug like she was ringing it out. She worked her hips back in a rhythm until her cheeks made a clapping sound against King's flat stomach. As he lay on top of her thrusting his hips in the air and then back down deep inside her, King leaned next to her face and took her lip in between his teeth, sucking it, then tongue kissed her slowly and deeply. Bouts of electric pleasure shot up and down Keisha's slippery body.

King's dick was a perfect combination of thickness and length. He was knocking the bottom out of Keisha's pussy.

"King, I'm going to cum all over that fat black dick; please don't stop, please don't stop, daddy."

With that, King's love-making went faster and deeper. Both were dripping sweat mixed with coconut oil. It was a beautiful sight.

"Right there baby, shit, right there, I'm bout to cum," Keisha moaned. She was at her limit. King reached under her from behind and gently caressed her clit. Keisha convulsed and had the most intense orgasm of her life.

"Ah, ah, ah, ah." Keisha's head shook from side to side. Three more thrusts, and King was filling Keisha with his seed.

"Oh shit!" King growled as he stiffened his muscles and exploded. King's body was a masterpiece. His arms, shoulders, chest, and stomach were ripped and defined. His muscles were pumped and bulging from his effort.

Keisha was face down with King on top of her but he was holding his one hundred ninety pounds of body weight off of her just enough so that he didn't crush her. For minutes, Keisha couldn't form a single thought. She just knew that she was content and satisfied in every way. King wiped the sweat from her face, kissing her gently on the cheek and forehead. In less than five minutes, Keisha could feel King start to grow hard again. Her own pussy responded by getting that wonderful heartbeat in her clit.

"Oh my God!" Keisha thought. This is going to be the best night of my life. King rolled over, pulling Keisha on top of him; it was time for round two.

Chapter 46

ROAD TO RECOVERY

[Past]

I had passed out. When I woke up, I was in a plush bed, and I was heavily bandaged on the head, stomach, and leg. I had lost a lot of blood. I had nine staples in the back of my head from banging my head back against the cinderblock. I would need graft surgery to replace the missing skin on my stomach and the back of my leg. I didn't know where I was but I could hear waves clapping on the shore through an open window. There was a fresh glass of water on a nightstand next to me, so I grabbed it. My mouth was sticky and dry. I tried to swing my feet off of the bed, but it caused a sharp burning pain throughout my body, that doubled me over. I let out a deep growl. A pretty Latina in her early twenties came walking in shortly after.

"Señor King, please, you are in no shape to be out of bed yet. You are still in very bad shape." She picked my legs up at the feet and placed them back on the bed. Then she fluffed some pillows up behind me so that I could sit up.

"Where am I, señora?" I groaned.

"You are in a safe place. I am Claudia, El Señor's oldest daughter. I'm a registered nurse in San Diego. My father called me here to take care of you. You've been unconscious for two days, and I have you heavily medicated because your wounds are very severe."

She had kind eyes. I nodded and then looked down at my heavily bandaged stomach. The bandage was soaked with blood. I placed my hand on the wound.

"You are very lucky, señor King. We had to put staples in your stomach. When you got here, your intestines were coming out of the lining of a hole in your stomach. I could see your guts hanging out when they drug you in. My father keeps a very sophisticated medical facility here for his friends in need." I was the friend of the most powerful drug kingpin in all Northern Mexico, I thought to myself.

"My father will return shortly; in the meantime, I will have food prepared for you. You need to eat for your strength; and so that the antibiotics don't make you sick. After that, I will clean you up and change your bandages." Claudia smiled and walked out.

I was starving, and I ate two helpings of eggs, potatoes, and bacon. I also had strawberries, kiwi, and orange slices that tasted like life itself. Claudia came back in shortly after I was done eating.

"Ok, Señor King." Claudia started off with a somber tone, and she looked like she had bad news for me.

"Please, Claudia, call me King," I said. Claudia nodded.

"It is time to clean your wounds. I can give you morphine for the pain before I do it if that will be better for you," Claudia asked. She seemed curious about what kind of man I was. No doubt she'd seen some tuff mutha fuckas in her dad's organization.

"Nah, let's just do it, I said quickly. I don't fuck with opiates. I mean, I don't need pain meds!" I corrected myself. This was El Señor's daughter, and respect was mandatory.

"Ok," Claudia said, looking pleased.

When your business is supplying junkies, the last thing you want is a junkie in your organization. I was certain that she'd tell El Señor that I had refused pain meds.

First, she unwrapped the bandage on my head and cleaned around the staples, before rewrapping it. There was a dull throbbing on the side of my head, but the pain wasn't too bad. After that, I leaned back on the pillows, and Claudia propped my leg up at the foot, so that my thigh was off the bed, and raised into the air. Claudia began unraveling the bandage on my thigh slowly. When it was down to a single layer, I winced and tightened up. The wound was healing and sticking to the bandage.

Claudia reached out, placing a soft hand on my hard stomach. She looked up slowly as she left her hand there a little too long. We locked eyes briefly as she slid her hand just a little towards my chest. I looked away. There was no way I would cross that line, but I couldn't deny that Claudia was gorgeous. A flawless Latina. She had jet black hair, sleepy almond eyes, and curves that couldn't be hidden. She coughed shyly, and then removed her hand.

"Ok, King, this is going to hurt a little bit because the blood has absorbed the bandage into the wound." I nodded and tried to relax my mind, breathing deeply and slowly. It hurt almost as bad as it did when Mano tortured me. My face broke out into a sweat. Claudia wiped my forehead with a cool towel. I growled deep in my throat, but didn't cry out.

"Very good soldádo," Claudia beamed. She was her father's daughter, nurse or not.

"Now is the most serious injury, King. You need to sit all the way back against the headboard so that I can unwrap your stomach bandage." I scooted back, using my arms to lift myself up as I slid.

"Ok, now lean forward just a little bit so that I can get my arms around you. The bandage is tied in the back." Claudia commanded softly.

I leaned forward. Claudia and I were chest to chest. Face to face. Her breasts were caressing my chest, and her light brown cleavage was breathtaking. Her perfume filled my nostrils, mesmerizing me. She slowly began unwrapping the bandage. A few moments later, a pain gripped me at the core of my soul. I bit down hard on my lip. Sweat started dripping down my forehead and chest in large droplets. Claudia looked sympathetic but kept going.

"Ok King, almost done," she whispered. I nodded, unable to speak.

"Now it's time for the part that is directly over the staples." She paused to look into my eyes. "Do you need a moment to relax, first King?" she asked. She seemed to be genuinely concerned.

"Just finish please," I said between clenched teeth. The wound was in my stomach, but the pain was in my soul, and I was anxious to be done with this.

"Ok," she said while wiping my face and chest. I thought about Mano, the mutha fucka who did this to me and rage filled me. He shouldn't have left me alive, I thought to myself. The pain momentarily resided as my rage built. It's amazing how powerful emotions can be.

"Done King!" Claudia announced.

I looked down, and I wasn't prepared for what I saw. A portion of my stomach was gone. At the deepest part, the tissue was just starting to heal over the muscle, but it was still raw meat. The staples were holding this part of my stomach together, and there was blood, and raw flesh caked up around the metal. It wasn't pretty.

I looked up at the ceiling. A single tear rolled down my cheek, but it wasn't from pain or sadness. The thought that I was momentarily helpless, had me in a rage. That I had no outlet for my rage was a pain of its own.

"King, King," Claudia whispered, bringing me back. "Listen to me, King." I looked at her. "It's not what happens to a great man that defines him; it's how he handles what happens to him." I nodded. "Your wounds will heal. You are young, and you are strong, but you must know that you will never heal completely until your enemies blood flows. The person who did this to you must look into your eyes, and he must see that he didn't break you. He must feel every ounce of your rage." She sounded like El Señor, and I knew that she was right.

"Now get some rest, King. Soon you will need all of your strength." Claudia kissed me on my forehead and walked out. Soon after, I was asleep.

Chapter 47

REJUVENATED

[Present]

The time in Tahoe did King good. He and Keisha made love, went shopping, and walked on the beach. King was tentative to Keisha's every desire. She was in love. King cared deeply for her, but with what King knew he was about to have to do, he knew that this was no time for being preoccupied with a female. He'd have time for that once he found out who his hidden enemies were; and then killed them all! Once back in Sacramento, King made preparations. Telling Keisha and Alisha that he had to go out of town on business; King packed his bag. Not just clothes, but several pistols, two sub-machine guns, and some "specialty" items that he planned on using when a situation required a personal touch. His out of town

killers would be arriving tomorrow. King would be prepared.

Chapter 48

BETRAYAL

[Present]

Cash was driving in the south area, checking traps. The last week had been hectic. Jamille was dead, and Capone had been tortured and murdered. Cash's plan to overthrow King had taken a few unexpected turns because Jamille couldn't keep his mouth shut, and it was just a bit of luck that Capone hadn't mentioned Cash's name before he died. This would have never worked if he had. King would have already been out to kill him like he'd done Jamille.

"Fuck him; he deserved to die." Cash thought. The good news is that King doesn't suspect me yet. He had put it on thick when King told him and Rico about Jamille at the meeting the other night. It was lucky for Cash that Rico didn't act mad.

That was just how he was sometimes, too laid back, but that made King suspicious of Rico instead of him. He could use that to his advantage later. Cash said that he'd body Jamille for King, but he knew that he wouldn't have to when he said it. King would take care of that on his own. Cash was almost ready to make his move! Things were falling into place. He had a cool dope connection out of Stockton and a couple of young killers ready to take over the blocks that King controlled. Most importantly though, would be cutting the head off the King. You cut the head off, the body dies.

"Cash, what's up my nigga?" One of Cash's lil homies, PJ, answered Cash's call.

"Shit blood, bout to pull up on you in a few, you dressed?" Cash asked impatiently.

"Yea bra, I'll be ready, pull up!" PJ responded.

"Ok bra, bring your banga and your mask; we got a mission."

"Yep." The phone clicked. PJ was a real soldier. He didn't ask questions.

Cash knew that in order to execute his plan, he had to be on his "A" game. King was a chess player, and he thought several moves ahead. King saw the whole picture and he wasn't easily fooled.

Cash knew that King would rely on him to help exterminate the nigga's that he thought were disloyal. Cash knew everything that there was to know about King. King's inner circle was super small. With Jamille dead and Rico under suspicion of being disloyal, it would be Cash that King turned to for support. Cash was going to do something to make sure that King turned to him for help.

"Sup Brodie." PJ was all business.

"Get in," Cash replied. "I got a lick for us. It's at least half a bird, at a house over in Greenhaven. The two young nigga's over there is flossing; they need to be got blood."

"Fasho, fasho!" This was what PJ lived for, so he didn't ask questions. If Cash was putting him up on a lick, then it must be official.

"Here's the thing though lil bra." Cash would see now how down PJ really was. "This a murder- robbery! No witnesses, no retaliation." PJ's eyes didn't blink. He had no problem adding another body to his count. Especially for that much dope. He had killed nigga's for way less.

"Yep, yep!" was PJ's only response.

What PJ didn't know was that this was King's spot and that the young nigga's inside had to be killed, so that they couldn't identify Cash. They all knew him! PJ also didn't know that the one running the spot was King's nephew. He was only seventeen. Once word got back to King that the spot his nephew ran had been robbed and his nephew murdered, he'd reach out to Cash. Once the King was out, he was vulnerable. King wasn't the only one that played chess.

"Ok, look blood." Cash started talking again once they got close to the trap house. Once we in here, nigga's get dropped, no playing, no delaying! I already know where the dope is."

"Yep, yep," said PJ.

"Alright nigga, mask up, let's go."

Cash led the way, jogging up the stairs and to the front door. He knew that it would be unlocked because he had called telling Jamarius that he was sliding through and to unlock the door. It would be open. Cash turned the doorknob and pushed in. His dreads with blonde tips were poking out the bottom of his mask. PJ was right behind him. The first nigga was sitting on the couch in the living room with his head down as he cut up some dope. When he heard the door and looked up, Cash's hamma' spit fire, putting a hole in his chest the size of a silver dollar. The round lifted him; making him sit up, before he slumped over dead.

The second nigga came out of the kitchen. PJ leveled three rounds from his 9mm Ruger into his chest, before standing over him and putting one in the top half of his forehead. He was the real reason that this trap house was picked. Cash knew that the little nigga PJ had just downed was King's nephew, Jamarius.

This would start the war that Cash planned to use to bring King out. King would take this shit personally. Cash would be at his side like he'd always been, until the time came that he could catch King slipping. Cash chuckled to himself, thinking about how it was King who had taught him that the element of surprise could end a war before it began. It was King who taught him to play and love the game of chess. Cash grabbed the coke from the hidden stash spot, and him and PJ left.

Now all Cash had to do was wait. King hadn't been answering his phone for the last few days, but before the night was up, he knew that King would hear about the robbery and murder of his nephew. Cash didn't want to be the one to tell him; King would sniff that out. Once King heard about what happened, he'd reach out to Cash. After that, PJ would have to be sacrificed. He was only a pawn in a game much bigger than himself. Cash needed to show King that he was the only one who was still loyal and rocking with him. This was the only way that he'd ever get to the throne.

At a safe house that no one knew about, King was waiting for his out of town killers to arrive. KC had been out of the pen for a year and had been trying to link up with King. He was on his way in from Missouri. Bheef was coming in from Watts. Most importantly, El Señor had agreed to send his number one henchman, Paulo, to assist with what was needed. Murder was an art to Paulo. His instincts and guidance on the situation would be invaluable. King still wasn't sure who could be trusted. He did know better than to assume anything about anyone; it could be anyone. His phone rang.

"What's good?" King answered. It was Rico.

"King, my nigga, the spot in Greenhaven got hit." Rico hated to be the one to have to tell King the bad news. He knew how King might look at it.

"Fuck!! The feds or local?" King automatically assumed that the police had hit the spot.

"Nah brodie, a lick, but there's more blood!" King looked at the phone, like it was the one talking to him. He knew that something bad was coming.

"Jamarius is dead big bra! Three to the chest, one to the head! All the dope was snatched. I will get more info to you brodie, as soon I get it." There was silence over the phone.

"King," Rico said.

"Yea, I'm here." King couldn't think.

"I'm sorry, blood, we'll figure out who did this," Rico said as he hung up. There was really nothing that Rico could say to help, so he was anxious to get off the phone. He had been in situations like this, and usually people say really stupid shit that they think is helpful; the truth is that nothing is helpful!

King felt like the wind had been knocked out of him. This was an act of war. What really got to King was that this was his safest trap house. That's why his nephew was working there. There was only an upscale clientele going to that spot. They sold powder cocaine only, no rock. This was an inside job, King thought. Maybe it was the nigga on the phone with him who just delivered the news. Nigga's is known for doing shit like that.

"Yea, alright Rico, get back to me, bra." King said as he hung up. Venom and rage were flowing through his veins. King called Cash.

Chapter 49

DECISION TIME

[Present]

Keisha was still floating from her time in Tahoe with King when her phone rang.

"Yes, I'm calling to confirm a pizza order." A female voice said over the phone line. Alisha was in the other room watching TV, so Keisha stepped outside before answering.

"Yea, medium pepperoni," Keisha said, answering with a little attitude.

"One moment Agent Johnson." Came the response over the line. Keisha sucked her teeth as she waited.

"Agent Johnson?' It was her supervisor, Agent Vargas.

"Yes, sir." Keisha said sarcastically. He didn't catch it.

"Look, we think we may have gotten a break." Keisha's supervisor was breathing heavily over the phone like he'd been running.

"Ok?" Keisha wanted to know what he was talking about.

"There was a double murder at a house we've identified as belonging to King." Agent Vargas said.

"So, you think King killed two people in one of his own spots now, Agent Vargas?" Keisha shot back. Not attempting to hide her sarcasm this time.

"I'm not saying that, but we've got good reason to believe that one of King's top lieutenants was responsible. We don't have a positive identification yet, but a witness saw the suspects leaving, and one of them had dreads with blonde tips, like Cash. Cash's body type and size also matched the witness's description. What we don't know is why? Why would one of King's top lieutenants hit one of their own spots and kill the two teenagers inside? There's something going on here that we don't know about, and if I know King, it's going to get worse before it gets better."

Damn, Keisha thought, King was being attacked from all sides. No wonder he seemed preoccupied for much of their trip in Tahoe. She needed to buy him some time.

"So, what do you have planned?" Keisha questioned Agent Vargas, trying not to appear too concerned.

"Well, we don't have enough for murder charges on Cash yet, but we've got someone on him watching him. If we get the chance, we'll bust him on something lesser, see if he flips."

This was Keisha's chance. For the first time in her life, Keisha lied to a superior officer. "Sir, I've got King right where I want him. He's supposed to be taking me on a buy in seventy-two hours. Don't do anything that's going to spook him. This buy will be enough to put King away for life. I've worked hard on this case sir, and I'm close."

Keisha sounded convincing; the DEA trained her how to lie, but Agent Vargas was still suspicious. "Why hadn't you notified me before now, Agent Johnson?"

Keisha lied again. "He just told me this morning sir. I had to make sure it was safe to call and I hadn't had time yet."

Alisha was at the living room window finishing up her makeup when she thought that she heard Keisha talking on the phone outside. Alisha inched her face closer to the window, and it was open just enough so that she could hear everything that Keisha was saying.

"Agent Johnson, you have seventy-two hours; make good use of it," Agent Vargas finally acquiesced.

"Yes, sir, King's on his last leg," Keisha said as she hung up. She needed to figure out how to help King; to warn him at least!

Alisha was thinking the same thing. She needed to help King. Alisha could barely comprehend what she had just heard. This bitch Keisha was the police, and based on what Alisha had just heard, she was about to bust King. She needed to figure out what to do.

Chapter 50

HAPPINESS MUST BE TAKEN

[Past]

"Success will often depend on extraordinary persistence and a willingness to endure hardships." Theodor Roosevelt.

When I woke up, I could hear El Señor talking in hushed tones with Claudia. I couldn't hear every word that they were saying, but she was telling him what had happened when I woke up earlier. Probably about our conversation and my unwillingness to take pain medication. Not wanting to seem like I was eavesdropping, I coughed loudly so that they knew I was awake. El Señor walked in, smiling broadly shortly after.

"King, I'm so glad you're up. We were worried about you for a while," El Señor said. Paulo walked in behind him, and that was the first time that I'd ever seen the stone-faced killer smile. He nodded at me, then turned around and left. El Señor started talking again.

"Claudia tells me that you ate well and that she replaced your bandages and cleaned your wounds. I am proud of you for refusing the pain medication, King. People spend their whole lives running from pain, but life is pain. Pain's to be embraced; not endured." I nodded at the wisdom that El Señor was imparting on me.

"Anyway." El Señor's mood went from serious to excited. "I have many wonderful surprises for you King, once your health permits it." I didn't ask what. He would tell me when he was ready. "Until then, I leave my most valuable possession with you." He looked towards the door and to Claudia as he said it.

"Claudia." El Señor whispered her name. "She will nurse you back into tip-top shape. It is obvious that she has taken a liking to you King, and that's ok, but you are family now. You have proven your loyalty and you will be rewarded for it. There's nothing you can't ask of me, but I'll only say this once King, Claudia is off-limits." I nodded. "Do you understand what I mean by off-limits, King?"

"Si, El Señor," I responded.

"Very well, my son. I have business to tend to in other parts of Mexico that will take several weeks. Claudia assures me that you'll be sufficiently healed by the time I return from my trip. It is then that I will inform you of your good news."

"Gracias El Señor," I replied.

"De nada." El Señor said as he turned and left.

I spent the next six weeks recovering and healing. Claudia was magic. It wasn't just her medical skill; it was her! She lifted my spirits. She read to me. She fed me. She bathed me.

She cleaned my wounds. She made me feel strong! She was Latin fire. Claudia was beautiful and naturally seductive.

Claudia was off-limits, but the bond that we formed and the chemistry that we had was undeniable. Once she began hinting at her attraction towards me, I knew that it was time to go. It was already hard enough to keep myself in check. I was up and moving around pretty well now, and I just had a little limp that I could manage with a cane.

"Do you know when your father is scheduled back, Claudia?" I asked.

Claudia's mouth pouted. "Why, King, are you bored with me already?" She shot back with a hint of attitude.

"No, Claudia, I just thought El Señor said that he had something special for me." I couldn't tell her how I really felt about her. It wasn't a smart business move. It wasn't safe for my health either.

"He'll be back tonight. He called earlier to see how you were getting along." I nodded and smiled. Claudia was in her feelings, shit, so was I, but what choice did I have? She was off-limits.

El Señor got to the compound about eleven that night. He didn't come in; he just sent for me, so I limped down to his SUV.

"King, very good to see you up and moving. Claudia took very good care of you, I see?" El Señor eyed me suspiciously.

"I owe my life to you both, El Señor. She is a very intelligent and honorable woman. She is definitely her father's daughter." This seemed to appease him. He smiled.

"Very good, King. Let us now go to your first surprise. I was in the back of the SUV with El Señor. Paulo was the front passenger; somebody I'd never seen was driving. There was a pickup truck in front of us, and the back of it was loaded with henchmen. The bulky SUV lurched forward.

I recognized the house immediately once we pulled up. It was one of El Señor's torture houses. I thought that I'd fucked up for a moment, a torture house wasn't normally a good place to be pulling up to, but El Señor was in too good of a mood. If there were a problem, I would have sensed it. As El Señor opened his door to get out, he waved me around. Once I got to him, he put his arms around me, and spoke softly.

"King, you are family. I take care of my family. I will die for my family. If anyone harms my family, I will kill for my family." We walked inside the house as he talked to me. My eyes had to adjust to the darkness. When they did, what I saw was the best gift anyone had ever given to me.

Mano was there, stripped naked and handcuffed. His hands were hooked and cuffed above him to the ceiling on the metal beams. His mouth was duct-taped and his face bruised, but otherwise, he was fine. When he saw me, his eyes widened. He must have thought that I had been killed at the compound.

He wasn't expecting to see me alive. El Señor walked to my side.

"Nino, this is the man that mutilated your body. This is the man that would have me killed in an instant if he could." El Señor was surprisingly calm. "It is up to you, King, to decide his fate. You decide if he dies fast, slow, or walks out of here alive."

If I told El Señor to let him walk out of there alive, he'd have us both killed. This was a test, and there was only one right answer. Mano could only leave this house one way, dead as fuck.

The torture room already had the tools of the trade in it. Everything that was needed to bring immeasurable pain was there. I asked El Señor if he could leave me an assistant. I wanted to take my time with Mano. El Señor smiled brightly, then left.

For the next forty-eight hours, I dissected Mano piece by piece. Starting with needle-nose pliers, I pulled out all of his pretty teeth, top and bottom, that he had smiled at me with only weeks earlier. His teeth clattered to the floor like falling dominos, and his mouth filled with blood. He screamed until he had to keep spitting out blood to keep from choking on it.

I worked in silence; only talking to instruct my assistant! I looked over the "tools" with a careful eye. I wanted something that would bring maximum pain, slowly. Mano needed to suffer. With each hour that passed, with each agonizing scream that came out of Mano's mouth, a certain healing took place for me. Claudia was right. I needed this in order to become whole again.

On the morning of the third day, El Señor returned. He was pleased with my viciousness. Mano was hanging on to life by a thread. He was in and out of consciousness. The room was splattered with his blood, bone, feces, and tissue. His ears, toes, and fingers were littered around the room; scattered on the floor like children's toys. I bandaged his hands and feet so that he wouldn't bleed to death. It wouldn't help him with the pain.

El Señor put his hand on my shoulder, then handed me a beautifully crafted marble chess piece. "Finish this mijo, we have business that needs handling," El Señor said as he walked out.

It was time to go, but a message needed to be sent to our enemies. Plus, I wouldn't make the same deadly mistake that Mano had. He was dying today. I took a six-inch serrated steel army knife and approached Mano. I proceeded to carve a hole an inch deep into Mano's breast bone, big enough to shove a chess piece in. He shook violently and twitched as the metal blade sliced and cracked through his breastbone.

Paulo stood in the doorway watching as I finally wrapped guitar string tightly around Mano's throat, twisting with all my power. The string melted into his neck like a hot knife through butter and almost severed his head clean off. The next day Mano's mutilated body was found hanging from a light post. He still had the black King chess piece sticking out of the hole in his chest, for all to see.

Chapter 51

BETRAYAL

[Present]

Cash had just finished fucking one of his side bitches when King called.

"Sup, big bro, I been tryna tap in but you ain't been answering. Everything good blood?" Cash asked, doing his best to sound concerned. It was hard for him. Sometimes he didn't even understand himself why he hated King so much. King had been nothing but good to him.

"Yea, my nigga, I've just been getting my thoughts together. There's been a lot of shady shit going on lately. Did you know the spot in Greenhaven was hit?" King asked. Cash immediately acted surprised by the comment.

"The police hit it? Did they find the dope?" Cash asked, playing dumb.

King sighed. "That's the thing; it wasn't the police. Some masked nigga's pushed in. They killed my nephew." Cash cut in before King could say more.

"What!! On bloods? It's time to start choppin' nigga's down King. You point me in the direction and I'm murking everything moving. You know that brodie!" Cash growled, wanting to be convincing.

The problem was that two things had been bothering King. First, the door to the trap spot hadn't been kicked in, them nigga's just walked right in. How? Why? Jamarius knew to dead bolt the door after every customer. Two, the house wasn't ransacked, but the dope that was hidden in a special compartment behind a bookcase was gone. Only a select few people knew about that tuck spot. Cash was one of them. King would play along until he had all his moves in order. The fact of the matter was that until King knew who he could trust, he wouldn't trust anyone.

"You right Cash, it's time to put in work. I got word that it may have been some nigga's from the Eastside. I'll get all my info together, and I'll tap back in with you. Just be ready blood."

"I'm ready brodie, I'm made for this shit. I owe everything I got in this game to you. I'll have some of the brodies see what the streets is saying while I wait to hear from you." Cash ended his charade and he hoped that King had bought his act. His power move depended on it.

"Aight bet! In a min." King said as he hung up.

Cash smiled at the thought of King thinking that it was some nigga's from the East that robbed the spot and killed his nephew. Cash knew that King would want blood for this act, but Cash had his own plan that would make PJ, his accomplice, a casualty of war.

Cash would down PJ and get the dope back for King all at one time. He told PJ to hold the dope for a few days. Once Cash got the dope back from PJ, King would see that he was the only one that could be trusted. When King least expected it, he'd blow the back of his head off. Shit was going better than Cash had planned.

Chapter 52

BUSTED

[Present]

"What's this bitch's problem?" Keisha thought. Ever since she'd come back in the house, Alisha had been acting weird as fuck.

"Bitch what's up wit you?" Keisha asked. Alisha ignored her the first few times while staring blank eyed at the television. "You ain't said nothing in over two hours."

"Yeah," Alisha finally responded. "I get like that when there's fake shit all round me." Keisha's stomach dropped. She left the bedroom and walked into the living room, where she saw that the window next to the door was slightly open. Alisha had heard the conversation she'd had with her supervisor. That had to be why she was acting like that.

Fuck, Keisha thought. What am I going to do about this bitch? I can't have her fuck my relationship off with King. I love the nigga. A panic came over Keisha. Think, think, Keisha said to herself as she was going back in the house to the bedroom where Alisha was. Keisha needed to figure out just how much Alisha had heard. Maybe she was overreacting. Alisha was just getting up when Keisha appeared in the doorway.

"Hey Alisha, you and I are like sisters. Anything on your mind you can tell me. We can talk about it." Alisha spun around sharply, staring Keisha in the eyes. Keisha could see the hurt, anger, and disappointment on her face.

"Look bitch," Alisha started, "There's really nothing to say. I texted King. I'm waiting for him to call me back. When he does, I'm going to tell him that you're the fucking police bitch."

This was Keisha's worst nightmare coming true. She had already decided to tell King everything. She just needed to figure out how and when to do it! She had no intentions of betraying him, but this bitch could ruin it all. The only chance she had at keeping things together with King was for her to be the one to tell him. Shit, that would be hard enough. He would be hurt and suspicious. She would have to do something to prove to him just how loyal she was. Keisha had to act fast.

"Turn around, put your hands behind your back Alisha!" Keisha shouted before she even thought about it. "You're under arrest for interfering with a federal investigation." Alisha looked shocked. Her mouth was wide open. "Bitch I'm not playing." Keisha snapped. "Turn the fuck around; I'm taking you in." Alisha finally turned around slowly. She was suspicious and hesitant, but she'd been raised to obey law enforcement, and she really believed that Keisha was the police. Keisha cuffed Alisha's hands behind her back, and then took her to the garage and stuffed her into the trunk of the Mercedes AMG. It was a tight fit.

Keisha drove Alisha across the California/Nevada border which was an hour and a half away. Taking Alisha's body to a different state would slow up the investigation. When Keisha finally found a secluded spot in a wooded area in the mountains, she pulled over and parked. She made sure she was in a spot that couldn't be seen from the highway. Keisha grabbed the six-shot .25 cal pistol King had given her. She got out and popped the trunk. Alisha was yelling at the top of her lungs.

"What the fuck you doing putting me in the fucking trunk bitch? Are you crazy or something?" Alisha couldn't have known that Keisha had in fact, snapped. Keisha replied coolly. Too coolly!!

"You can talk to my supervisor about it. Get the fuck out the trunk. I'm taking you to him right now." Keisha talked in her most professional DEA voice now.

"Where the hell are we at??" Alisha asked, looking around nervously.

"Just get out of the trunk. The command center is down the trail. Hurry the fuck up." Keisha still had the pistol concealed. Alisha got out and started walking, but it was clear that she felt that this didn't seem right. But she was handcuffed. She had no choice. As they walked down the narrow trail in the Sierra Nevada Mountains, Keisha pulled the chrome .25 cal from the small of her back. Just as Alisha was about to turn around to say that she didn't see any command center down the trail, her mind went blank. It was Alisha's last thought.

Chapter 53

OT KILLAHS

[Present]

King was meeting Paulo, KC, and Bheef when Alisha texted him nine-one-one. He didn't call back right away, but when he did her phone was going straight to voicemail. He called Keisha and her phone was ringing and then going to voicemail. Fuck it, King thought. I've got more important shit to deal with right now. It was time to get his nigga's doing what they did best. King called Bheef.

"King, what's the play blood?" Bheef answered excitedly.

KC joined in. "Yea King, I came all this way to knock a nigga dick in the dirt. Where these pussy ass nigga's at?" KC loved and respected King. He saw his gangsta in the pen when the odds was stacked against him, but also King was a real nigga. Once he got out the pen and KC was still locked up; King sent him a little money each month. Shit, his own blood family didn't do that for him. As far as KC was concerned, King was family.

The problem was that King still didn't know exactly who needed to be killed or if the treachery went so deep, that he'd have to body everyone and start over. He would do it if he had to, but it would be bad for business.

Talking to both KC and Bheef King said, "That time will come soon enough, but I didn't call ya'll out here to be on no crash dummy shit. It would be disrespectful for me to take advantage of ya'll friendship and loyalty like that." Bheef and KC nodded in agreement. "Let me get the war plan tight. When we strike, we hit hard and mercilessly. Until then, my nigga's, ya'll kick back. I got plenty of kush and backwoods here for ya'll. The fridge is stacked with food and drink. It won't be long. I've almost got all of the information I need." KC's hungry ass was up and opening the fridge in no time. He liked what he saw; a refrigerator full of food. He turned around, smiling.

"Oh, I can work wit this King. You hungry Bheef? KC asked. Im about to whip up some links and omelets."

Bheef nodded his head up and down fast. "Yea! Hell, yeah, blood, hook that shit up."

King had already spoken with Paulo privately. Paulo told him that El Señor said that he needs to make examples out of his enemies. Whoever they may be. Sometimes bullets were too generous. He sent Paulo so that he could help strike terror into those who crossed King. Send them all to hell; God could sort out the innocent later.

Chapter 54

DOUBLECROSS

[Present]

Rico sat in his Lexus, dazed and confused by what he had just heard. The lady across the street is sure that one of the guys who robbed the house in Greenhaven was Cash. She had seen him over the months when he'd go there to pick up the trap money from King's nephew, so she did know who he was.

Rico was skeptical because the nigga's who robbed the spot was masked up, and Cash wasn't the only nigga in the town with dreads with blond tips, but then the neighbor described a car. It was an old model Toyota Celica that Rico knew was one of Cash's bitches cars. The lady described a dent on the front driver's side panel that made the car stick out. That couldn't be a coincidence. Cash's bitch had a dent in the same spot. But why? Why would Cash do some shit like that Rico thought. We were all balling and we owed it all to King. Cash was his brodie. He'd just tap in with him and see what he said. He couldn't see Cash doing no shit like that.

The phone call that Cash got from Rico that morning had caught him off guard but he'd handled it like a "g". By the time the call was over, Cash had Rico feeling bad that he even thought he was capable of some shady shit like that. It was clear now though, that Cash would have to kill Rico.

"Come on my nigga, you know me better than that. That's that disloyal sucka shit." Cash told Rico convincingly when he called asking about the robbery.

"I know blood," Rico responded. He was already feeling bad for having those thoughts. Him and Cash had been through hell together, so he wanted to give him the benefit of the doubt.

"You didn't tell King no bullshit like that did you brodie?"

Cash asked and tried to sound disgusted at the thought of it. He needed to know how much had been said. Rico could fuck his whole plan off if he started running his mouth.

"Na bra, dats why I'm hollering at you," Rico said.

Good Cash thought. He needed to make sure that Rico didn't fuck off his plan to take over King's organization.

"Look, I got my ear to the street. I'm seeing who just came into a lot of dope all of a sudden. You know it won't take long for me to get word back. When I do, it'll tap in wit you asap." Cash listened closely to see if Rico was convinced.

"Ok, I'll do the same thing blood. Whoever did that shit gotta get bagged! Period!" Rico said feeling better about the whole thing now.

"Ok bra, in a minute blood," Cash said as he hung up.

Cash sat for a minute, thinking about what his next move should be. This was unexpected, but that's just the way shit played out sometimes in the streets, shit in life really. He'd have to adapt. King taught him how to play chess and in chess you always had to be prepared for the unexpected. It was time for Cash to call King.

"King, what's good blood gang?" Cash asked as King answered.

"Shit bra, out here in Reno. I'll be back later tonight." King lied! He didn't know who could be trusted so he wasn't trusting no one.

"Ok, ok, well check game, I found out who hit the spot and killed your nephew. It wasn't nigga's in the East, it was right here in the South."

"Is dat right?" King asked suspiciously.

"Yea blood, I already tapped in with Rico. Once we get all the info we need, we gonna move on it. I just wanna be sure the info is right cause I'm murking everything moving blood."

"Yea make sure the info is solid." King said, playing along. He had already got a description of the nigga's who ran up in the spot. To him, one sounded a lot like Cash, but he couldn't figure out why. "Tap back in as soon as you know blood, I want the nigga's responsible put on they ass."

"Fasho, fasho," Cash said as he hung up. King had been all but certain that it was Rico who was shady. Shit, Capone had said the nigga's name right before he died. Now he wasn't so sure. There were a lot of moving pieces on a chessboard. It was never smart to assume your opponent's next move.

In his mind, Cash was playing King like a guitar. King wasn't as smart as he acted. Within the week, I'll be controlling this nigga's blocks, Cash thought. The King will be dead. What Cash didn't know was that he was a pawn in his own game. His new connect in Stockton was using him to weaken King's organization so that he could move in himself, kill King, and take over his organization. Not just for the money, or power, but revenge; a much stronger motivator.

Omar "Murda" Murdock, the son of Fat Leon has been waiting his whole life for this opportunity. He knew that he had to get his money up before he went to war. The hustle was in him. He got it from his dad. It was in his blood. Now at the age of twenty-three, he controlled Stockton, California's coke game.

Now it was time for him to get revenge on the nigga who took his dad from him so many years ago, forcing his mom to move out of Sacramento alone to Stockton with a young son.

It was a stroke of pure luck when one of King's top lieutenants, Cash, came to Stockton looking for a plug on bricks. Cash was a jealous and disloyal nigga, one in a million, and Omar hated him. Omar "Murda" Murdock was just going to use him to weaken King's organization before he came in to annihilate them all. The enemy of my enemy is my friend, Omar thought as he laughed out loud to himself. Omar was an avid chess player, and he had a patient game. His time was coming.

Chapter 55

THE BOSS

[Past]

The second surprise El Señor had for me was almost as good as the first. Torturing Mano was soul cleansing. On the way to our next destination in the back of the SUV, El Señor clicked open a black briefcase and handed me a small stack of court papers. Eyeing them over, I couldn't believe what I read. It was a plea agreement from the Clark County District Attorney guaranteeing me probation and time served on my robbery charges. I would need to sign the papers and then turn myself in at an agreed-upon date and time, but I wouldn't do any real time. I was shocked. El Señor looked me over before speaking.

"King, I have been assured that you will not be in custody for more than seventy-two hours." I smiled. I didn't ask how he'd done it. He's El Señor!

As I finished reading the papers, we were pulling onto a gravel road up to a warehouse that I'd never been to before. It was huge with a chain-link fence. It had barbed wire all the way around the warehouse. At least thirty guards walked the perimeter and the inside compound. All of them were armed with semi-automatics and submachine guns. When we pulled up to the gate, we were waved straight through the armed checkpoint. El Señor suddenly took on a serious demeanor. This was his livelihood; his business. There would be no smiles or laughing now. El Señor had already made it clear to me that business and friendship could not and should not mix. No one could ever question whether or not El Señor was deadly serious about his money.

"King," he said. "You are about to see something that very few people have. Only my closest associates are trusted with the knowledge of this location. Even then, I move it ever so often. Do you know why I move it ever so often even though I say that these men are my closest associates, King?" I had an idea, but El Señor was giving me priceless wisdom, and I didn't want to interrupt. I just stared at him, so he continued.

"Because even my closest associates are just men, King. They are susceptible to envy, jealousy, and betrayal." El Señor stared at me intently as we walked through a set of iron double doors into the main warehouse. More armed guards patrolled. Some had chunky Rottweiler's on leashes. What they were guarding was unreal. It was unbelievable. There were bricks of cocaine stacked so high it looked like a snow mountain. No shit, it reminded me of when I got off the bus at Ely State prison. It looked like snow. I couldn't hide my amazement. It showed in my eyes. El Señor smiled at me momentarily before he went on.

"This is one of my many supply warehouses!" El Señor said. Fuck, I thought, one of many?

"From here, I distribute cocaine all over the United States. The American government pretends to want to stop the introduction of drugs from Mexico, but then they make as much money as I do off of the business. It's just not in their best interest to shut it down." I looked confused.

"I see you don't understand yet, King. Let me explain." El Señor spoke in a fatherly tone. "First, the US government makes billions of dollars a year sending poor people to prison when they catch petty drug charges." I nodded. I knew first-hand about that. "Then, when they want to seem like the kind-hearted government that they are not, they set up mandatory drug treatment programs, and parole and probation systems that they pretend are designed to help people. These programs keep people trapped in the system, and the government makes billions of dollars a year off of them.

Incarceration is a business in America." It was becoming clear to me now. Then, El Señor went on, "Your country's big pharmaceutical companies come out with trillions of dollars'worth of prescription drugs that are supposed to help addicts get off of drugs, but in reality, only get them hooked on your government's prescription drugs. Did you know that they actually treat heroin addicts with "prescription" opiates? The pills emulate opiates so that the addicts still get high. In fact, those drugs are harder to get off of than the illegal ones. They just want people using their dope.

At the end of the day, King, a capitalist government will always approach things from a business mindset. A business is about money, period! They only arrest and kill the kingpin because they know that someone will immediately fill my spot. It won't stop the business." He looked at me to be sure that I followed. I did!

"That's why I was able to deal with your legal matters. You and your case were not more important than money King. You were just business to the district attorney. All that was needed was to find out how much the business was worth and to whom the fee needed to be paid to. I just found out how much and who." El Señor smiled at me. Even his smile could be unsettling; this was a very powerful and dangerous man.

"Gracias El Señor," I replied. He waved a hand in my direction, dismissing the thank you.

"Nino, it was one of the best bargains that I've ever had. You are to become my sole representative in all of northern California and that's just to start. I have big plans for you. Come now, let us walk and talk."

For the next hour, we walked while El Señor laid out his plans for our future. It was wilder than my wildest dreams. Only a few blacks in the history of our country had ever had a connection like this. It would still be up to me to build my organization, control my blocks and enforce my will over the nigga's who were already established. No one willingly gives up millions of dollars' worth of territory, but my time in Mexico with El Señor had prepared me for what was to come.

Without me knowing it, El Señor had been grooming me for this for over a year now. I was ready.

Chapter 56

THE SET UP

[Present]

Cash was playing a deadly game, but like all bitch ass nigga's, he justified his disloyalty by telling himself that he deserved to be "the man." He was willing to betray and even kill his closest comrades, the nigga's that he's known since childhood to fulfill his fantasy of having that ultimate power.

"Rico, where you at brodie?" Cash asked as soon as Rico picked up the phone.

"Out here in Elk Grove chilling with Sasha, what's good?" Rico responded.

"I got the info that we talked about blood. I told you I'd find out who ran up in the spot." Cash listened for any suspicion in Rico's voice as he told Rico the lie that he had rehearsed all morning. There was none. Rico only said, "Tell me what happened, blood."

"Yea blood, a lil smoker bitch told one of the young brodies that she went to buy some dope at a trap spot in the south when she seen the young nigga pulling coke out of a bird that was wrapped wit King's label." Cash needed to put it on extra-thick now. "Plus, she said dat jus days ago the same little nigga was hustling twenty rocks on da corner. No way he should have that much dope, that fast!"

"Ok nigga, I'ma suit up! Meet me at the Food for Less on Mack Road in thirty minutes. I'ma hit King to let him know what's popping," Rico said. Cash jumped in immediately.

"I just got off the phone wit King and he wants us to move on this one alone," Cash lied. "We're supposed to meet him at the safe house in Elk Grove after we take care of this shit."

Cash held his breath. This had to work. He didn't need Rico talking to King right now. Who knows what they might end up talking about? It took a second for Rico to respond.

"Alright blood, I'ma get ready and be on my way," Rico finally said. Cash smiled and let out a sigh of relief.

"Bet," Cash said as he hung up the phone. Next, he called PJ, the one holding the coke. It was time for PJ to become a casualty of war.

"What's up big bro?" PJ answered. Cash had put him up in a cheap studio apartment downtown so that he could keep tabs on him and so that he had him waiting like a sitting duck when it was time to set him up him.

"I'm on my way thru nigga, go ahead and pull the dope out so we can split it up when I get there."

"Yep, yep," PJ responded.

"I'm a bring you some dro too," Cash said for good measure. He wanted to make it sound extra good so that PJ wouldn't become suspicious because this wasn't the plan that they had discussed initially. Sometimes it amazed Cash that nigga's could be so gullible.

"In exactly thirty minutes, unlock the door, so I don't have to knock or wait when I get there," Cash finished.

"Yep, yep," PJ mechanically replied.

Cash was high on his own treachery. He was feeling good. Today he'd be killing two birds with one stone. He'd be proving to King that he was the only one that could be trusted, and he'd be getting Rico out of the way. Rico was too loyal to King, and he'd never go along with Cash's power move so he'd have to be killed at some point anyway. Might as well do it now while I can make it look like Rico was the one that robbed the spot and killed King's nephew all at the same time, Cash thought.

Chapter 57

SNAPPED

[Present]

Keisha couldn't believe what she had just done. Really, she could barely remember doing it! Something inside her had snapped the second Alisha had said that she'd texted King. She didn't regret blowing Alisha's brains out. It just meant that she was committed to riding shit out with King, no matter where it led.

Keisha went home and packed up all of Alisha's shit. Then she wrote a letter to King from Alisha, forging Alisha's handwriting as best she could. She'd taken a class on forgery as part of her DEA training, so the fake signature was pretty good. The letter told King that Alisha couldn't handle this lifestyle anymore. She finished by saying that she didn't want to share him with another woman. She said she had quit her job at the DMV and to please don't try to find her. Keisha knew King, he wouldn't try to find a bitch that said that she didn't want to be found. This would at least buy Keisha some time to think and figure things out.

Now she needed to figure out how to warn King that Cash was on the DEA's radar. King needed to know that Cash was about to be busted and flipped, but she couldn't just come out and say it. It would be too much to explain, and there wasn't a lot of time. Plus, she didn't know for sure that Cash would fold once picked up and interrogated by her boss. This would be tricky. King cared for her, but no doubt he would kill her if he felt betrayed.

Chapter 58

BACK STABBED

[Present]

"Ok brodie, that's the apartment right there!" Cash said, pointing out the apartment to Rico where PJ was stashed with the dope. They were sitting in a car across the street.

"I don't know if the door is unlocked," Cash lied. "But I'll creep up the stairs and try the door first. If it's not unlocked, we'll kick it down. King said he wants everybody dead." Cash lied again.

That had been bothering Rico. Over the years, whenever they had dirt to do, King was with them, or he was communicating with them every step of the way. This was the first time that him and Cash went off solo. He felt like he should have talked to King. Something didn't feel right.

"Aight blood, mask up, check your clip!" Cash spoke softly.

"I'm good, let's do it," Rico replied.

They crept up the stairs. Cash first, Rico right behind him. Cash acted like he was checking the door, but he knew it was unlocked. He turned the doorknob and pushed the door open at the same time. PJ was sitting in the living room with all the dope out in plain sight. He looked up confused. The only one that knew about this spot was Cash! The only one that was supposed to be coming here was Cash. PJ wouldn't have time for anymore thoughts. As soon as he looked up, Cash put several rounds from his Glock 17 into PJ's chest and face. It would be hard for his momma to have an open-casket funeral. By the time Rico came in, Cash had killed the only connection between himself and the murder of King's nephew.

Rico looked around and saw King's dope on the floor and the dead body on the couch. Cash looked up at him.

"I told you blood, the smoker bitch was right," Cash said excitedly. Rico nodded but couldn't help but to think that this shit seemed almost too perfect. He looked around more. Then he noticed the gold chain the nigga was wearing. He'd seen it before. Cash interrupted his thoughts.

"I'm going to check the other room real quick to see if there's more dope," Cash said. Rico nodded as Cash went to the back room. While in the room, Cash pulled out the .357 revolver he had hidden under his sweatshirt. He walked quietly back into the living room. Rico was bent down over the corpse looking at his chain and medallion. Now he remembered, this litlle nigga used to be with Cash.

Cash leveled the burner at Rico's chest from behind as he walked back into the living room. "Nigga, stand up!" Cash yelled. Rico stood up calmly and turned around. What he saw broke his heart.

"Nigga, it's like that?! We played on monkey bars together," Rico asked. Cash stared at him coldly.

"You got no vision blood; you got no vision." Cash told Rico as he put two .357 hollow point cop "killah" rounds into Rico's chest. The power of the rounds lifted Rico off his feet. He landed on the floor at the feet of PJ, who lay dead on the couch.

Cash had to move fast now. He packed up the dope and then slid Rico's body closer to the front door. Then came the hard part. Cash lowered the .357, aiming it as his own foot and then pulled the trigger. "Ohh shit." He yelled as the bullet shot through the tongue of his Jordan, but his adrenaline was flowing so he kept going.

He wiped the .357 clean, then hobbled over to PJ placing the gun in PJ's still warm hands! Cash would tell King that PJ had killed Rico when they busted in and shot him in the foot during the shootout. It wouldn't be hard to believe. Some nigga's get killed in shootouts, and some get wounded. Cash smiled as he hopped back to the car on one leg. He had a good feeling that this was going to work. It was time for him to call King.

Chapter 59

CLOSING IN

[Present]

Special Agent Vargas had been trying to contact Agent Johnson now for twenty-four hours. She was off the grid. He wasn't worried, he had already been preparing. To him, it seemed like Agent Keisha Johnson had been acting strange for quite some time now. She wasn't reporting as scheduled, and when she did report, it was never anything of value that could be used against King.

Agent Vargas thought that Keisha had been compromised. It wouldn't be the first time that an undercover officer had been taken in by their target. The only reason the DEA hadn't pulled her out already is that they didn't have shit else to go on. They had nothing concrete to use against King. Agent Vargas had a hunch that his luck had just changed.

There was a double murder downtown. One of the deceased was Rico Calhoun, another one of King's top lieutenants. Agent Vargas was called in on the case by homicide because a small amount of coke wrapped in King's insignia, the Black King, was found on the murder scene. It wasn't that, that had caught agent Vargas's attention though. They already knew that King supplied ninety percent of the city's dope.

What stuck out to Agent Vargas was that it was clear that the crime scene had been staged. It was someone's amateur attempt to confuse detectives. It only took the seasoned agent a few short minutes to put together a more accurate picture of what had really happened in the small apartment.

The entry wounds into Rico Calhoun weren't fired from someone who was sitting down on the couch as the staged scene was trying to suggest. The angle was all wrong. There was also blood smearing on the carpet. Rico's body had been dragged. His hunch was confirmed when CSU detected a third source of blood. Someone else had been there. Agent Vargas was willing to bet his career that it was Cash. Agent Vargas told the crime scene investigators to put a rush on the blood results. Once he got the results, Agent Vargas thought that he'd have enough to arrest and charge Cash. Then he'd use Cash to testify against King.

Chapter 60

ROOK TAKES ROOK

[Present]

King was just thinking that it was strange that Rico hadn't tapped back in when Cash texted him nine-one-one. King hit him right back. When Cash picked up, he was breathing heavily.

"Nigga what you doing? Fucking?" King asked, irritated.

"Nah bra, I got shot getting them nigga's that hit the spot and killed Jamarius." Cash said, trying to sound frantic. Now he had King's attention.

"What happened? Why you didn't tap in first?" King asked suspiciously.

This was where Cash needed to be careful. Cash staged the murders to make it look like PJ shot Rico, but that was just so the police would be confused. He needed King to think that Rico was the one behind the treachery in the organization and that it was Jamille and Rico plotting all along. This would make King trust him completely.

"Big bra you not gonna believe it. I was parked in theToyota, just watching the apartment where the nigga's that robbed the spot were supposed to be. After about thirty minutes, the nigga Rico came out the apartment. I was shocked blood."

King was quiet. So, Cash went on.

"At first blood, I thought Rico had just got to the nigga's first and had downed them before me, but Rico went to his car and then headed back up to the apartment. If Rico had just set them nigga's on they pockets, he wouldn't have been heading back up there, ya feel me?" Cash wanted to make sure that

King was buying what he was selling and that he understood exactly what he was saying. This was a matter of life and death, so every word counted.

"Go on!" King said impatiently.

"So, I sat there for another thirty minutes and then I got mad blood. I started feeling like it was some shady shit going on so I grabbed the Glock and pushed up the stairs. I was at the top step when the door cracked open. I could hear Rico telling somebody that he'd be right back. He told them that they did good the other day and that soon he'd have his own block!" Cash paused. "I was right outside the door and could hear every word."

King didn't say shit but Cash could feel his fury through the line. Cash pushed on! He had to seize the momentum. Cash knew that anger was a powerful emotion that often overpowered peoples logic. If he could get King furious about the situation, he might make a mistake.

"I pushed through the door blood and caught both of them nigga's off guard. I pointed the Glock at Rico so he backed up with his hands in the air. He tried saying some sentimental shit with me blood, saying to hear him out and that we been rocking since monkey bars!" Cash mixed the truth with his lies. "But I looked around blood and saw the dope on the table that I knew came from the lick. From there I didn't have time to put more pieces together because the other nigga on the couch reached for a burner. I downed him where he sat."

"As I turned, Rico was pulling his banger out of his waist trying to raise it at me. I had no choice but to slump blood. Even after I shot him, he got off one shot that hit me in the foot. That shit hurts like a bitch blood. I grabbed the dope and dipped. I texted you as soon as I left and was on the way." Cash hoped his story rang true. It could mean the difference of King killing him or him getting to King.

King sat silently thinking about everything that Cash had just said. It sounded crazy but the game was crazy. Shit, he'd been through wilder shit himself. King believed Cash. King had never told Cash that when he tortured Capone that he had said Rico was plotting to knock him off his throne. So, it made sense that it was Rico. Cash had no way of knowing any of that. Cash said he'd heard Rico tell the nigga that he'd have his own block soon. Why would he say that if he hadn't been plotting on King, if he wasn't at the root of this disloyalty and treachery? Finally, King spoke.

"Good shit brodie, how's the foot?"

Cash smiled. King had bought the story.

"It's fine, the bullet went through and through. The homie is bandaging me up, I couldn't go to the hospital with what had just happened, the ops would have booked me quick."

"Aight, take a little time, I'm bout to clean house." Cash knew what King meant. He was about to start murking shit. Cash wanted to be in on it. That's how he planned to catch King in the open; vulnerable. When bullets started flying, anything could happen. Everyone knows that bullets ain't got no names.

"Blood, just give me an hour or two, you know that I'm rocking wit you." Cash pleaded.

"I'll tap in if I need you bro," King said as he hung up.

Cash had been counting on King needing him to put in work , but he didn't seem to need him. Cash would have to wait a little longer to get King out in the open.

King knew what he had to do now. When part of the body is infected, you have to chop it off. Since King didn't know exactly who Rico had recruited to help him, he'd have all the hustlers and gunners associated with the blocks that Rico ran killed. Then Rico's mom, sister and thirteen-year-old brother would simply disappear. This would be a message to any others who had sights on King's throne. It was time for his out of town killers to get to work.

Chapter 61

STRATEGY

Omar "Murda" Murdock kept a close eye on things as shit heated up in Sacramento. It was clear that a war was jumping off cause bodies was popping up like pimples on a teenage boy. These wasn't normal hood murders either. This was King making an example out of nigga's.

One young nigga wasn't just shot. His head had been bashed into the grass of his mother's front lawn with a sledgehammer. They found some of his teeth over twenty feet from his body. Another nigga was found in the front seat of his girl's car in the morning when she left for work. His throat was cut from ear to ear.

Omar just got word that one of King's most reputable and loyal hitters had been found on the side of the road asshole naked. He'd been tortured with some kinda chemical that eats straight through skin, meat, and bone. All he had on was one of those paper Burger King crowns on his head. If that wasn't King sending a message, he didn't know what was.

Omar had heard of King's gangsta. He wasn't taking him lightly. What Omar did know was that at last count, thirteen of King's soldiers had been downed. These was young nigga's known for busting they guns. It didn't matter how powerful King was, this would weaken the nigga's strength. Murdock would continue to wait while King destroyed himself. Then he'd crush him and take his throne.

Chapter 62

Going Crazy

[Present]

Keisha was stressed. Her supervisor at the DEA had been blowing her phone up. She had been blowing King's phone up. He wasn't answering. She knew that he was in some shit. Everyday bodies were being found. They weren't just being killed either, it was over kill. It was the same kind of murders that her supervisors had shown her pictures of before she went undercover. The murders had King written all over them.

Keisha was pacing the living room floor. "Fuck," she thought. I need to warn him. I need to be by his side. But he thinks I'm just a pretty dancer. I'm his bitch, but if he's in business mode, he ain't gonna worry about checking in with me. He probably won't even answer his phone. "Fuck," Keisha screamed.

Then it hit her. A few months after she went undercover, she had placed a GPS monitor underneath King's BMW. She had never used it cause by then, she was already falling for the nigga, but this was important. If her bosses got a hold of Cash and flipped him before she could warn King it was over. If Cash testified, they'd probably give him a new identity and relocate him. "Nah, fuck that." Keisha thought. I'll track the nigga on the GPS and let the chips fall where they may. If I don't do something, I'll never be able to live with myself, Keisha said.

Chapter 63

BALLING

[Present]

King sat in the beemer with Paulo. Bheef and KC had made quick work of the hustlers under Rico's control. They'd come up with some creative ways to down the nigga's that would be remembered for a while.

The thing that would be remembered forever was how a whole household, Rico's entire family, down to the dog, had just vanished. With Paulo's help, King made sure that their bodies would never be found. His mortuary experience was still paying dividends. Sitting there with Paulo, King couldn't help but to think back to when El Señor had delivered the first one hundred keys to him. He had the time of his life, and much like when Rob had "put him on," King decided right then that he'd do anything necessary to keep his power.

(Past Reflection)

"You like that car, sir?" The Mercedes dealer asked, but he had a smirk on his face. "Well, it's a b-e-a-u-t-y!" He sounded it out. It was the Mercedes Delorean. It had a V-12, with the doors that opened up like bird wings. It was just under $300,000, brand new.

"Yea," I nodded. I walked around it, eyeing it. I sat in it! This was the sexiest car I'd ever seen. There was only one at the dealership. It was on the showroom floor; metallic silver with black guts. Hand-stitched Italian leather seats sculpted to my body.

"I want to test drive it," I told the cocky Mercedes dealer. He chuckled.

"Sir, I'm sorry, but this is one of only thirty made in the world. We don't just let anyone test drive it," the salesman said. He chuckled again while looking around to see if anyone else was paying attention to this young nigga who came in asking to drive their most expensive Mercedes.

Turns out, another salesman was watching and he wasn't so dumb. We locked eyes, and he tossed me the key. The first salesman had a "What the fuck look on his face." What he should have noticed was Cash standing next to me with a Louis duffle bag. The bag alone cost fifteen bands; inside was two hundred and fifty thousand; in cash.

I started the car, right there on the showroom floor. That bitch sounded like it had an airplane engine. It barked like a pit-bull who wanted to be let off the leash so it could fight. I hit the gas a few more times. The first salesman was yelling, "Sir, Sir," then he started screaming, "S-i-i-r, s-i-i-r!" I cut the car off. He was still screaming.

I nodded at the salesman who had thrown me the keys. He made his way over to me. Shoving the first punk to the side, I told him I'd be back later for the paperwork. He said ok and Cash tossed the salesman the Louis duffle. The salesman glanced inside it briefly, then nodded back at me. He'd just made a thirty thousand dollar commission in ten minutes.

That night me and the brodies did it B.I.G. We went to Old Sacramento, Club Niros, back to back in our cars. None of us was driving a car that didn't run at least a hundred thousand. Nigga's couldn't tell us shit. We parked all three whips right in front, then hopped out. Jamille, Cash, and Rico was Gucci'd out from head to toe. I was draped in Louis. The whole line outside the club was silent. Sacramento had never seen no shit like this before.

"Sir, you guys can't park there, sir you'll get towed." The doorman said as I reached in my pocket handing him ten fresh $100 bills. He slid to the side without saying another word and let us walk in.

Inside the club, we had it our way. We bought out the bar. Every drink was free for everybody there. Even the hating ass nigga's drank for free. We blew kush. I had a VIP section roped off. Bitches flocked to us by the dozens.

This was my first taste of what this kind of money could do. It could open up doors where no doors could be seen. Me and my day one nigga's drank and got fucked up. I had my pick of the baddest bitches in the club. I told the two baddest bitches to go sit on the hood of the silver Mercedes right out front while me and my nigga's toasted. That night, where it all began, we toasted to money. To loyalty! My nigga Cash stood up, held a glass in the air, and said. "To King, we owe this all to our brodie. Death before dishonor." Everyone cheered and toasted.

That night I was on cloud nine as I left the club with two bad bitches. One was super chocolate with green eyes and said she was Haitian. The other was Latina. They were both students at the local college. On the way to the hotel suite, it started to pop off after I turned on that Game, "Start from scratch."

"If I could start from scratch! I wouldn't change shit! Same Red Bandana! Same Fo Fifth! Same g wagon! Same hood rat bitch! Workers in the kitchen! Cooking up my shit!"

Latin mami in the front seat got on her knees facing the chocolate goddess in the back. Her skirt hiked up when she bent over so that I could see her pink thong. She started moving her hips slowly and seductively; staring at me. Her thighs were thick but tone. I reached over while driving and grabbed her round ass, trailing a finger right over her pussy. It was hard to keep my eyes on the road.

I could feel the warmth of her mound. She moaned, then began kissing the Haitian in the backseat. She cocked over on her knees in my front seat. Moving her panties to the side I stuck a finger in her already wet pussy. Her walls gripped my fingers like a suction cup. "Oh, fuck," I thought. I punched the gas.

Once in the hotel suite, the action picked right up. This was about to be my first threesome, so it was "on-the-job training." Latina baby took the lead.

"Papi, sit down," she said, pulling my brick-hard dick out! "Oooh, papi." She whispered as she stroked the full length of my manhood. I groaned as her warm wet mouth took me in. The Haitian wasn't going to be outdone. She put her face next to the Latinas as they went back and forth with my dick in their mouths. The Latin mami slid down and began gently sucking my balls while Haitian baby worked my throbbing dick.

"Suck that shit," I groaned. The visual of this scene alone was enough to make a nigga bust. "Get up and turn around," I whispered. Latin mami got up and bent over and began rubbing her own pussy.

"Papi fuck me! Fuck me. I've never had a black dick before." She said as she rocked her hips. That's why her pussy gripped my finger like that, I thought. As I slid into that Latin fire, she let out a growl that was mixed with pleasure and pain. She reached her hand back, placing it on my stomach. "Despacio Papi (slow down)." I grabbed her hips so she couldn't run from the dick. Slowly, inch by inch, she gave all of herself to me. Her moans and cries in Spanish filled the suite.

"Sí papi.", "por favor," "o dios," "aye papi", "si aye." Her round brown ass sliding back over every inch of my shaft was a beautiful sight. Haitian baby was tongue kissing Latina mami while I pounded her tight pussy. The Haitian got up and slid underneath me while I was on my knees fucking doggystyle. She began licking Latin mami's clit and sucking my balls while Latin mami's fat pussy lips gripped my dick. This threw Latin mami into a frenzy. Her body shook as Haitian baby feasted on her clit.

"Por favor don't stop, por favor papi. Oh, shit King," Latin mami screamed.

"Cum on this big black dick," I growled.

At the sound of my voice, Latin mami exploded. Her eyes rolled into the back of her head as I stroked her deep and at a rapid pace. I knew that I would cum soon, so I pulled out and sat on the couch. I was still rock hard with Latin mami's juices all over my glistening dick. Haitian baby bent over, and sucked me clean before sliding her thick chocolate ass on top of me. She slid down slowly, adjusting to the length and curve of my dick. Her pussy had a whole different feel to it.

As she found her rhythm, Haitian baby rode me hungrily. Placing her hands on my chest for balance, she rode to the tip and back down. She was moaning and making a deep gurgling sound the whole time. Latin mami sat up and began kissing Haitian baby as she furiously rode my shaft. She rode my dick like she was mad at it. Working herself into a frenzy, she began clapping her fat ass down hard on my thighs. Now she was taking my full length deep into her stomach.

"Don't stop," I commanded. "I'm bout to bust."

Haitian baby didn't stop. Latin mami took one of Haitian baby's firm titties in her mouth while she was pouncing on my manhood. This did something to her. She shot forward, straight down, and chest to chest with me while still working her shapely hips. She began convulsing as she felt the erotic eruption of her orgasm. I exploded at the same time. I couldn't help but to think of my favorite movie, "Scarface."

"First you get the money, then you get the power, then you get the bitches."

Chapter 64

THE VOID

[Present]

Cash took a quick trip out of town to sit down with his new connect. He wasn't ready yet to grab the amount of keys that they had agreed to, but he wanted to let "Murda" Murdock know that it was still all good. He met "Murda" Murdock at a strip club in Stockton where the baller was having lunch. Cash had no idea of Murdock's history with King.

"What's good Cash?" Omar asked as he chewed on a juicy looking steak.

"Earned it." By the Weekend was playing as a tall blonde snow bunny worked the pole.

"Same ole shit, just gettin' everything in order. Things got a little hot, so I wanted to get out of town for a second. I also wanted to holla at you."

Cash didn't know just how hot it had really gotten. A few hours after Cash had left Sacramento, Agent Vargas and his team hit his baby momma's house with a federal search warrant.

"Shoot," Omar said calmly. "What's on your mind?"

Cash looked around nervously. "I just want to make sure that we are on the same page. It's gonna be a large void to fill when we start doing business."

Omar smiled slightly. "However much you need, I got. It won't be a problem," Omar said while still chewing his steak.

"That's what I wanted to talk to you about. I may not have the whole amount I'll need to buy them straight out." Omar acted like he was thinking, he cocked his head to the side and looked up at the ceiling, but he already knew what he'd say. He would agree to whatever Cash wanted because once Cash served his purpose, he'd be dead anyway. These nigga's kill me, Murdock thought. This snake in the grass, disloyal backstabbing ass nigga is really sitting here acting like he on some solid business shit.

"This is what I can do for you, Cash." Omar said. He leaned in and whispered for effect. "For every bird you buy, I'll give you one on consignment." Cash lit up like the Fourth of July. He had some money put up but nowhere near enough to replace what King supplied. Once King was dead, the Mexican connect was cut. Cash was trying to cover all bases. With this plug at this price he'll be able to get what he needs.

"That's what up bra; I appreciate that." Cash smiled. "I do good business, and I'm loyal as fuck." Cash said. Now it was Omar's turn to smile at the irony of that statement. He just nodded.

They sat around for a minute making small talk and watching the bitches when Omar asked, "Say, man, what happened to your foot?" Pointing at Cash's heavily bandaged foot.

Cash said the closest thing to the truth that he's said in a while.

"It's nothing. I accidentally shot myself." Omar accepted this lame answer because he didn't care. He knew that for the moment, him and Cash were on the same side. They weren't friends, but they shared a common enemy.

"Nigga, be more careful; we got millions to make!" Murdock said instead. He knew what Cash wanted to hear. Some pieces on the chessboard can only move in one direction, so you always know what to expect. A jealous and disloyal nigga was just that, a piece that only moved in one direction, so Omar knew exactly how to have Cash eating out of the palm of his hand.

Chapter 65

NOW WHAT?

[Present]

King was dropping Paulo off at a small executive airport where he'd be flown back to Mexico. Not much was said on the ride, Paulo was a man of few words. King knew that Paulo would report to El Señor that the problem in his organization was under control, and that those whose loyalty was in question had been dealt with and dealt with mercilessly.

Shit, King had murdered Rico's entire family, and he'd grown up with the nigga. Rico's family had been placed in a casket and sent through the cremation flames at a local funeral home. King didn't have a choice, he thought. Maybe if he would have killed Rico once Capone had initially said his name, his nephew would still be alive.

When Cash confirmed that Rico was in on the lick and murder in Greenhaven of his nephew Jamarius, there was no more doubt. Knocking off Rico's family was the hardest thing that King had ever had to do. They had been like a second family to him; but it had to be done.

It was clear to King that Cash was the only one left he could trust. He'd have to meet with him soon to explain what had been done and why. Not because he had to, but because now, since Jamille and Rico were gone, Cash would have to play a bigger role in running things until King could find nigga's he trusted. He'd tried to get KC and Bheef to stay, but they were both anxious to get home. King gave them both fifty bands when they parted ways.

King had that old haunting feeling that has been with him since his mom left in his childhood. He felt alone. It didn't seem to matter how many people surrounded him or how much money he had, loneliness was his only consistent companion. "Fuck it," he thought. "This is the life I chose."

Pushing the thoughts aside, King started thinking about how to rebuild the parts of his organization that he'd had to destroy. He had no way of knowing that the real war hadn't even begun yet.

Chapter 66

SNOW PACKED

[Present]

One hundred fifty miles to the north, in the snow-packed Sierra Nevada mountains, a snowmobiler came across a badly wounded female. She was bleeding heavily from the head. The snowmobiler was a part-time paramedic and he could see that the woman had been shot in the back of her head. No doubt, he thought, the snowpack had chilled the woman's blood, slowing her heart rate and saving her life so far. It was amazing that she was still alive and barely conscious.

"Young lady, what's your name?" he asked. Alisha opened her mouth but could only make sounds that he couldn't understand. "Don't try to talk," he said as he took off his scarf, wrapping it tightly around Alisha's head. "I'm going to get you to a hospital. Stay with me, stay with me! You didn't make it this long to die now!"

Alisha couldn't talk, but her mind was working. She played the days events back to herself. Being at the house arguing with Keisha. Being handcuffed and thrown in the trunk. Being walked down the trail. That's when her mind went blank and it felt like she got hit in the head with a bat. Alisha started to lose consciousness again as the snowmobile revved and hummed over the snow towards the hospital. Her last thought was of Keisha. That bitch is the police.

Chapter 67

PRESSURE COOKER

[Present]

Cash was posted at his side bitches spot, losing his patience. He had even started smoking Newport's again over the last few days. The stress of the situation was getting to him. Why hadn't this nigga King reached out to him yet? He knew that King was directly responsible for all the bodies that had been found murked in the city. They were all the litlle nigga's that ran with Rico.

That let Cash know that King had believed his story about Rico being in on the plot with Jamille. The question was, why hadn't King reached out to him? Why hadn't he called on Cash to help send them nigga's to the next life? Who was King using to do all these murders? The young hitters from the other blocks in the east and north hadn't been used either. Shit, most of them was laying low, not knowing how far King's vengeance would stretch. Cash had bet all his cards that King would reach out to him. That would be the only way for him to knock King down clean.

I'm running out of time. Cash thought. Soon, Omar would start thinking that he was full of shit. Initially he'd told Omar that he was ready to do business, but some unexpected events had slowed his progress. By now, he thought he'd already have blown King's brains out. Should I call the nigga? Cash thought. Na, he replied to himself. I can't seem like I'm desperate to meet up with him. I'm just gonna have to keep Omar waiting until my chance comes. Fuck it. Cash said, cheering himself up. It will be worth the wait. When all is said and done, I'll be King.

Chapter 68

TRACKING KING

[Present]

Keisha was busy trying to track King on her DEA-issued GPS system. The system had one flaw though; it tracked the car to a radius of five hundred yards. It would get her close to King, but then it would be up to her to find his car or him. So far, she'd gone to two locations and had just missed him. One was a soul food restaurant on Martin Luther King Blvd, and the other was a small airport on Freeport Blvd. She hoped that King hadn't caught a plane somewhere, then her chance to warn him and to help him would be lost.

Keisha watched the tiny monitor as the red dot representing King's beemer finally stopped blinking on the screen. He had stopped. Keisha punched the steering wheel when she saw that he was now nineteen miles away. It was almost five o'clock, so traffic would be a bitch. Keisha dialed King again. No answer. Hopefully, his black ass will stay put, Keisha said out loud as she pulled out of the parking lot, intent on getting to King.

Chapter 69

BAD BLOOD

[Present]

King was on the phone with Cash when Keisha called. He'd have to hit her back. King had been giving it much thought, and it was clear that Cash was the only one that he could trust. His other day one nigga's were dead, and it took time for King to trust anyone. Just like he'd had to prove his loyalty to El Señor, he expected the same thing from his inner circle.

King knew that in an organization as big as his, there was always going to be nigga's that couldn't and shouldn't be trusted. It was his inner circle that he was most concerned about. These were the only ones that would have direct contact with him. This also made them the most dangerous; they knew the most about him. He'd known several other boss nigga's who'd been ratted on by their closest associates. Shit, he even knew a few who'd been killed by their closest folks. That's why he'd waited before he got back at Cash and why he didn't get at Cash to help knock down Rico's family and his crew of young hitters. Finally, King was convinced that Cash was loyal and solid.

"Blood, wats good brodie? A nigga been worried about you." Cash said as he picked up the phone.

"My bad, my nigga. You know how I get when I need to clear my head. I had to figure a few moves out, but shit smooth now." King replied.

"Ok bet, bet! So, what's brackin now?" Cash knew what had been done to Rico's family and crew, so there had to be some changes coming. He felt his spirits lift.

"Look blood, we gonna holla tonight? Meet me at Arden Fair Mall at ten, right there by the movie theater. I'll lay it out for you then, aight?"

"That's wats up blood. What car you gonna be in?" Cash asked. This is my chance, he thought. I'll have King out in the open tonight.

"The white seven series, don't be late!" King said as he hung up.

Chapter 70

DIRTY COP

[Present]

Downtown on J street at the building that the DEA shared with the FBI; agent Vargas was briefing his team. They had hit three spots looking for Cash. They had him dead bang now. His DNA was at a double murder scene, but agent Vargas wasn't after Cash because he wanted to lock him up for murder. Cash was just an ends to a means. Agent Vargas just needed Cash so that he could bring King and his organization down.

The DEA had only seen a few drug kingpins in the US whose organization ran like King's. Spanning over six states with ties to two others, the DEA estimated that King's organization moved over a hundred kilos a week. However, King wasn't your typical drug dealer. He cushioned himself with layers and layers of workers who didn't know anything about him.

King's estimated worth was one hundred and eighty million, but he lived like he made a hundred thousand a year. Most of his money is kept in offshore accounts, and up to this point, he's been untouchable. Agent Vargas was obsessed with bringing King down. Now with Cash in his sights, he figured that he'd have the info he needed to do it. I need to find Cash now, he thought. I'm running out of time.

El Señor had paid him a lot of money to make sure that King got arrested and convicted. Agent Vargas was on El Señor's payroll. El Señor was not the kind of man you let down. Vargas knew that El Señor's reach was long. He could surely have had King killed, but he obviously didn't want that. Maybe he wanted worse for King. Life without the possibility of parole in a maximum-security federal prison was a slow death sentence and worse than death to many. No matter what, he thought, I've got a job to do.

Chapter 71

BALLING OUT OF CONTROL

[Past]

Over the next three years, I had it my way. What I had learned from my time in Mexico with El Señor gave me a blueprint for setting up my organization in California. It took six months of recruiting young killers, hitters, and gunner's to my squad before I was prepared to move in and take over. When your'e making a move like I was making, you best to be ready for war.

It took another sixty days of what was called the "Bloody Summer," in Sacramento where the remaining nigga's who wasn't trying to join the squad, got dead. Nigga's had two choices; they could get bread or get dead. Since I was able to get them nigga's purer coke for cheaper prices, the smart ones got on board. They ended up making way more money than they were before, and most of them became somewhat loyal to me. Regardless, it's always nigga's who gotta learn the hard way. The squad was ruthless when dealing with them nigga's. After the opposition was wiped out and the blocks I wanted cleared, shit went smooth.

Me, Cash, Jamille and Rico lived it up. The dough was coming so fast that we had to make up ways to spend it. The jewels and cars wasn't shit, so a I copped a few pieces of property. We took trips all over the country. New York, Florida, Las Vegas, and a dozen places in between. I wanted to travel out of the country but because of my record I had to wait five years.

It was nothing to spend thirty thousand in Vegas over a weekend. I came into the game for riches, to ball out, and I had it all. What I didn't have was a plan to make my money last. I didn't have an exit strategy, and that's a recipe for disaster. That is until Faith got back in contact with me. I had done her wrong when I got out of prison and went on the run to Mexico, but she still loved me.

"Hello," I answered without recognizing the number. I rarely answered a number that I didn't recognize, but today was different for some reason.

"Hey, King." Faith said in a timid voice.

"Who is this?" I shot back sharply, not recognizing the voice and thinking that it was one of my bitches calling from a different number because I hadn't been answering her calls.

"Wow," Faith said. "I never thought that you'd forget my voice."

"Stop playing games, girl; who is this? I'm about to hang the phone up!" I snapped back.

"It's Faith, King."

I was silent. I'd thought about Faith a lot over the last few years. She was a good girl, and when I left for Mexico, she was pregnant, but I'd never tried to contact her. Not even once I came back to the states. I didn't know what to say.

"Damn girl, long time no speak," I said it like it was her fault that we hadn't talked.

"Look, King, I'm not gonna pretend like I understand why you left me like you did. I went through hell and back because of you and don't want to relive it. I forgive you though and I've moved on. I'm calling to see if you want to see your daughter." Damn, I had a daughter and I didn't even know it.

"Yea fasho I do! Why are you just now reaching out to me?" I asked, making it seem like it was her fault again. She laughed out loud but didn't answer the question. She just changed the subject instead.

"Ok, well, I'm going to the Bay Area this weekend to visit family. I'll call you when I'm there so that you can come see her." Faith said.

"Ok that's what's up. You going out there to see some nigga?" I asked.

I'd taken this girl's money, disappeared on her without saying a word, and left her pregnant. I hadn't talked to her in several years, but since I was that "nigga", to me it was no big deal. It was just too hard to acknowledge that I was wrong.

"Bye King, I'll call you Saturday." Faith said as she hung up.

Over the next two days, I thought about having a daughter. How would I feel when I saw her? What would I say? I had a lot going on in these streets. My squad of young goons was running Sacramento. The name "Rilla" was ringing bells. We was the realest. The realest when it came to gangsta shit, hustling, and macking bitches. This was my life. The life I had dreamed of. This was the life I'd built and this street shit was where my heart was at. Was there room in my heart for my daughter? I didn't know. I wasn't even sure that I was capable of love.

The day that I met my daughter for the first time, I was frustrated. She didn't seem interested in me.

"Come here lil mama." I said as my daughter ran back and forth past me. "She won't come to me," I said, looking at Faith. Faith rolled her eyes at me.

"First of all, King, her name is Terri." I hadn't even asked my daughter's name.

"And secondly, she doesn't know you. You're a stranger to her." Faith finished, staring me in the eyes. That shit had me heated. I was used to having things my way. Everything! I shifted my attention and asked Faith a question out of the blue.

"So, who you fucking with Faith?"

"Are you being serious right now King?" Faith shot back.

"What?" I said, acting shocked. Like I had a right to ask that question.

"You pull up here in your expensive car, jewels, and shit and don't even ask your daughter's name. You bring these nigga's with you." Faith pointed at Cash and Rico, who were standing by my car. "They carrying guns out in the open like the shit is legal to my aunty house, and you worried about who I'm fucking?" Faith teared up. She really was beautiful. "King, I hope you know what your'e doing! I've been hearing about you, and I know who you've become, but do you have anyone around you who loves you for you? Or is it just people who are around you for what you can do for them? That shit don't last, King. I hope you're putting money away for a rainy day, but by the looks of it, you're not," she said, while cutting her eyes at my car and jewels.

"I love you King, I always will. But do you love yourself?" Faith asked softly as she turned to walk away.

The shit cut like a knife, but probably not in the way that she intended. It made me start thinking that if I loved myself, I'd start stacking my money as tall as the empire state building. Fuck spending all that dough on bottles, jewels, whips and trips. That shit didn't hold value.

That day, thanks to Faith, I changed my mentality in regards to money. Unfortunately, I was too caught up in my own wants to change my mind in regards to being a father. Nobody changes until they're ready.

After less than an hour with Faith and my daughter, I was ready to get back in the streets.

"Here," I said. I was trying to hand Faith a roll of about two thousand dollars. She looked at me sadly shaking her head no.

"I don't want your money, King." She picked Terri up and began turning for the front door of her aunt's house. "Oh yeah." She paused. "By the way, you have a son too. He's three months older than Terri." I looked at Faith, confused.

"JuJu." She said rolling her head. "The police were trying to get both of us to turn on you for the robberies in Las Vegas, so they brought us together, hoping that one of us would feel betrayed and say some foul shit about you. She's a good girl too, King. She stopped prostituting when she found out that she was pregnant and went to nursing school." Faith searched my eyes to see if I gave a shit.

I just sat on the hood of my car watching her. I didn't know how I felt.

"She named him Prince," she said as she walked into her aunt's house. Faith walked away, thinking that every time she saw King, he broke her heart.

Chapter 72

COST TO BE THE BOSS

[Present]

In Tijuana, El Señor was dealing with treachery and betrayal of his own, and this time there wasn't' a whole village that he could have killed to deal with it. It all started once he had forbidden Claudia from seeing King, even though she was pregnant with his child. El Señor tried to get her to have an abortion, and she refused. "It's my fault." El Señor thought. I should have never sent her to pick up a payment from King in California, but I'd told King several years ago that Claudia was off-limits. King had been like a son to me. To dishonor me in this way was unforgivable.

El Señor couldn't just kill King. Claudia would never speak to him or see him again. He'd decided to get rid of King another way. El Señor had sent Paulo to California to make it look like he was helping King, and he did help him kill mutha fuckas, but Paulo was really there to make the first payment to Agent Vargas.

El Señor had paid Agent Vargas a large sum of money to arrest King. El Señor would use the American legal system to dispose of King. This way, Claudia couldn't blame him. If King got arrested and sent to prison for life, that wasn't El Señor 's fault. Claudia would be heartbroken but at least she couldn't blame him.

"El Señor, the plane is approaching." His driver was standing outside the limo, looking towards the sky with a pair of binoculars. El Señor nodded from the backseat of the limo. It was a clear and beautiful day, but El Señor still heard the plane before he saw it begin it's descent to land.

After the plane landed, the driver waved as Paulo got off and started to walk the hundred yards to where the limo was parked. The driver waited for Paulo to get into the limo, and then opened and shut the limo door for Paulo as he got in. The driver paused. Something caught his attention. It was something bright, like a mirror reflecting off of the sun.

While in the process of opening his door to get in the limo, the left side of the driver's face exploded. Blood, tissue, and brain matter splattered against the window and hood of the car. The driver slumped to the ground. A bloody crater was all that was left of his skull as the side of his head hit the ground with a thud.

Immediately after, heavy machine-gun fire erupted from several directions towards El Señor's limo and his bodyguards pickup trucks. El Señor's henchmen in the car in front of him and the ones behind him didn't stand a chance. The trucks that they were in might as well have been tin cans against the heavy artillery. They were chopped down like grass under a lawnmower.

Paulo grabbed El Señor by the shoulders, pushing him to the floor in the backseat of the limo. Unlike his henchmen's cars, El Señor's limo was armored, but the fifty caliber machine gun rounds wouldn't be denied for long. One tire had already been blown out and the back passengers side window where El Señor's head had been only seconds ago had a million tiny cracks in it like spider webs. Even the bulletproof glass wouldn't hold forever against a barrage like this.

Stay down El Señor." Paulo yelled as he jumped from the back of the limo and into the front, hoping that the driver had left the keys in the ignition. The rounds bouncing off the limo sounded like big balls of hail bouncing off of a tin roof . It sounded like someone was beating on the outside of the limo with an aluminum bat.

The keys were in the ignition, so Paulo started the car. He put it in reverse while punching the gas. He didn't know which way to head; he just knew they were taking heavy fire right there. If they stayed there, they were dead. Paulo cut the wheel hard to the left, the limo hydroplaned, spinning around in the opposite direction because one of the tires was flat.

El Señor was thrown on the floor from one side of the limo to the other. Rounds were still pinging off the limo but there were fewer than before. It wouldn't take long though, before the hitmen repositioned themselves and found their target again.

"Stay down El Señor." Paulo screamed as he saw his potential escape. It was the only entrance and exit to the small airfield. The same reason that the airstrip was secure and safe, was now the reason that it was a death trap. Paulo punched the gas. He had no choice; not to move was to die. The limo shot forward. It was a race against time now.

Paulo was eyeing the narrow exit. He felt that they would make it. Once outside the airfield, the hit squad would be useless. Paulo was already thinking about who might have been responsible for this betrayal and how they were going to suffer when a garbage truck came speeding out of nowhere, smashing into the rear end of the limo spinning it like a bottle top.

El Señor had the wind knocked out of him from the impact. He was disoriented. More shots began finding their target; the limo.

"El Señor, we have to get out of here," Paulo said as blood dripped down his forehead and into his eyes. He had split his forehead on the two inch thick bullet proof windshield. "We're dead if we sit here."

El Señor couldn't think clearly. He was in shock. Not because they were under attack, but because only two people in the world knew he'd be at the airfield today. One was in the car with him, and Paulo was trying to save his life. It couldn't be Paulo responsible. El Señor couldn't finish his thought.

The limo shook and thumped before shooting straight up in the air like a flipped coin. The limo had just been hit by a rocket-propelled grenade. The heavy armor prevented the limo from disintegrating, but when it landed, it landed on its roof and was smoking like a crack pipe. El Señor wasn't going anywhere; he was trapped. How could she do this, El Señor thought as he began to lose consciousness.

Chapter 73

BIG MISTAKE

[Past]

Anybody that says money, power, and bitches ain't addictive is a mutha fucka that ain't never had money, power, or bitches. Period! And since I've been keeping it one thousand since the beginning, I've got to keep it one thousand now. I didn't just like the lifestyle; I was addicted to it. What's an addict except for someone who has lost control of their ability to make a different choice. I've seen crack addicts cry real tears behind how fucked up their life is now because of crack. They lost their jobs, wives, kids, houses, and all self-respect. They hate themselves for it, but before their tears dry up, them mutha fuckas are trying get a dub for fifteen.

By all rights, I had everything that I'd set out to acquire. My bread was stupid long. I owned three houses and six whips.

I should have quit while I was ahead. I could hand the reigns over to one of my top nigga's.

I could have been one of the few nigga's that make it in the game. To make it in the game, means to make it out the game. To go through all the bullshit that I had; the jail, prison, violence, murder, and torture, and to make it out would be a miracle.

I could have switched to legit business or invested. Anything! I had more options than I knew possible. But I'm going to say what these fake ass nigga's won't. I'm an addict. I'm addicted not just to the things that the game brings, but to the lifestyle as a whole.

I came into the game at a young age with a clear set of standards, guidelines, and principles. It's the "g" code. When the money and the power came, those lines blurred. I owed my success to one man. One man that without his guidance, support, and plug, I would have died or been homeless in Mexico. El Señor had saved my life.

I had two responsibilities when it came to dealing with El Señor. The first was to have his money in full and on time. The second was to remember that Claudia was off-limits. The first was easy. The money was never an issue. The product moved itself. The second turned out to be more difficult, and like with all bad choices, there were repercussions. El Señor called me out of nowhere one day.

"King, how are you my son?" El Señor sounded excited when I answered the phone.

"I'm great El Señor, all is well. I wasn't expecting to hear from you until the end of the month. Is everything ok?" I asked.

"Yea, yea, nothing like that. Everything is fine. I just wanted to see if you could do me a favor?"

"Of course, El Señor, anything!" I answered eagerly.

"Ok good King, my daughter Claudia is coming out to Sacramento to look into a few business ventures for me." El Señor said.

"Ok, ok," I responded.

"Well, I want you to take care of her. Show her around, see that she's situated and comfortable. I figured that since she's coming to your area, it might as well be you to make sure that her trip is smooth.

"That's fine El Señor, I'd be honored. When will she be arriving?" I asked.

"At the end of the week, I'll get you the details soon. She'll also be collecting your investment money. Will you be ready by then?" Now I understood, El Señor was sending Claudia to collect payment for the last shipment he had sent. She must be taking on more of a role in El Señor's Cartel now. It would be good to see her. I'd thought about her often since I'd last seen her.

"Of course, El Señor, my investment money is never late," I told him.

"This is true, this is true!" El Señor said chuckling. "Very well, King, I'll be in touch in a few days," he said as he hung up.

I couldn't lie; I was excited at the thought of seeing Claudia again. I wasn't the same bandaged and wounded animal that I had been when she first met me. Her dad was "the" boss, but shit, I was a boss too. It was gonna be fun showing her how far I'd come. Here's the thing though; she was off-limits. That didn't stop me from wanting her anyway. So the boss nigga in me started to override the loyal nigga in me. I owed El Señor everything, but still, the one thing that he had said was off-limits, I wanted more than anything. No wasn't something that I was used to hearing over the last few years.

"Hey Claudia," I said. I picked her up from the airport in my sexiest whip, a black-on-black Bentley GT coupe.

"Hello, King," Claudia responded. She had changed too. She didn't look like a nurse anymore. She had on a beige Fendi business suit with burgundy Prada heels. Her jet back hair was pulled back into a ponytail, showing off her delicate neck. It was her eyes that had seemed to have changed the most though. She had the eyes of someone who was used to giving orders now, not taking them. I smiled!

"What are you smiling at, King?" Claudia asked.

"Nothin, just checkin you out. Last time I saw you, you was in your whole little nurse mode, and now…" I wasn't sure how to word what I wanted to say.

"Now what, King?" Claudia asked and smirked at me.

"Shit, now …." I stuttered. "Now you look like a CEO or something."

"Well, you're not looking so bad yourself King." Claudia eyed me up and down. "I'm sure all the little chica's out here are throwing themselves at you huh King?"

"Ha, look at you!" I smiled, "Really tho, no one that can keep my attention."

"That's because no one knows what you've been through and what you go through to keep it all together. It takes a queen to know a king," Claudia responded.

Fuck, I thought, I'm in over my head right now. Here I am with the bosses daughter who he trusted with me, but she's never left my mind since she nursed me back to health. The thing is, all I push on my "Rillas" is loyalty. I've had disloyal nigga's knocked off. So why am I sitting here having disloyal thoughts? El Señor would have me killed if he found out that I fucked Claudia. Shit, she coming on to me though, I thought to myself. A nigga will always find a way to justify some fuck shit if that's what he really wants.

"So, where are you staying, Claudia?" I asked.

"I thought that you were taking care of all of that King! Isn't this your city? I'll be staying wherever you take me papi." Now she was clearly flirting; and I was clearly falling for it.

"Ok bet! Well you might as well crash at my spot, that way, I can keep a good eye on you." I said.

"Just your eyes on me, King?" She asked seductively as she caressed my hand before leaning back in her seat and closing her eyes. We were on the way to my house, and I was on my way to betraying El Señor.

Chapter 74

MURDER IN MOTION

[Present]

Omar "Murda" Murdock had just gotten a call from the nigga Cash. Cash was meeting up wit the nigga King later tonight at Arden Fair Mall. Stockton was less than an hour away from Sacramento so that gave him an hour to get his goons together. This was an opportunity that he couldn't miss. After slumping King and Cash, the "Rilla" would be open for the taking, and Omar could tell his momma that he avenged his pop's murder.

"Say man, get the squad together, we headed to sac in an hour," Omar said. He was talking to his most blood-thirsty young killer.

"Bet that! Light work or heavy work?" the young gunner asked.

"Bring the big toys, I don't want no slip-ups on this one." Omar responded.

"Yea dat. I'll get everyone together and meet you on the block in thirty minutes," the young killer said and was about to hang up.

"Nah, meet me at the McDonald's off the ninety nine in forty-five minutes. I don't want all you nigga's on the block dirty like that. We'll leave from McDonald's. I'll follow behind you on the way to sac so that the police can't get behind you," Omar ordered.

"Aight, in a min!" They both hung up.

Within the hour, Omar "Murda" Murdock would be on his way to sac. His plan was to wait until King and Cash were in the car together, and then have his hit squad come out of the cuts with the AK's. They'd chop the car to pieces. Omar would be across the street at the gas station watching it all unfold. He smiled at the thought that Cash had given him the information that would lead to his own death when he was plotting on getting his own patna King. It was a cold game, and Omar was a cold chess player.

Chapter 75

DELUSIONS OF GRANDEUR

[Present]

This was it, he thought. He'd played this scenario in his mind a hundred times. I'll be King; it's all Cash could think about. Now all that he needed to figure out was how to kill King and get away with it clean. Should he wait for King to pull up in the parking lot and just start busting? Should he get in the car with King, play it smooth, and then down the nigga? No matter what, he wasn't letting King leave this meeting alive. He would only get one shot at this. Better to be safe than sorry. It was time for the young nigga's that he was going make his top lieutenants earn their pay. They'd been waiting to prove themselves, and this was the time.

Marquise looked down at his phone screen and he saw Cash's name pop up.

"Wuz up Cash a million?" Marquise answered.

"Where you nigga's at?" Cash shot back. This was a business call.

"We over here on the block, just posted up!"

"Ok bra, I need you nigga's tonight. Something that can't be fucked up."

"Aight blood, lace my boots!" Marquise answered. He was excited.

"Tonight, I'm meeting with the bitch ass nigga King, he's not gonna leave the spot breathing. Ya feel me?" Cash kept it short and sweet.

"Now you talking my talk blood." Marquise really did enjoy murder.

"We gonna be at Arden Fair Mall by the movie theater. You know what that nigga's white beemer looks like right?" Cash asked.

"Yeah, we see the mutha fucka sliding through the hood sometimes." Marquise loved that car. He couldn't say that to Cash right now though.

"Ok listen, I'm a get in the nigga's car and chop it up with him for a few minutes. That way you can see me walk to the car to know exactly which one it is."

"Bet." Marquise said, indicating that he understood.

"After a few minutes of sitting in the car with the nigga, I'm going to tell him that I left my phone in my car and that I'm going to hop out to grab it. When you and Levelle see the passenger side door open, and me about to get out, y'all walk up on the driver's side."

"I thought King was your nigga blood," Marquise asked before thinking, cutting Cash off.

Cash snapped. "Bitch ass nigga, shut the fuck up. Is you tryna ball out or do you wanna stay curb serving? Listen and do what the fuck I tell you!"

Marquise relented. "Aight bra," was all he said.

"Now what kind of banga's you and blood got?" Cash asked.

"I got a chunky .40, and Levelle got a beefy .45, both with extendo's."

Good, Cash thought. That should get the job done.

"Now listen nigga, don't start shooting until I'm out of the car. You hear me blood?" Cash wanted to make sure that he didn't get shot on accident.

"Yeah," Marquise answered, still a little hurt by the way Cash had just belittled him.

"I'll get out, take a few steps, and then turn around with my hammer. I'll open fire from the passenger side. Y'all light up the driver's side. Simple little nigga's. No way he can survive gunfire from both sides like that. Anything you don't understand?" Cash asked.

"Nah, we good!" Levelle and Marquise answered simultaneously.

"Aight, I'll hit y'all in about two hours. Make sure y'all answer the phone."

"Yep." Marquise said.

Marquise hung up thinking to himself that Cash was one fucked up nigga. He didn't know everything about King, but the whole town knew that King put Cash on back in the day. Cash wouldn't be shit without King. Fuck it, he thought, Cash promised him his own block.

Chapter 76

REVENGE

[Present]

Omar "Murda" Murdock was in his 2017 Chevy Tahoe following behind the van with his gunners in it headed to Sacramento. He picked up his phone and hit the speed dial button.

"Yea." Came the answer from the other end of the phone.

"What the fuck you mean yeah? Nigga slow the fuck down. Highway patrol is all on the highway, and you driving six nigga's, three of them ex-felons with choppers and pistols all in the fucking car. Slow the fuck down nigga and don't go two miles over sixty-five."

"Aight cuz". Omar's hitter knew better than to upset his boss when he was in murder mode.

Omar had been waiting too long for this moment. He was balling out there in Stockton, but until he got revenge on the nigga that killed his pops, all that shit was irrelevant. No matter what was going on, and no matter what he was doing, that shit was always in the back of his mind. Thinking about how King had dressed up as a homeless man and gunned his pops down had been the cause of many sleepless nights for Omar. Once he knew that King was dead, he would get the first full night of sleep that he'd had in years.

Chapter 77

MOMENT OF TRUTH

[Present]

Keisha felt like she was having a nervous breakdown. About halfway to the location where the GPS detected King, it cut off. Either King had found it and disconnected it or her supervisor had it disabled because she hadn't reported. Either way, she was fucked. She sat there with her head slumped forward on the steering wheel. Tears were streaming down her face. Her phone started to vibrate. It was King.

Keisha answered. "Oh my God, King, I've been trying to call you all day."

"My bad ma, I've been handling business! What's good tho, you aight?" Keisha didn't want to say what she had to say over the phone. "Yes….no…. I just need to talk to you, King."

"Ok ma, I've got to handle one more thing today, then I'm all yours. Why don't you meet me at the movie theater in Arden Fair Mall at about ten? Theres a bunch of new movies out at the theaters; it had been two years since the last person had tested positive for covid, and Hollywood was making movies left and right.

Fuck, she wanted to say something, but how do you say, "Babe, I love you, by the way I'm a DEA agent, and there's a good chance your main nigga Cash is about to be busted and flip on you. But I love you, and I want you to trust me." It would be a lot for anyone to take in at one time. The thought of how King would react brought butterflies to Keisha's stomach.

She settled for, "Ok babe, for sure, right!?" King laughed, not understanding why Keisha seemed so anxious.

"Yea fasho, it's a date! I'll already be in the area."

"Ok King, I'll see you in a little while! "King?" Keisha spoke softly.

"Yeah!"

"I love you," Keisha said.

"I hope so, girl. I've built my life around you." King answered and changed the topic quickly. "Say, have you seen or heard from Alisha?" King asked.

"No." Keisha lied, "But I haven't been home all day. I'll go home before the movie and check, ok?" Now it was Keisha who wanted to change the subject.

"Ok, ma, see you in a few," King said as they both hung up.

Chapter 78

CLOSING IN

[Present]

Earlier that day, through sheer persistence, Agent Vargas got a lead on Cash. After confirming who Cash's baby mama was, Agent Vargas went to her apartment to see if she knew where he was. Once he got there, he would have to get her to cooperate.

"So, you're telling me that you haven't seen or spoken to him?" Agent Vargas asked Cash's baby mama.

"That's exactly what I'm telling you," she spat back! She had an attitude now, but that would change. Agent Vargas had not played his trump card yet.

"Ok, that's fine." Agent Vargas smiled as he looked around the living room. There were three kids there under the age of seven in the living room. "Are these all Cash's kids?" he asked.

"No, just the boy, why?" she answered, rolling her neck.

"Because I wonder how those beautiful little girls' fathers are going to feel when they find out that you got your daughters taken trying to protect a murdering drug dealer. Who, by the looks of things," Agent Vargas paused and looked at the shabby apartment for effect, "doesn't give a shit about you." This got her attention; no woman wants to lose her kids. Especially over a nigga who she know's that at the end of the day didn't give a shit about her.

"What you mean by that?" she asked. It was time for Agent Vargas to play his trump card.

"Well, I'm in the process of getting a warrant for your phone, and as soon as I discover that you've lied to me, and that you have heard from, or been in communication with him, then that's interfering with a federal investigation." Agent

Vargas stared at her intently. "You go to jail and the kids go bye-bye." Agent Vargas waved his hand for effect. "There's not a judge in America that's going to say that you're a fit mother. Child neglect and child endangerment for starters." Agent Vargas got up to leave. "So good luck. I hope Cash is worth it."

"Wait!" Cash's baby momma yelled. Agent Vargas wiped the smile off of his face before turning around.

"Yes." He said, turning around slowly.

"Look, all I know is that he's supposed to be buying his son some shoes from Arden Fair Mall tonight." She finally acquiesced.

"What kind of car is he driving?" Agent Vargas asked. He wasn't going to let her off the hook that easily.

"Agghhh," she yelled out. She was frustrated because she knew that she had no choice but to cooperate, "Some bitches

Toyota Celica. Now please get the fuck out of here." She tried to get some of her toughness back.

"Ok, if you're not lying, you'll keep your kids. If you are, I'll be back very soon," Agent Vargas said walking out.

At the control center downtown, Agent Vargas briefed his team. He was holding up a picture of Cash towards each member. The picture he was showing had Cash with long dreads and blonde tips.

"This is the target. He's a murder suspect as well as a key player in "Rilla." We've got credible intel that he'll be at Arden Fair Mall tonight. I've already sent a team undercover to the interior of the mall to start surveillance. We will secure the exterior, including the parking lot."

An agent interrupted, "Is he expected to be armed?"

"We have to assume he is, but let me make this clear. We want him alive! He could be the key to bringing down King's organization, "Rilla." I also guaranteed El Señor that I'd have King arrested soon, agent Vargas thought to himself.

"Not until we have a definite identification on him will we move in. Team one will be in the cable company van. Team two will be in the phone company truck."

The team members did the final checks on their gear, fastened their vests, and triple-checked their clips. They ended the briefing as they always did, with a quick prayer.

Chapter 79

POWER MOVE

[Present]

El Señor was handcuffed and thrown into the back of the Federale's pick-up truck face down. A thin black burlap bag was thrown over his head.

"It couldn't have been her," El Señor thought. "But it had to be," he told himself right after.

El Señor couldn't see a thing, but he could hear. He was face down in the back of the pick-up truck with a heavy boot pushing down on the center of his back, pinning him to the bed of the truck. He knew better than to talk or ask questions. Nothing would come of it. Plus, these were professionals; they came to do a job. Nothing more, nothing less. He could ask questions until his face turned blue, but he would get no answers.

El Señor tried to pay attention to the sounds, smells, and bumps in the road. He knew Tijuana like the back of his hand, and he thought that if maybe he had an idea of where he was, it would come in handy later. He needed to stay calm and thinking clearly because if he lost his cool, he'd be dead for sure. He could smell the clean air after about twenty minutes in the truck. That let him know that they had hit the coast from the airfield.

The only way to hit the coast in twenty minutes was through Fundádores. Five minutes later, he smelled the strong stench of fresh fish. The fish market is halfway between Tijiana and Rosaritó.

They came to one of the toll plazas that were posted all along the highway. His kidnappers were waved through immediately. No words had been exchanged. It took official authority to be able to do that. Had he been taken by the police? If so, why hadn't they taken him to the local municipality in Tijuana? Fear crept into El Señor 's mind. They had tried to kill him initially. Only the armor of his limo had saved him. Or did they know that the limo was armored and were only out to capture him the whole time? Calm down, he thought. These questions were unanswerable, so it was a waste of time and energy to try and figure it out now. He needed to stay in the moment.

A list of his enemies began to play across his mind like scenes from a movie projector. The problem was that it was a never-ending movie. Men such as El Señor knew of certain enemies, but there was no way that he could know of them all. He'd killed too many people and had even more ordered killed. He had been responsible for ruining thousands of lives. It could be someone's relative seeking vengeance! Not to mention the hundreds of rival cartel members that dreamed of seeing El Señor in a position like this.

The thought that only two people knew he'd be at the airfield that day kept creeping into his mind like a snake stalking its prey. He'd push it back, but it always came slithering back up.

The truck veered off the paved road and was now bouncing up and down as it navigated it's off-road course. I'm on a dirt road, he thought, and we're going uphill. His body weight was pulling him down towards the tailgate. Only the boot on his back kept him from sliding down. They drove for another few minutes. El Señor thought about Paulo, his longtime number one guard, and henchman. He had to assume that he was dead, but the only person besides Paulo who knew about the airfield….

"Alto," came from a voice above El Señor . They were the only words spoken on the entire forty-five-minute drive. The truck came to a screeching halt. El Señor could smell dirt and dust through his mask. They were somewhere off the grid, secluded!

The tailgate slammed open, and a burly hand reached between El Señor's handcuffed arms snatching him up like a rag doll. He was half carried and half dragged in the dirt, ruining his fifteen hundred dollar Louis loafers. A door opened, and another one slammed shut. El Señor found himself in a dark, damp room. His only companion was the sound of his own heavy breathing.

Several uncertain minutes passed. Finally, the door swung open, casting a small amount of light inside. The sound of a woman's high heel shoes clacked across the floor towards the most powerful and ruthless drug Kingpin in all of Mexico. Nothing could have prepared El Señor for what he saw when the sack was removed from his head. His mouth dropped open, and his eyes bulged in their sockets.

Chapter 80

FROM THE ASHES

[Present]

"I told you I can't remember," Alisha said as she lay in a hospital bed at Lake Tahoe Mercy. Doctors and detectives filled her room.

"Well, is there anything that you can tell us, ma'am? We really don't have much to go off? Do you remember how you got to those mountains? Let's start with that." It was the fat detective with jelly donut stains on his shirt, that was asking the questions.

"Look, I want to remember; I just can't," Alisha lied. "Everything seems like a dream, and I can't tell the difference between the dream or reality." The Detective got frustrated.

"If you don't give a damn who shot you in the back of the head, that's your business, but I've got a job to do, and this type of shit doesn't go down in my county."

Alisha dropped back in her bed looking exhausted. The doctor intervened, putting both of his hands in the air.

"Gentlemen, gentlemen, that will be enough for the day. She has been through a very traumatic experience; there's no guarantee that she will ever remember what happened to her but trying to force her to remember at this critical stage in her recovery certainly won't help. I'm going to have to insist that you gentlemen leave. You can check back in a few days."

The two detectives sulked out of the room like two scolded children. Alisha was grateful. She needed her rest. She needed her strength. She needed to think. Alisha believed that the one thing that had kept her alive was rage. Rage and a desire for vengeance. Of course I remember what happened to me, she thought.

That police ass bitch Keisha shot me in the back of the head. A seven-inch gash down to the scalp and through the skull on the crown of her head would be her lifelong souvenir as a result of the encounter. Turning her head to look back at Keisha to ask where they were going at the exact moment that Keisha fired the shot had saved Alisha's life. A fraction of an inch to the left, and she would have died instantly.

Alisha was not ready to leave the hospital yet, but that didn't stop her from planning the ways that she could make that bitch Keisha suffer. I hope it's not too late, Alisha thought. I hope that King found out before it was too late, but for now; she would plan. Plan for vengeance. Plan to put herself in a position to never have to work at the DMV again. She had learned a lot about the game from King.

Alisha drifted off to sleep with a smile on her face. There was freedom in not giving a fuck. Facing death and beating death made her feel more powerful and alive than she had ever known possible.

Chapter 81

COMING CLEAN

[Present]

Keisha had a million things on her mind as she got ready to head to the mall to meet King. It seemed to her that a million things could go wrong, and that's what worried her. What if King couldn't accept what she had to tell him? In her mind, she had said fuck her job and her old life as she knew it for King! She had killed because of her love for King. She was going to take Alisha's letter to King and hope that it bought her some time. This was a delicate situation, and Keisha was nervous as shit. Mostly though, she didn't want to lose King. The rest could be figured out later.

At home, Keisha showered and got dressed. She grabbed Alisha's forged "Dear John" letter for King and grabbed her

Sig Sauer .22 and put it in her purse. She didn't know if she could shoot King if he was trying to hurt her for what she had done, but the weight of the pistol in her purse gave her comfort. Keisha looked at herself one more time in the mirror, promising herself and God above that no matter what, tonight she'd tell King the truth. After that, she was going to have to figure out which direction her life was heading because the DEA was no longer an option.

Chapter 82

IN POSITION

[Present]

"That's a go, team two?" the agent said. He was talking into his wireless earpiece.

"Gotcha loud and clear!" team two responded.

"Interior team? Are you there?"

"We're in position, sir!" came back the response.

"Ok, good! Mike and Jimmie? You guys copy?" Agent Vargas asked his two most senior agents.

"Ten-four boss, in position."

"Now, look." Special Agent Vargas added. "Everyone stay on high alert. We don't know exactly when or where he'll turn up, but we can't miss him when he does. Whoever spots him first, notify me immediately. I'll decide how to proceed from there. From here on out, we go silent, no radio chatter."

Vargas took off his headset and took a deep breath. He needed this to go right. Not just for his career, but because he couldn't afford to let El Señor down. It was already bothering Vargas that El Señor hadn't returned his last two calls. Once El Señor decided that someone was no longer reliable, he usually also decided that they were no longer needed. Once El Señor decided that someone was no longer needed, they ended up dead. Beads of sweat trickled down Vargas's forehead.

Come on Cash, you son of a bitch! Come to me you son of a bitch, he thought. There was nothing left to do now but wait and watch.

Chapter 83

FINAL INSTRUCTIONS

[Present]

Across the street in the parking lot of a Chuck E. Cheese's, "Murda" Murdock was giving the last instructions to his young gunner's. This wasn't the first time that they had put in work, but it was their first time doing it on foreign soil. Murdock could sense their nervousness.

"Check it out my nigga's." Omar looked them all in their eyes before he began to talk. "This is just another day! Another nigga that needs to be downed! Ain't nothing special or different bout this shit, so get that look off y'all face." They all nodded their heads up and down. It seemed like they were getting courage from their boss, and each other.

"When y'all pull across the street, park the van right there between the Best Buy and the movie theater," Omar ordered. Park with the other cars and just wait. I'll hit y'all as soon as I see the nigga's. Once you park, don't move the van or get out of the van till I hit you, y'all dig?" Omar raised his eyebrows questioningly. He wanted to make sure that they understood what he expected. They all nodded. They were in murder mode now.

"Aight now check your clips. Once y'all start busting, don't stop until the car got more holes in it than a chain link fence."

With that, Omar got out of the van and into his Mercedes. He had a perfect spot to watch King, the nigga who had killed his pops, get smoked. Tonight was going to be a good night. Murdock smiled to himself at the thought of it all.

Chapter 84

PARKED

[Present]

Keisha passed right in front of "Murda" Murdock while she was looking for a spot of her own to park, so that she could think. She was early for the movie, but she just wanted to get out near the mall so that she could play things over in her mind before she met up with King. One thing that the DEA taught her was that things very rarely go exactly as planned.

Keisha thought to herself, he could be understanding or he could he flip out and try to hurt me. He could tell me to get the fuck away from him and walk out of her life forever. The thought of that made her sick to her stomach. Sicker that any of the other possibilities. She just hoped that she could find the right words to explain to King that she loved him and that there was nothing that she wouldn't do for him. Yeah, she was a

DEA agent who had been sent undercover to build a case against him that would send him to prison for life, but that was before she got to know the man he truly was. She knew now that he was not the man that the DEA had painted him out to be. Without knowing it, Keisha parked two cars down from "Murda" Murdock. One of them was out to end King's life. The other was out to save it.

Chapter 85

DREADLESS

[Present]

Cash was feeling himself. He was in a great mood. He believed that this was going to be a fresh start for him. As the new King!! He went out earlier that day, bought a new iPhone, and in a split-second decision, he decided to cut his dreads off. "New look for a new time!" he told himself.

"Sir, can I help you?" the cashier asked.

"Yea, let me get these Jordan's in size six for kids." Cash told him.

"Yes, sir, I'll be right back." Cash looked at the kid's Jordan sweatsuits while he waited for the clerk to return with his son's shoes . "Here you go, sir," the clerk said as he handed him the shoe box. "Anything else?"

"Put this wit it." Cash said, handing the salesman a dark gray sweatsuit to match the J's that he'd just bought for his son.

"If you'll follow me, I'll ring you right up, sir."

Cash followed the clerk, but his mind was on the meeting that he was about to have with King. There was a lot going through his mind but he had come too far now. Marquise and Levelle were already in the parking lot waiting to hear from him. Everything was set. Cash just needed King to show up as planned.

Cash paid for the shoes and sweatsuit, and then decided he'd go upstairs for a Cinnabon while he waited on King. As he left the Kids Foot Locker, he noticed a stiff-necked, crew-cut wearing white boy with an earpiece in his ear, walking in front of him. Fucking mall security, think that they the fucking FBI now, Cash thought laughing to himself.

Agent Sampson didn't give Cash a second glance since the main thing that he was looking for was a black male who had dreadlocks with blond tips. No one knew that Cash had cut his dreads off earlier that day. The agent had just walked past his murder suspect.

Chapter 86

KINGS OUT

[Present]

King was at a stoplight on Florin Road in the beemer. A carload of young bitches pulled alongside him, trying to get his attention by waving their hands out their car window, smiling. King smiled as he rolled his window up. The driver was cute; she had brown skin with dimples. This wasn't the time though, King had other things on his mind right now. As he pulled off when the light changed, he nodded at the driver, and she mouthed, "I love your car."

"I bet you do." King thought as he sped up.

It was crazy now how the smallest things could trigger the strongest emotions from the past. Those words made King think about his mom. About his failed military experience.

About all the choices that he'd made throughout his life. It wasn't that he had regrets. Regret was for bitch ass nigga's. The past was the past, and it was done. But that didn't mean that a nigga shouldn't learn from the past. Especially past mistakes.

When the bitch with the dreads said she loved his car, it immediately made him think about Faith and his daughter again. That had been happening a lot lately. When he went to the Oakland to see Faith and his daughter, she had asked him if he had anyone around him who loved him for him and not for what he could do for them. That question had played over and over in King's mind since then too. The answer to that question led King to the biggest decision of his life.

"Hello.' Faith answered on the second ring.

"Sup ma? How are you and Terri doing?" King asked, in a somber tone.

"We are good! I just got off work a little while ago. I fed her and gave her a bath. She's in bed now. Are you ok, King? What's the matter?" Faith asked.

"Yeah, I'm good, I'm good," King paused. "I just wanted to apologize to you for doing you like I did you back in the day. I was young, immature, and I know I hurt you. For that I am sorry." The phone was silent. King had never apologized to anyone. "I hope that you can forgive me. I also want to tell you that I'm going to do better as a father. Not just helping financially, but actually being there. I'm going to call JuJu tomorrow and tell her the same thing. I want to be in Terri's and Prince's life."

King had recently been spending a lot of time with his son Prince and JuJu. They were the main part of why King had been having these kinds of feelings. Spending time with his son, and being around JuJu, the one woman he knew he could spend his life with, had changed his perspective about what's important.

Faith was stunned. She didn't know what had come over him, but she wasn't going to mess this up by asking questions.

"King, that makes me very happy, and your daughter is an amazing little girl. She's smart as I don't know what, just like you." King smiled over the phone. It felt good and it was a genuine smile.

King continued, "I know you're wondering, so I'm just going to go ahead and say it. I'm also getting out of the game!" Faith pulled the phone away from her ear and looked at it. She didn't see any of this coming, but this last news was a bombshell. She never thought that King would leave the lifestyle, ever! Knowing that once King made his mind up, God himself couldn't get him to change it, she knew he was serious. There was no need to ask him if he meant it. Tears started streaming down her cheeks.

"I'm happy, King," Faith finally responded after a few quiet moments. King sighed and took a deep breath.

"Alright ma, it's getting late. I just wanted to let you know what was on my mind. I'll hit you in a day or two. I'd love to come and see Terri!"

"Ok." Faith said softly.

With that, King felt like he had a ton of bricks lifted off of his shoulders. He had already been planning to move away with JuJu and Prince. All that was left to do now was to meet with Cash in a little while to tell him that he was handing everything over to him.

The thought of seeing Cash's face when he told him, made King smile. Cash always act's like he don't want me to step down, King thought, but he has always been very ambitious and I know that he wants to be the boss. It wasn't an easy decision to make, but ultimately, King had decided that he had already beat the odds. By all rights he should already be dead or in prison with a life sentence. It was time to turn a new chapter in his life.

As King got on the freeway headed towards the mall, he felt like a new man. "Shit, I'll plug Cash in with El Señor and I'll take my millions and go legit," he thought. "Maybe even go back to school or something. A new chapter in the life of King."

King called El Señor again for the third time. For the third time, El Señor's phone went straight to voicemail. Fuck it, I'll catch him later, King thought as he turned up that old school Jeezy the Snowman. The eighteen-speaker Harman Kardon system in the seven series took him into his thoughts. "This is it," King spoke out loud to himself as he often did when working out difficult decisions. After I meet Cash, I'm through! I'm out!

King felt light. He felt free. Like any addict who's recently kicked an addiction. He would no longer be an addict to the streets. It would be up to his last loyal, remaining lieutenant to hold it together now. Sink or swim Cash, sink or swim. Either way, I'm done. There was something liberating about finalizing a tough decision. King headed to his meeting feeling happier and more relaxed than he had in quite some time.

Chapter 87

MY OWN BLOOD

[Present]

El Señor was feeling anything but relaxed. He hadn't even had time to process what he'd just seen when two gringos rushed in, lifting him up off of his feet and placing a different hood over his head. He could only briefly see his kidnappers but this hood allowed no light to penetrate the fabric. He could see nothing but darkness after the hood was placed on his head.

His heart was beating out of his chest, and his tongue was so dry that it felt like an old carpet. His kidnappers now spoke English. The ambush was a snatch and grab, but who were these Americans, El Señor thought. He knew that many cartel members spoke perfect English, but these were gringos. These were straight G.I. Joe military-style pútos. They had big, clenched, square jaws, with short haircuts and blank expressions on their faces.

El Señor took comfort in the thought that if they had wanted him dead, he'd be dead already. I'll find a way out of this, he thought. As long as I'm not dead, I'm alive. If it is the Americans, I'll find out who needs to be paid, and I'll pay. This thought gave him momentary solace, but still, the thought of who he'd just seen made him uneasy.

El Señor was rushed outside. He was bound by his hands and feet, and thrown in the back seat of a vehicle. He was squeezed between two burly bodies on each side of him.

"ETA?" came a crackling voice over the radio.

"Twenty minutes sir, assuming we don't run into any complications!" It sounded like the man in the front passenger seat had answered. El Señor couldn't tell if it was the driver or the passenger.

"Copy that! Stick to the pre-planned route. We have the caravan on satellite; we've got eyes on you!"

"On the move now sir!" the front passenger replied.

With that the car jumped forward on route to a destination unknown. This time, El Señor couldn't hear or smell anything. Not that he thought it mattered now. He had a sinking feeling in his gut. With all the uncertainty that he'd become accustomed to living with like the competition from other cartels and the disloyalty from within his own cartel, what he secretly feared most, more than death itself, was falling into the hands of American authorities. Keep thinking, he told himself over and over. I'm El Señor. I'll find a way out of this.

After a fifteen-minute race through the streets of Tijuana the front passenger got on his radio.

"Approaching rendezvous, two minutes out."

"Copy that. Eagle one waiting!" came the response from the other end of the radio.

Shortly after that the van screeched to a halt. When the door opened, the sound of a helicopter rotor spinning caught El Señor completely off guard. This van must be sound proof, he hadn't heard a single thing before the door opened. No doubt that the van had been bullet proof too, he thought. I'm definitely with the Americans, only they name their aircrafts, "Eagle." El Señor chuckled at this thought despite his current predicament.

El Señor was snatched out of the van. A big hand grabbed the back of his head pushing his face towards the ground while another arm pulled him forward at a swift pace. They raced El Señor towards the chopper. The wind from the chopper felt like a hurricane and puffed El Señor's shirt out making him look forty pounds heavier. The walk to the chopper was short. El Señor was hoisted up and into the chopper. He was strapped into a seat. Ear muffs were placed over his ears on the outside of the hood. After that there was only silence. No sound.

El Señor could tell when the chopper lifted off because his stomach churned. El Señor knew that he had been betrayed. This troubled him but he had more pressing matters right now. As long as I'm not dead, I'm alive he said over and over to himself to keep the thoughts of why she'd betrayed him at bay; even though he knew that she did it for King. As long as I'm not dead, I'm alive, he repeated over and over.

El Señor couldn't hear the pilot as the chopper lifted then banked to the right say, "Set course for C.M.S.F.P."

El Señor had no idea that he was headed for the United States most secure penitentiary. The Colorado Maximum Security Federal Penitentiary was built more than one mile under the earth and no one had ever been able to even attempt an escape from there. It was designed so that the inmates had no contact with other inmates and very little contact with the outside world or staff as a whole.

The penitentiary was fully autonomous. Doors opened and closed automatically. Trays on electric rails delivered the food to inmates, so even the correctional officers rarely interacted with the incarcerated. Even the most criminally connected people have difficulty getting anything done in this place. It was too secure; there was too little movement; and all correspondence was intensely monitored. No criminal organization would be run by El Señor from this place. At least, that's what was said when the decision had been made to send El Señor there.

Chapter 88

SHE'S A RUNNER

[Present]

Alisha was faking sleep in the hospital bed as the nurses did their nine o'clock rounds before taking their evening breaks. Alisha knew that this would give her about forty-five minutes to get the fuck out of there before they noticed that she was gone. Those detectives had been back all throughout the day trying to get her to answer questions. She was pretty sure that she had convincingly faked her amnesia but it was hard to tell if they were buying it. Earlier, when the detectives were in her room and thought she was asleep, she heard them whispering something about, "in custody" and "material witness". She wasn't sure exactly what they were talking about, but it was enough for her to decide that she wasn't going to stick around to find out.

She needed to warn King about what was going on and she needed to get to that police ass bitch Keisha. People say that killing someone changes you, and that may be true Alisha thought. What she knew for sure was that something had changed in her since being shot. Getting shot in the head had altered something in her brain and in her thinking. The constant thoughts of revenge along with the ways she'd enjoy seeing that bitch Keisha suffer filled her mind. Along with these thoughts though, was the fact that she knew she was willing and capable of carrying them out now, and those thoughts of violence gave her comfort.

The door to her hospital room opened as the nurse walked in. Alisha slowed her breathing and faked sleep. The nurse grabbed the clipboard from the foot of her bed then scribbled something on the chart. Alisha breathed softly and steadily. The nurse tucked in a bit of blanket that was hanging off the bed. Alisha heard the door click open, then shut shortly after. She waited for about a minute before she moved.

Alisha's clothes were folded and sitting on a chair next to her bed. There were still faint blood stains on her shirt but her clothes had been washed. Quickly she threw on her jeans and shirt, but couldn't find her shoes. Fuck, she thought. I can't run out of here without shoes!

Just as panic began to rise in her chest and her eyes darted around the dim room, Alisha spotted a shoelace sticking out from under the bed. Alisha got on her hands and knees to look under the bed. As she did, a spell of dizziness shook her and she had to stay there, on her hands and knees, before it passed.

Finally, she grabbed her shoes, slipping them on before tip toeing to the door. She opened it slowly looking towards the right, to where the nurses station was located. The nurses were eating and caught up in girly conversation.

Alisha slipped out to the left and down the stairs that led to the parking garage. She didn't have a plan for what to do once she was outside. All she knew and all that mattered to her was getting to King. Getting to King and killing that two-faced police ass bitch Keisha.

King was on the freeway about two miles from the Arden exit. On his right was Cal Expo, where the last rides for the state fair were being dismantled. Something about the vacant roller coaster and tilt a whirl seemed depressing. They looked like dinosaur skeletons. He shook the thought away and began focusing his thoughts on his meeting with Cash. There were certain details that would need to be worked out, like introducing him to El Señor and Paulo but King was more determined than ever to step down as King of "Rilla". Cash was capable of taking the reins, and if he fucked it all up, who gives a fuck, King thought. I'm out! This will be Cash's reward for staying loyal through it all.

King had already begun rearranging his finances and making preparations so that he could be closer to his kids. He was committed to making sure that neither one of them had to, or decided to make the kinds of choices that he had. He'd done his share of dirt, that was a fact. It was time to give the other side of the coin a try. One thing I've learned, King thought, it ain't material possessions that keep a person happy. Shit, I have it all and I still always have a feeling that something is missing inside of me. A constant sense of unease, anxiety, and worry is always with me no matter what whip I'm driving, what jewels or clothes I'm wearing or who I'm around. All the shit that I thought would lead to my happiness; didn't. Don't get it twisted, there was definitely some happy moments in there, but then the emptiness would return almost immediately.

Exiting on Arden, King felt in his soul that he was doing the right thing. He was uncertain where the future would take him, but fuck it, who knew the future? For the first time in many many years, King said a prayer. Not a prayer asking for anything, but a prayer just to say thank you. Thank you to whatever power is out there, for the fact that through it all, he'd made it. He'd get a chance to be in his kids lives and maybe even do some other good shit along the way. King was smiling when his phone rang.

"What's good Cash?" King answered.

"Shit bra just tappin' in. Everything good?" Cash wanted to make sure that King was still going to show up.

"Yea blood I'm about five minutes from the mall. I'll hit you in a few, to tell you where to meet me."

"Ok bet." Cash was about to hang up.

"Hey Cash," King said, his voice getting suddenly serious.

"Sup my nigga?" Cash felt momentary unease not knowing where this was headed. King was not to be taken lightly or played with.

"I got some good news for you," King said.

Cash smiled and breathed a sigh of relief. Nah nigga, I got something for you, he thought to himself!

"Aight, in a minute bra, I'll put these bags in the car and wait for your call." Cash couldn't think of what news could be better or what he wanted more than to take what King had but, when Cash hung up the phone he wondered what news the nigga had for him. Fuck it, he thought, it's too late. Cash called Marquise and Levelle.

"Cash-a-million, what it do blood?" Marquise answered.

"Remember," Cash said forcefully, he wasn't in the mood for small talk or games. "Wait till I get out of the car; when you see me draw down, walk up on the driver's side and open fire on the nigga."

"Yea dat," Marquise replied.

"Y'all changed the plates on the whip, right?" Cash asked. He wanted to make sure that all bases were covered.

"Yea, I stole some earlier," Levelle said proudly.

"Ok, I'll tap back in, in a minute". Cash paused for effect. "Marquise??"

"Yea!?"

"Don't fuck this up!" Cash said as he hung up.

Chapter 89

THEY ARE ALL HERE

[Present]

The big black nigga parked two cars away from Keisha had caught her attention. She couldn't just cut her police training on and off and this nigga looked nervous and suspicious. For one, he was chain smoking Newports back to back to back and throwing the butts out of his window. What really caught her attention though, was that he kept lifting a pair of binoculars to his eyes and looking across the street.

Keisha tried to figure out what he was looking at but all she could say for sure was that he was looking across the street towards the mall. Towards the movie theater where she was meeting King. Probably spying on his bitch or something, Keisha thought. But as soon as she thought it she knew that it wasn't true. It didn't feel right. She started the car, backed out, memorizing the plate number as she drove behind Omar's car.

Omar didn't notice her because he was caught up in whatever he was trying to see. Keisha pulled out of the Chuck E. Cheese's parking lot and waited for the light to turn green before driving across the street and into the mall parking lot.

Agent Vargas was sweating profusely even though the air-condition in the van was blowing on high. He tried to tell himself that it was all the gear and bulletproof vest that he was wearing that had him sweating like that. The truth was that he was nervous. He had everything riding on this bust. Not only would he look like a fool for using all of the DEA's resources for nothing, but if he didn't deliver soon for El Señor, his life may be in danger too. None of the team members had spotted Cash yet and the mall closed at ten; in only fifteen minutes.

Not just that, Agent Vargas thought, even if I can bust Cash and arrest him there's no guarantee that he'll fold. Most of them do when they're looking at life sentences, and Agent Vargas was counting on Cash to be like most of them.

When it's their lifelong freedom on the line, most suspects snitch. But not all! Agent Vargas got butterflies once he started thinking about all of the things that had to go right in order for this to work out the way that he needed it to. He wiped the sweat off of his forehead and calmed his breathing. In his earpiece a voice said.

"Sir. I think you oughta see this!"

"What is it?" Vargas snapped. All he wanted to hear was that someone had spotted Cash.

"ELRS just got a hit sir!" ELRS was a new technology. It looked like a small cable satellite dish that mounted on top of the van and it was the "Electronic License Plate Recognition System". It read any and all license plate numbers that passed within its radius, alerting the agent if it picks up one that's on the "hotlist".

"Who is it?" Agent Vargas asked impatiently.

"Well I can't say who it is in the car for sure sir, but the car is registered to King." Agent Vargas sat up straight, his eyes darting from side to side out of the heavily tinted side door windows of the van. My luck has finally changed, he thought, my luck has finally changed. In an instant, his butterflies disappeared. In its place, adrenaline. It couldn't be a coincidence that King was here. He knew in his gut that something big was about to take place.

"Look, nigga look!!" One of Murdock's young killa's was pointing out the window excitedly at a short thick bitch with braids, wearing spandex and flip flops who was coming out of the Best Buy.

"Damn nigga," the other one said, smiling and punching his patna's shoulder.

"She is thicker than a mutha fucka. I'm bout to go holla."

He hopped out of the van, egged on by the others. The sexy little female made him forget that Omar had told them not to get out of the van. He took off his beanie, that was really a ski mask rolled up as he walked fast towards little mama. He also left his pistol.

"Excuse me miss, excuse me! Can I holla atcha real quick?" The young thug yelled out as he approached her.

Chapter 90

ALL ABOUT TIMING

[Present]

King pulled into the mall parking lot and found a spot by Barnes and Nobles in the same area as the movie theater and Best buy.

He texted Cash, "I'm right here by the Barnes & Noble, pull up, I'm a roll a blunt." One minute later came the reply (text), "Bet!"

Keisha was looking for a place to park when she spotted Kings car. She could see that he was inside but he had his head down. Probably rolling a blunt, she thought. I'll find a parking spot and then text him. I'm not supposed to meet him for another thirty minutes anyway. Keisha smiled for the first time that day. At least she knew that King was safe. This is all going to work out, she said out loud as she backed into a spot giving her a good view of King's car.

———————————————

Cash popped the trunk on the car and tossed the Kid's Footlocker bags in the back. While bending over he pretended to be looking in one of the bags, and he checked the clip on his hammer. He glanced behind him quickly before sliding the pistol into the small of his back.

Cash had been anxious all day, but at this stage in the game, he was as cool and calm as could be expected. He had done too much to turn back now. That didn't mean that a little part of him wasn't feeling fucked up for what he was about to do.

The fact of the matter was that King had been nothing short of the best friend Cash had ever had in his life. King had never let him down. He had bailed Cash out of jail three times with his own money and hired private attorneys to represent him each time. That kept Cash from going to prison. When Cash's mom passed away from breast cancer, King paid for all of the funeral arrangements and services, then sat up with Cash all night, listening to him cry and reminisce about his mom. King never tried to make Cash feel like he was a peon and King was the boss. He treated Cash like family.

They were like brothers and even though Cash had fucked off a lot of dough over the years, King had put him in position to make more bread than he knew what to do with. All that King had asked for in return was loyalty.

For all that, Cash was about to have King slumped in cold blood, and even now King had told him that he had good news for him. This is not time to be soft, Cash said to himself. This is the game and fuck what nigga's say, the only rule to the game is that it ain't no rules to the game. Cash pushed the doubt out of his mind and started the car. It was only a short drive across the parking lot to where King was parked; waiting for him.

"I see it, I see it!" Agent Vargas replied excitedly. "Team two, move your van a little closer to the target vehicle. See if you can get a confirmation on the driver."

"Yes sir," team two leader responded. "Moving now."

Chapter 91

A NUMBER TO A GUNFIGHT

[Present]

"So just take my number! Come on you got me all out here in the parking lot like this. I promise I'll make sure you don't regret it."

Omar's pistol-less gunner was trying to close the deal and get the phone number of the girl that had walked out of Best Buy.

"Gimme your number nigga. I might call, we'll see," she said smiling as she put her hand on her hips, cocking her fat ass out and up, taunting the young thug.

Chapter 92

POSITIVE ID

[Present]

"Sir, the car is occupied times one. It appears to be King sir. Just give me one second, his head is down."

"Copy that! We're going to move closer. Let me know as soon as you have a positive ID," Agent Vargas said.

"Yes sir." the subordinate responded.

Chapter 93

NO TURNING BACK

[Present]

I know that van, Keisha thought to herself as she watched a phone company truck slowly pull into a stall behind and to the left of King's beemer. It looks like a normal phone company truck except for the "satellite" dish on top. That was a piece of high tech law enforcement equipment. Her old boss was here. He must be going after King, Keisha thought. Shit, shit, shit! Keisha punched the steering wheel.

I can't just pull up to him and warn him. For all I know, Vargas had a warrant issued for me too. At the very least for obstruction of justice. I'm not going to jail today, Keisha thought. And I don't have answers for why I went rogue. Uncle Sam and the DEA weren't going to accept the fact that I fell in love with the drug dealing, murdering, monster I went undercover to bust. "You guys just have to get to know the King I know and you'll understand." No, that wouldn't work!

Just as Keisha picked up her phone to text King. Some nigga in black jogger sweats, red and black Air Max and a matching red and black hoodie walked up to the passengers door of Kings car. After a brief pause, the passenger side door opened and he got in.

Chapter 94

WHO'S WHO?

[Present]

"Team two, team two, do you have an identification on the unknown black male who just got in King's car?"

It never crossed agent Vargas's mind that it was Cash. This guy had no dreads under his baseball cap. It was clear that he had short hair.

"We're on it sir! We got a partial face shot and were trying to run it through the facial recognition system now. "You find out who that is! I need to know yesterday!" Vargas snapped.

"Yes sir," the subordinate replied.

"Nobody moves until I give the word. Everyone stand down. We need to find out what's going on and who that is. I don't want to blow this by jumping the gun."

Agent Vargas's heart was beating a million times a minute, but he did his best to remain calm. The rest of the team didn't know just how much he had riding on this. For him, it was much more than a bust. It was a matter of life and death. Agent Vargas had no idea that El Señor had been abducted and was on his way to federal prison.

When Cash got in the car, King blew out the indica smoke he had been holding in and handed Cash the Backwood. Cash nodded and took two long pulls of the weed, then sat back into the plush leather seats of the beemer.

"What's up my nigga? Cash said as he sat down. You looking like you just hit the lottery and shit. You glowing like a mutha fucka."

Cash was smiling and chuckling as he said it. He handed the Backwood back to King and sat silently staring at him. The energy inside the car was peaceful and serene even though Cash had come to the meeting with betrayal and murder on his mind. King's energy was so positive and genuine that Cash felt it immediately.

Outside of the car, no further than one hundred feet away all hell was about to break loose. Agent Vargas and his agents were pretty much in position, but they were frantically trying to figure out who got into King's car and whether or not it was King in the driver's seat. The last thing that they wanted was to move in too early, only to discover that it wasn't King in the car. King would hear about it and they would never get the opportunity again. King was too smart to slip up twice.

Chapter 95

PAST LIFE

[Present]

Thirty feet behind Agent Vargas to the left, Keisha was staring intently at King's car while she checked the clip of her 9mm Taurus. She was on high alert but her mind was blank, and as calm as an empty lake. She was out of choices and now the circumstances would determine her next moves. All she knew was that something was going to give that day. Tonight, her past life as a DEA agent, as one of the "good guys" would officially disappear. Keisha continued to watch and wait.

Chapter 96

TWO-SIDED ATTACK

[Present]

While parked right between the Best Buy and Barnes & Noble Marquise and Levelle could clearly see the passenger's side of Kings white beemer. They saw Cash get in the car and now they were waiting for him to get out of the car. Once he did, they'd move in, and between them, King's car would be filled with no less than thirty hollow point rounds. They sat in silence watching the car.

Chapter 97

POOR PLANNING

[Present]

"Murda" Murdock's young killers were parked almost right in the middle of it all. They were three car stalls back, directly in front of the Best Buy. They were the most heavily armed, but they also had the least discipline. One was punching his cell number into the females phone which she had finally handed to him for that purpose. He held the phone smiling like it was some kind of trophy.

The driver was on his Instagram, messaging a bitch that he was trying meet up with later that night when they got back to Stockton. Murdock had lost sight of his squad from across the street and he was getting worried. He started the car thinking that he should head across the street so that he could see things unfold from up close.

Chapter 98

TOO LATE

[Present]

King looked at Cash long and hard and then turned the music down a little using the volume button on the steering wheel. He knew that it wasn't going to be easy just turning everything over to Cash but he hadn't anticipated getting emotional either. Nevertheless, the decision had already been made.

Not only had King given sweat, blood and tears to building his empire but he had also built some amazing relationships that would last a lifetime. He had seen the lowest of the human condition. The crack addicts living life for their next hits; stealing, robbing, and prostituting for a fix while their young kids sit at home going hungry. However, he'd also seen the resourcefulness and strength of the human will and spirit too. He'd seen the same dope fiend who had long ago hit, "rock bottom," bounce back with the help of other amazing people. Sometimes these people were little more than strangers. They were just people who believed in other people. On a few occasions, King has seen these ex-drug addicts go on to accomplish remarkable things.

King had witnessed, dished out and been a victim himself of the kind of violence that would make the most hardened man squirm. He knew firsthand how cruel, merciless and evil men could be. He also knew how kind, generous and loving a man could be. His life as King, King of "Rilla" had given him a life perspective that few could match.

What had him emotional right now in the moment was the gratitude that he felt inside for the lessons that the game had brought and taught him. To make it out, and to make it out with the level of success that he'd reached, still intact, was unheard of. King could tell that Cash sensed something, he just couldn't put a finger on it and this made King smile. The way that he was feeling on the inside was being reflected through his aura, energy and appearance. Which also meant the most important thing; that it was real!

"Cash." King started talking. "You've been my day one, since day one my nigga."

"Off top blood, you know I'd spill blood and shed blood for you King," Cash replied. King stared at Cash for a long moment, hit the Backwood, and continued.

"Bra let me just tell you what's on my mind real quick. I'm meeting up with Keisha soon to watch a movie." Cash nodded. "I've given this a lot of thought." King paused; Cash shifted in his seat, putting his back against the passenger's side door. King and him rarely had these kinds of deep conversations. Cash knew it was something serious.

"I'm getting out the game bra," King finally spit it out.

"What you mean getting out King?" Cash shot back sharply but King raised a hand silencing him before he could get too worked up.

"Listen, I didn't call you here to go over all of my reasons or to get myself worked back up. The decision was hard enough and in the months to come we'll get to sit down and chop it up about why! But for now, the reason I called you here was to let you know that I love you bra. I love you like a brother and just because I'm stepping away, don't mean that I'm stepping away from you. You'll always be able to call on me like I've always been able to call on you." Cash began sweating profusely. "Second, I brought you here to tell you that it's all yours now my nigga." King was looking at Cash but he didn't get the kind of expression or reaction that he was expecting. Cash looked confused. He looked scared.

"The blocks, the houses, the plug, it's all yours my nigga. I'm not going to just drop it all on you and disappear though bra. Wipe that look off your face," King said. Cash forced a smile. "I'll stick around for few months to make sure that your transition goes smooth. You've always been ambitious blood, and I've always known it. I know that I wasn't always the easiest nigga to deal with." King chuckled. "I know that I can be stubborn and shit, but you stayed solid, true and loyal through it all. You checked your ambition and were guided by your loyalty instead. This is your reward my nigga. We gonna show these nigga's how it's done. Loyalty pays, ya feel me?"

Cash just stared at King wide eyed. All of a sudden, every bit of guilt that Cash had been brushing aside welled up inside of him and threatened to overwhelm him. In a matter of a few short seconds the magnitude of what he'd set in motion had dawned on him. It hit him like a ton of bricks. He thought of everything this nigga sitting next to him had done for him. Every way that King had had his back over the years played before him like the scene of a movie as he stared at the nigga who had been nothing but solid to him. The nigga who that because of his own greed; he had set up to get murdered. It was never an issue of whether or not Cash had a conscience or good heart. The truth of the matter is that most nigga's that do fuck shit in the game, do have good hearts. The problem was that King read one thing wrong. It was the one thing that had just recently changed in Cash. This was also the one thing that was bout to cost King his life. Cash's misplaced ambition overrode his desire to remain loyal.

"Say something nigga." King's eyes glowed as he stared at Cash. He's overwhelmed, King thought. Cash snapped out of it and without thinking said, "I gotta make a quick call."

Cash opened the door of the beemer, and stepped out, reaching his hand in his pocket for his phone as he did. His only thought was to call Marquise and Levelle to tell them to stand down and to go home; it's over!! What happened instead would trigger a chain of events that would forever alter the lives of everyone involved.

Chapter 99

THE HIT

[Present]

Marquise was first to see the passenger's side door pop open; and even though he was supposed to wait until he saw Cash draw down, he didn't. As Cash opened the door to get out, Marquise and Levelle opened theirs. Both were wearing all black; they pulled their baseball caps low and put their pistols down at their sides. They started trotting towards King's beemer. Cash had pulled his phone out and was about to dial their number's when he looked up and saw them coming. He froze.

Chapter 100

BACKFIRE

[Present]

Agent Vargas saw them too.

So did Keisha.

"Armed hostiles two o'clock, I repeat, two armed hostiles two o'clock," the Agent said over the radio.

Before Marquise and Levelle could close the distance to the beemer, they had three DEA agents pointing pistols at them.

"Drop the fucking gun, drop the gun," the first agent yelled.

Cash looked up. One agent pointed his nine at him. "Don't you fucking move," he commanded, shaking his head no.

"Marquise and Levelle looked to Cash for direction but Cash was like a deer in the headlights; he was still frozen.

Keisha started the Mercedes.

King looked behind him out the rear window to see what all the commotion was about.

"Team two, team two, south side parking lot now." Agent Vargas was yelling through the radio in the van. More agents would be on their way.

Everything was happening so fast but it felt like slow motion. A million thoughts were crammed into a split second.

In that same moment a beat-up car that was driving down the street with a bad muffler backfired, "Pop, pop, pop!" ...... All hell broke loose!!!! It sounded like gun fire.

Marquise and Levelle were the first to get hit with hot lead. Neither one ever had a chance to raise their pistols. The DEA's government issued Berettas hit them both center mass with three shots to the chest. One round blew out a chunk of Marquise's throat as he fell. The impact from the slugs lifted Levelle off of his feet, pushing him up and back before slamming his body to the pavement with surprising force.

Chapter 101

SHOTS FIRED

[Present]

Cash jumped down on the ground against the side of King's car. He fumbled to pull out his pistol but his hands were shaking like a motorbike and he couldn't get it.

The agents began to close in.

"Flat on your stomach you son of a bitch, face down," one agent shouted. He was looking but from where he stood, he didn't have a visual on Cash.

King hit the push button start on the beemer, keeping his head as low as he could, and prepared to back out of the parking lot.

Chapter 102

UTTER CHAOS

[Present]

"Murda" Murdock's young killer's heard the first shots and jumped from the van. They hadn't been on point like Omar would have wanted but as long as they got the job done, it would be cool. The driver stayed in the van. The young hitter that had been talking to the female that had come out of the Best Buy, hit the ground and pulled her down to the ground with him. He didn't have his gun on him. The other two pulled their masks down as they exited the van. They pulled and locked the slides on the AK's and started making their way between the cars; headed towards King's BMW.

Just as King was about to pop the whip into drive, his rear windshield shattered into thousands of pieces. The AK's distinctive "CLACK, CLACK, CLACK, CLACK" is all you could hear in the nights air. Cash laid flat on his stomach. The DEA agents dove to the side away from the direction of the assault rifle fire.

Murdock's young gunners were walking casually between the cars, closing in on the beemer. They were still about thirty yards away. The agents knew that they were outgunned and they were trying get back to safety.

Chapter 103

THE KING'S DOWN

[Present]

The beemer was being shredded with bullet holes the size of quarters. The hood flew up on the beemer and smoke and steam hissed from the engine like an angry cat. The first chopper round that the beefy seven series engine didn't stop, ricocheted and caught King in the right shoulder above the collarbone. A chunk of flesh ripped from his body as the round pushed straight through.

King yelled out in pain but couldn't be heard over the "CLACK, CLACK, CLACK" of the AK 47's melody. The young killers were closing in and were only twenty yards away from King's car now. As they came out from in between the cars and into the open, an engine revved. Before anyone could react, tires screeched and rubber burned as Keisha lurched forward in the Mercedes.

"Murda" Murdock's killers looked to the left, towards the sound of the engine and screeching tires, but they were too late. Keisha plowed into them. Both of their bodies bounced off of the hood of the Benz and then the windshield, before hitting the ground with an astonishing force. The AK 47's that they were just holding, clanked to asphalt with a sound that might make you think they were toys if you didn't just witness the carnage they'd produced. For a moment, the night was silent.

PROLOGUE

BLACK TESTAMENT TRILOGY

BOOK II

"QUEEN'S GAMBIT"

Omar "Murda" Murdock slowed to a crawl in his silver S550 Mercedes. As he began to make the right turn to enter into the mall parking lot, he was able to see what he couldn't see from across the street. Omar recognized King's car parked to the right, but who the fuck were these three nigga's standing in the middle of the parking lot; frozen like statues?

The one closest to the back-passenger's side door of the BMW was flamed up; he had almost all red on. That wasn't surprising, Omar thought, the realest nigga's in the city are "Rilla's" and they almost always wear red.

What Omar couldn't figure out was what the other two nigga's were doing. They were about twenty feet away from

King's car, and they were dressed in all black. They had masks pulled down over their faces but they were frozen in place like they were caught up in a fucked-up game of "Simon Says". They kept looking toward's the nigga in all red standing by King's car, and then off to the left. Their heads were moving, but their bodies looked like they had been super glued to the ground.

Oh shit, now Omar saw it. Two white boy's had gun's drawn on the two nigga's with mask's on; and one white boy had the nigga in all red in his sights. Omar couldn't hear what was being said, but it was clear that the white boy's were the op's. Fuck, Omar yelled. Where's my nigga's at? I don't want them walking into no shit like this.

Right then, one of the police started circling around wide to his right so that he could get a better angle on the two masked gunmen. That's when Omar saw the bright yellow letters of DEA on the back of the white boy's blue windbreaker. Omar's stomach dropped. He hadn't gotten to where he's at in the game by being stupid. He was a boss, a kingpin in his own right, and if he wanted thing's to stay that way, then he knew that it was best to stay off of the DEA's radar.

The scene that was playing out before his eyes made him feel like he was on the set of an action film. The last of the mall's shoppers were leaving the mall but they were walking into some gangsta shit that their minds couldn't comprehend.

Some saw the DEA agents with their guns drawn and were curious; they just stood there frozen. Other shoppers pointed or grabbed their cell phones to take pictures or call the police. Omar noticed a group of shoppers standing in the direct line of fire of the officers. If the officer's busted on them nigga's with the masks on, the shoppers were sure to get hit too. Stupid mutha fucka's!

One bitch looked like she had just started screaming. The nigga in all red standing by King's car momentarily looked in her direction. Now other shoppers were starting to get frantic and it looked like people were just a second away from panicking.

Where the fuck my nigga's at, Omar hissed to no one in particular. Omar grabbed his phone and was about to call them to see where the fuck they were at and to tell them to get the fuck out of there. He pulled the number up and was about to hit send when a "pop,pop,pop" sound from behind him scared the shit out of him.

Omar jumped in his seat and his phone dropped to the floor. Fucking backfire!! Omar could barely finish the thought before the unmistakable sound of gunfire erupted. Omar stayed down. He counted at least five or six shots.

When he finally dared to look over the dashboard, he couldn't see any of the nigga's anymore. He couldn't see the nigga's in the masks or the nigga in all red. What Omar did see was the DEA agents circling towards the passenger's side door of King's car. I wonder if that's King in the all red, Omar thought. If it is, I hope they killed his ass.

Omar looked in his rearview to see if he could back up and out of the parking lot, but by then there were several cars that had pulled in closely behind him; he couldn't reverse. He needed to get the fuck out of there. Omar turned his steering wheel hard to the left but there was a black Honda Accord coming from the opposite direction, attempting to leave the mall parking lot. As soon as it passed, Omar could whip the slick Mercedes around, and get the fuck out of there. "Hurry the fuck up!" Omar yelled out his window. The Honda had slowed down to try to figure out what all the commotion was about.

The Honda was just about passed and out of the way when, "CLACK, CLACK, CLACK, CLACK, CLACK" shattered the momentary silence. Omar knew that sound anywhere; the C-H-O-P-P-A!! It had to be his young killer's. Omar looked out of his passenger's side window of his Mercedes and saw his young killers making their way between the parked cars. They were shooting at King's BMW. The 7.62 cal rounds of the AK were tearing through King's car like a hot knife through butter. He could see holes in the car big enough to stick his finger in. Each hole had little puffs of smoke coming from them.

Omar looked around but he could no longer see the DEA agents. In fact, he could barely see anyone. Everyone had taken cover; gotten the fuck out of there. For an instant, Omar felt a sense of pride. His little homies is with the shit and he had raised they ass. Omar bred them nigga's to be killers.

"CLACK, CLACK, CLACK, CLACK, CLACK!"

The hood of King's white beemer shot up like a bottle rocket. Smoke and steam billowed from the engine like smoke from a fireplace. Two of the tires on the car had busted, popped, and exploded, making the car tilt to one side like an old ship that had taken on too much water.

Made in the USA
Middletown, DE
29 May 2023

31026070R00309